NEMESIS

THE ALLIANCE SERIES: BOOK TWO

EMMA L. ADAMS

This book was written, produced and edited in the UK, where some spelling, grammar and word usage will vary from US English.

Cover design by Amalia Chitulescu
Stock photographs purchased from Shutterstock.com

To be notified when Emma L. Adams's next novel is released, sign up to her author newsletter.

1

KAY

"Nobody told me the goblins would be invisible," I said to Ms Weston.

This wasn't the oddest conversation I'd ever had with my boss, but it was close. First ambassadorial mission and I'd managed to break my third communicator in a month, this time because it had fallen out of my pocket when chasing down a horde of ravegens, or goblins, as Earth people called them, from the world affectionately known as the cesspool of the Multiverse.

Ms Weston narrowed her eyes at me in her usual disapproving stare. "We'll definitely look into that next time." She rested her hands on her meticulously organised desk. "That blasted Campbell family... we need a reliable way to track down who they sold the bloodrock to. This is happening far too frequently."

Yeah. It was inevitable, now the family who'd been in charge of the illegal bloodrock trade on Valeria were dead or imprisoned, that there'd be an upsurge of activity on the black market, but even I hadn't guessed I'd spend my first week as Ambassador tracking down goblins across three universes only to find they'd got hold of a substance that could create a camouflage effect, and used it to cross Valeria and cause havoc. Admittedly, I'd always wanted to ride one of those hover bikes, so as far as first missions went, it could have been worse. But I hadn't intended to crash it into a wall and break my communicator in the process.

Okay, perhaps it was typical of the way my luck usually went. For the past ten minutes, Ms Weston had lectured me about disrespect for Alliance technology—and offworld technology, come to that, considering the hover bike—and she was finally coming to the point where she remembered I had, technically, caught the culprits. Even if the Alliance had had to fork out for property damage.

"Anything else I should know about?" I asked. "Before the next job?"

Ms Weston sighed. "If you insist on getting into these situations, Kay, it might be an idea to look up how to operate Valerian transport beforehand."

She had a point. Valeria prioritised style over a system that made sense. I did have an Earth motorcycle licence, not that I actually owned one—*yet*. I was planning on rectifying that now I had the full use of my hands again. A wyvern had destroyed my car, and I'd find a one-to-one fight with another more appealing than London's public transport system. But assuming the same rules applied on another universe was never a wise idea. Valeria's technology revolved around magic, and people continually found ways to use it to cause trouble.

And I was a magnet for both.

Ms Weston turned and walked to the window, which overlooked London from the south of the Thames. Beyond the car park below, the river glittered amongst the towering office buildings, a markedly ordinary sight after Valeria's capital. Now I'd been promoted to an Alliance Ambassador for Central, I'd be spending more time offworld than on Earth, which suited me just fine. Even with the invisible goblins.

"Point taken," I said. "I didn't expect it to get out of hand so quickly."

"Things have a habit of doing that wherever you're involved, Kay. You didn't use magic, did you?" She turned her scrutinising stare on me.

"No, I didn't." I knew better. Now the Balance had shifted back to normal, virtually all traces of magic on Earth had disappeared and the other worlds had stabilised, but that didn't mean it wasn't dangerous.

"We could do without the damages," Ms Weston muttered. "Especially considering the recent refurbishment."

"I'll write a cheque in the Walker name," I said.

For the first time since I'd worked here, Ms Weston looked genuinely surprised, which was saying something, considering we'd once been ambushed by a wyvern outside Central. "Do you think your father will mind the Walker accounts being charged for offworld property damage?"

"Honestly?" I said. "I doubt he'd notice."

That, at least, was true.

"Very well," she said. "Carl will give you a new communicator. Again." She waved a hand in dismissal, and I left the office with the feeling of having narrowly avoided stepping off a cliff.

"Do I really want to know what happened this time?" asked Carl, head of Central's guards, as I met him in the guard office downstairs. The floor space in the office was the size of a cupboard, because the entire room was taken up by a large padlocked adamantine cabinet along the back wall containing weapons and any magic-related things that hadn't yet been classified. A foot-long reptilian claw was mounted to the back of the door, which I strongly suspected belonged to the creature to which Carl owed the scar on his face.

"Would you believe me if I said it involved invisible goblins and a hover bike?" I asked.

"Because it's you, Kay, I would. Try not to break this one." He handed me another of the Alliance's standard communication devices—advanced smartphones with offworld roaming, Internet and information storage on virtually every world in the Multiverse. On Earth, only Central's archives had a more comprehensive store of information.

I made a note on the communicator to check out Valeria's transport instructions as soon as possible, and pocketed the new device.

"Maybe the tech team should invest in wyvern-hide coverings for these," I said.

"How did you break it, exactly?" asked Carl. "It didn't involve magic, did it?"

"No." Why did everyone keep asking that? Carl, unlike Ms Weston, was unaware of the unusual nature of my ability, though he knew I was one of the Alliance's few magic-wielders, like him. "I crashed a hover bike."

"And your communicator took the fall?"

"Pretty much." I'd escaped lightly with a few bruises and caught both ravegens before they'd wreaked any more havoc. Not bad for a first mission, especially as I'd only been promoted two days ago.

And it had been two days since I'd last seen Ada. The distractingly pretty, fierce redheaded girl who'd caused the Alliance so much trouble and managed to both aggravate me beyond measure and impress me with her sheer goddamned stubbornness. She was starting work here tomorrow—well, evaluation—and considering the Alliance had almost cost her everything, it surprised me that she'd said yes so readily.

It surprised me even more that she'd *kissed* me. Damn if I hadn't relived the moment a hundred times since.

I'd thought she hated me, and I couldn't say I blamed her. Thanks to the Alliance, she'd been turned into a weapon and nearly died. I'd convinced the council not to order their arrests, but her family had lost their livelihoods. The least I could do was get her a job, but I hadn't had a clue how she'd take the offer. I'd half expected her to throw it back in my face.

Instead, she'd kissed me like I was the last source of oxygen on the planet, and for one brief moment, blanked out all the guilt and horror that had plagued me since the attack on Central—even before that.

"You're back," said a contemptuous voice from the hall as I turned to leave the guard office. Figured I'd run into Aric here. Aric had only two modes, self-satisfied and pissed off. Looked like the latter this time. He'd shaved his head military-style and stuck a metal stud through his ear, with the result that he looked more like a biker-gang dropout than a professional Alliance guard.

"Well observed," I said.

"Heard you had some trouble with goblins."

"And there I was, thinking you'd got past the stalking thing."

"Piss off, Walker."

"Eloquent as ever. I was just leaving, and you're blocking the door."

"Aric, quit stirring up trouble," said Carl. "If you want a chance in hell of getting a promotion yourself, then acting like a dick isn't doing you any favours."

"He speaks sense," I said, shouldering past. It took a herculean effort not to tread on his feet.

Aric had been an unwelcome presence ever since we'd both joined the Academy five years ago, and things had been even more strained since he'd set a wyvern loose in the Passages and almost got me and two other students killed. He was ever-so-slightly pissed off that I'd ended up at the centre of all the drama a few weeks ago and wound up getting a promotion out of it.

Talking to Aric always made me want to hit something, so I headed for the training complex after checking out. This was the place they tested new recruits, while the rest of us got in practise beating the crap out of monsters. Though the monsters weren't real, the simulations worked as a substitute until they'd let me out into the Passages again. This was offworld tech with restricted access, advanced enough to simulate virtually any situation and with total sensory immersion. Which meant: when the virtual monsters hit back, it hurt.

And right now, if I admitted it, I was also trying to distract myself from thinking extremely inappropriate thoughts about a certain future colleague.

A field of virtual corpses later and I left the training complex slightly less aggravated, though that changed when I had to sidestep a contingent of junior guards who kept glancing at me and talking in low voices. I heard the words "Walker" and "hero".

Oh, for god's sake. Apparently, that one was still going around. I'd told everyone the Alliance-approved version of the story, in which Ada and I just happened to be there when the Campbells' plan backfired, leaving them all dead. But rumours were hard to stamp out when I was the sole witness aside from Ada, and she hadn't been around to tell her side of the story. I still wasn't sure on parts of it. But in no way did it involve the word *hero*.

My communicator buzzed in my hand, and I flicked the

touch screen to unlock it and accepted the call from my boss. Ms Weston never seemed to leave Central, especially in the last few weeks. There was always some crisis or other.

"We need you to go offworld, tomorrow," she said, without preamble.

"Whereabouts?" I asked. Damn. I'd been intending to talk to Ada, because she didn't have the code for this new communicator.

"Aglaia. You should speak to Markos. Aglaia's in the middle of a crisis, and we urgently need an Ambassador to be there."

"Isn't Markos enough?"

"A non-Aglaian Ambassador. More than one. It seems the centaur king's been assassinated."

And there I was, thinking I'd be able to get through one day without someone mentioning murder.

"Damn," I said, moving away from the guards so they wouldn't overhear. "There's no way they'll let outsiders in."

"It's part of Alliance custom to oversee the change of leadership, as we're a neutral force I'm sure you already know Aglaia's history with the Alliance."

"Unfortunately," I said, with a glance at the dark shape of Central silhouetted against the perpetually-grey London sky. "Is Markos back on Aglaia, then?"

"He'll give you the details." There was a sound of papers being shuffled. "The peace treaty with the humans was due for renewal next week, so the timing makes it all worse. This could be perceived as an attempt to ignite old conflicts. At the very least, it will delay all plans, including consultations with the Alliance."

"You need someone who speaks Aglaian, right?" I was hardly experienced in this kind of diplomacy. Least of all with a volatile, high-magic world.

"Not just that," said Ms Weston. "We specifically need a magic-wielder. Just in case."

What? "Are you sure? I was under the impression centaurs hated magic." I retreated under the overhang outside the training complex. The last thing I wanted was anyone to hear me talking about magic.

"Yes, they do. But humans on Aglaia are all magic-wielders, and if it turns out one of them *did* have a hand in the centaur king's death, then it's better for us to be prepared. It goes without saying that you won't be able to reveal you are a magic-wielder in front of the centaur contingent, but considering Earth's lack of magic, they have no reason to suspect that you are."

Yeah, that's reassuring. "If you say so. The humans, though —they'll be trained magic-wielders. We aren't."

No. What I knew of magic, I'd learned on instinct when fighting for my life. And I couldn't forget that two streets away from here, it had almost caused a wave of destruction across London. Even the guards who'd fought in the Passages that day didn't know just how close Central had come to being wiped out. For all I knew, they were the ones who'd started the stories. People needed to believe someone had had the situation in hand.

Ms Weston paused before saying, "Actually, magic-wielders on Aglaia are relatively peaceful, at least with each other."

"It's the centaurs I'm more concerned about," I muttered. "Who else is going, aside from Markos?"

"A small team. You'll meet here tomorrow at seven."

"Right," I said, resigned. Aglaia was hardly an opportunity to pass up, but it felt uncomfortably like the conspiracy scenario I'd ended up mired in at the Alliance a few weeks ago. Assassination, magic, and aggravated centaurs? Still, nobody signed up as an Ambassador purely for the Valerian hover bikes.

"Good," said Ms Weston. "Best of luck. There are two aims. Reinstate a new monarch before certain disparate centaur groups take power, and find out who killed their leader, if possible."

"I'm pretty sure most of that is up to them, not the Alliance. They don't like humans meddling in their affairs."

Ms Weston drew in a breath. "Well, given the circumstances… Markos will tell you. Essentially, you'll be acting to stop a group of enraged centaurs from declaring war on humans."

"Great," I said. "No pressure?"

2

ADA

It was the evening before I started my new job, and from the look on Nell's face as she passed me in the corridor, I might have signed up to kick-start the apocalypse.

"Watch out," said Alber, my brother, handing me a tub of shoe polish through my half open bedroom door. "She's on the warpath."

"I figured," I said. "Shoe polish? Really?"

"Hey, you have to look the part."

"Yeah, when I'm not chasing monsters out of the Passages." I waved a hand in the direction of my new Alliance-issued guard uniform, laid out on my bed. Finally, I had my hands on their infamous magicproof gear, and if it wasn't totally vain to think so, I looked damn good in it.

One of the perks of working for the Alliance. Along with free entry to the Multiverse—if I passed their tests.

Alber stepped away from my room, hands in his pockets. We vaguely resembled one another though we weren't actually related, with the tanned skin and fair hair of Enzar, though Alber's hair was short and spiked, while I'd dyed mine dark red.

"You're making me jealous already. No more sneaking around. Hey, you'll be the one arresting trespassers."

"That's so weird." A month ago, I'd been arrested and taken into custody by the Alliance. Now, I was going to be working for them.

"It's a good thing," said Alber. "You've got to give us all the gossip on Central." He glanced down the corridor at Nell, who was now running through combat manoeuvres. Behind his half open door, our older brother, Jeth, sounded like he was on the phone but was probably talking to one of his computers. Alber himself had always preferred beating up monsters on video games to actually going out into the Passages, and maintained that he only wanted to travel offworld to have a ride in a hover car on Valeria. He was incredibly jealous of my hover boot experience, which was the one part of the worst day of my life I could look back on and not want to scream.

"I wanna go to a high-tech world," said Alber with a wistful sigh. "Do you reckon you'll be allowed to bring anything back?"

"Probably not," I said. "The Alliance is strict about that. They'd flip a lid if they knew half the stuff I've got in my room."

"Oh, yeah, you've got to play by the rules now." He smirked. "How will you survive without your daggers?"

"Shut it, you," I said. "I'll get proper Alliance-issued weapons. Wyvern-hide daggers. And stunners."

"Ooh, get you," said Alber. "That's a fancy Taser, right?"

"With magic." I'd had one of those stunners used on me, and it hurt like hell. Like an electric shock, but worse for me because I was a magic-wielder of the unconventional type.

And now I wished I hadn't thought about magic, because just that one word made the anxiety come clawing back.

"That's badass."

"Yeah." I managed a smile. "Guess it kind of is."

"Come on, Ada, admit it. You've spent years fantasising about running around with the Alliance guards."

"I have to pass evaluation, first."

From what I figured, it involved proving I had at least a rudimentary understanding of how the Multiverse worked, and could handle the unpredictable nature of patrolling the monster-ridden Passages. In the thirteen-odd years I'd helped Nell at her offworld shelter, I'd interacted with people from too many worlds to count. Nell had taught me three offworld languages and seven styles of combat from different worlds. And I'd battled my share of monsters. Even cut the tail off a wyvern.

But I was still nervous as hell about tomorrow. Nervous enough that I actually considered calling a certain someone on my (also-new, also-Alliance-issued) communicator.

"You'll rock it," said Alber. "You can run circles around them. They won't know what hit them."

At one time, I would have had the same level of confidence. But after that day, I couldn't even sneak into the Passages anymore. *It was for the best,* I told myself. That hidden door was where an army of dreyverns had almost killed Nell. Would probably have killed the rest of us, too, if not for...

I looked at the communicator lying on my bed for a moment, then shook my head and set down the shoe polish on top of a stack of books. I didn't used to get this nervous about life changes. As we'd lived under the Alliance's radar most of my life, every day had been about risk. But since waking from that coma, everything I'd once took for granted had suddenly seemed like it belonged to a different Ada. A more naive Ada who had no idea she carried a built-in weapon that could destroy the Multiverse.

Someone who never would have taken leave of her senses and kissed an Alliance guard.

Deal with it tomorrow. Once again, I repacked my bag and flicked the touch screen of my communicator. Fitted with offworld roaming up to five universes away, maps, information files and god-only-knew-what else, it had kept me entertained for two days straight trying to figure out what everything did. I was fairly sure it was worth more than our house.

"Hey, Ada," said Jeth, from down the hall, peering out of his room with his own new communicator in hand. "You figured out the night-vision button yet?"

"There's night vision?"

"Yep. They think of everything. If ever I want to know the temperature in Alvienne or the population of Klathica's capital, I know where to look." Jeth started work at the Alliance tomorrow, too, in the tech department.

"What're you taking?" I said. "Aside from the Chameleons? Your other projects?"

"Hell no. They're not getting hold of all my ingenious ideas, little sister. But this—" He waved the communicator— "is awesome. I've already thought of a few adaptations. There's a translator, right, but what if I made it into an earpiece? It'd mean people could communicate offworld if they didn't speak the same language. There are like fifteen thousand languages logged in here already, I doubt anyone on Earth speaks all of them. I know Klathica has some kind of device, but it involves cutting your head open and—"

"Yeah, we get it, you're a genius," said Alber.

I was glad at least one of us felt mildly prepared. But then again, the only jobs I'd ever had were crappy part-time shift work at supermarkets and once, a coffee shop (which had

had absolutely nothing to do with the free hot chocolate every hour). As I'd helped Nell at the shelter since I was eight, its absence left a gaping hole that hurt more than I'd expected. I knew the open Passage from Enzar to the New York Alliance would help more than I ever could, but my family was left jobless and sinking into debt. Being able to help people from my homeworld had made me feel like I had a purpose here on Earth. Stupid thing to think, really. Once I'd passed initiation into the Alliance, the first thing I'd do would be to ask my supervisor if I could help Enzar from here. Even if my new boss was singularly the most terrifying woman I'd ever met.

"Hey," said Jeth, glancing up from the communicator's screen. "It'll be okay, Ada. Just a new start, right? It's what you always wanted. The Multiverse."

He was right, of course. For all the years helping refugees through the Passages between the universes, I'd never set foot on another world—at least, not until the craziness a few weeks ago. If I got this job, then I'd be aiming for an ambassadorial position to help people in other worlds. I'd get to do what I'd dreamed of all my life. And yet...

I took in a deep breath. "It's just hard, you know? I have a feeling at least some of them won't trust me, after what happened."

"Then they're idiots," said Jeth, putting the communicator in his pocket and crossing the landing to give me a hug. "D'you think I'm not worried about the same thing? My world's not the Alliance's friend."

He had a point. Jeth was originally from Karthos, a world almost as volatile as Enzar, and Nell had adopted him like she had my brother Alber. She'd assembled our small family from broken worlds left to ruin, and since she'd smuggled me out of Enzar as a baby, she'd risked her life to keep the Alliance from finding us.

"You didn't cause a scene in front of a hundred guards," I pointed out. "Or break out of jail in the most dramatic way possible."

"I can think of worse things you've done when drunk."

I gave him a sarcastic look. "Thanks." My older brother was the sensible one. My younger brother was the recluse. And I'd always been the reckless one. Up until now.

"Hey, just being honest, Ada."

"Yeah, well, my wild party days are over." At school, I'd already stood out a mile thanks to my Enzarian heritage. If people remembered me as the girl who got shitfaced and danced on the table, I'd rather have that than anyone coming close to guessing I wasn't from Earth at all. Now it felt like everyone knew. Like walking under a spotlight.

"Quit overthinking things. You're gonna rock this job."

A disparaging noise told me Nell had caught the end of our conversation. Her mouth was pressed in a frown as tight as her hair, which was pulled in a bun. Like me, she had the tanned skin and deceptively delicate features of Enzar, but her natural eye colour was pale purple, now hidden by light blue contact lenses.

"What?" I said, more snappishly than I intended. Having to defend my life decisions to my foster mother didn't help all the doubts buzzing around my head like a swarm of mosquitoes. Unfortunately, Nell hated the Alliance for letting Enzar tear itself apart in war without intervening, and had blamed them for all of our problems. Even more unfortunately, she knew the name of the eminent council member who'd ruled that the Alliance would have no part in the Enzar conflict even to save the millions of innocents caught in the crossfire. Lawrence Walker, Kay's father.

It went without saying that a certain kiss shared in New York City had gone unmentioned in this house. No one else knew except for Simon, Kay's friend from the Academy, but

Nell had the uncanny ability to sense disobedience. I was twenty-one and more than capable of taking care of myself, but I'd put her through so much stress over the past month that she'd reverted into overprotective mode.

"Don't you 'What?' me, Ada Fletcher," said Nell. "You still haven't emptied the dishwasher."

"Taskmaster," I said, with an attempt to rekindle our usual family banter.

Nell followed me into the kitchen. "The Knights were asking after you," she said.

"Oh." They'd been Skyla's adoptive family. My heart sank.

"It turns out Skyla kept a diary. She wrote about experiments performed by the Alliance, at Central, on children. Did you know anything about that?"

The breath stopped in my throat. Crap. I'd managed to skate over that part of the story until now, but it had only been a matter of time before she'd run into the reason Skyla had betrayed us.

"Uh…" Delta had told me. But I couldn't name him. My former friend, who I'd killed.

"And you didn't think to mention it?"

Stop looking at me like that. "No, because it's the same thing that happened to me!" My voice shook, much as I tried to stop it. "Don't you think I'd rather forget about it?"

For an instant, sympathy warred with the sternness in her gaze. Then she shook her head. "Despicable," she said. "Experimenting on children."

"It wasn't all of them," I said, to no effect. Only a handful of people had been involved. It hadn't even been Alliance-approved, but because the council member in charge had been so important, it had been covered up and hardly anyone knew about it now. I only knew that much because…

The faces of two identical twins, boy and girl, flashed before my eyes, and the room momentarily swayed.

"Ada?"

I pushed the image of a warehouse from my head. "Yeah?"

"The Alliance's West Branch confiscated the Knight family's entire supply of bloodrock solution."

So much for her actually noticing I'd zoned out. Nell lived in her own head these days.

"Nell... the refugees will be fine now. They have somewhere to go." Before, Nell had made disguises for them using bloodrock stolen from Central's stores.

"Yes, assuming the Alliance don't go back on their word." Her nostrils flared. "And besides, we had to pay for that bloodrock from savings we don't even have. The only place *we're* going is bankrupt."

Again with the guilt-tripping. Yeah, I did feel guilty about it, especially as *I'd* been the one to steal the bloodrock in the first place, but well... stealing was kind of illegal. I knew we'd have had to pay for it eventually, whether I joined the Alliance or not.

"Jeth and I will take care of things. It's not like I'm working for nothing." Actually, the Alliance paid through the freaking *roof*, compared to the crappy part-time jobs I'd worked before. I'd have more money than I knew what to do with—something totally foreign to me. I supposed there had to be some incentive to risking my life in the Passages as an Alliance guard.

Nell tutted. "You'd better pass their tests, then."

"I'll take that as a 'good luck'," I said, returning to the dishwasher.

As Nell departed without another word, Jeth came into the kitchen. "Don't worry about her. She'll come around."

I sighed, following him out into the hallway. "Guess I shouldn't have expected her to take this lying down."

"Nell doesn't take anything lying down. She'd tear the

Multiverse apart for you, you know that, right? Same with all of us."

"Of course," Alber said from outside the door. "You're gonna rock it tomorrow. I won't be awake, but good luck, sis, okay?"

"Cheers," I said. "Not to worry. I've got this."

"Yeah, you have," said Jeth. "I'll knock on your door in the morning, all right?"

"Sure." I smiled at my brother. "You're both still first priority with me, right?"

"Always," said Alber, retreating to his room.

"Sure we are," he said. "Don't stay up too late, Ada."

"Now you're the parent?" I waved goodnight and went into my room. On the ceiling, the stars glittered. I'd painted them when I was younger, to represent the Multiverse. It would be mine to explore, at long last.

Everything else, I could handle. *I think.*

Sitting down on the bed, I picked up the communicator and scrolled through until I found the employee contacts section. One number leaped out. Kay.

Stop being a wimp, Ada, I told myself. *You were the one who kissed him.*

Yes, and he'd kissed me back, and just thinking about it made heat rush to my face. So why did the thought of seeing him tomorrow scare the living daylights out of me? I wasn't a teenager anticipating her first date. Those days were long gone.

I typed a "see you tomorrow" message and hit the button before I lost my nerve.

Message delivery failed. No signal? Was he offworld? He was an Ambassador now. It was what he wanted. That was one of the few things I knew about him.

But it was a long time before I found sleep.

~

A warehouse. Lights flashed on and off, reflected in the gleaming metal floor and ceiling. Laughter echoed, abruptly cut off when a body slammed into the wall. A girl screamed.

I'd watched this scene a hundred times. Maybe more. When I'd been in the coma, it had played on an endless loop. My subconscious was kind of a bitch.

Even though I knew what was going to happen, I wished I could tear my gaze away.

"Eddie!" screamed the girl.

I stood frozen, the breath caught in my lungs. Like someone held me in a chokehold, cutting off my oxygen supply. The heartbroken sobbing rang in my ears. I had to use magic—

I couldn't use it. Never again.

"Ada!" Hands grabbed my wrists, and I found my voice. I screamed, thrashing. A muffled *thump*, and a gasp of pain. The world righted itself. Jeth backed away from me, rubbing his arm. I must have kicked him.

"Ah—sorry." I flopped onto the pillow. Once again, I'd probably woken the whole house. The sky outside was still dark. "Jeth, I'm fine. Go back to bed."

"Ada, you really shouldn't be coming to Central tomorrow."

I groaned. "Not fair. Don't argue with me when I'm half asleep."

Jeth headed towards the door. "You should talk to someone about it."

"About what?"

He raised his eyebrows. "I know you felt obliged to say yes, but it's obviously too soon after what happened."

"I didn't feel obliged to do anything," I said. "I wanted it. I've always wanted it."

Jeth sighed. "Have you even spoken to… Kay? He offered you the job, right?"

"I can't reach him."

"Typical," said Jeth. "Just like those Alliance types. They only appear when they want a favour."

"You sure were quick to say yes when he offered *you* a job," I muttered. "Double standards?"

"We need the money." He sighed. "If they make me do anything I don't agree with, I'm out. But you, Ada, you're not ready for something like this. And I'm not trying to be a dick," he added. "I know you feel like you have to prove yourself to these people. But… you're not sleeping. Is it worse?"

"Same old," I said. "Just nightmares. Guilt. The occasional good old-fashioned panic attack." I tapped my head. "It's all rainbows and fluffy bunnies in here."

"It's not funny," said Jeth. "And—well, you know what Nell's like, but maybe you want to talk to someone about it? If you're suffering post-traumatic stress—"

"Like I can tell anyone the truth?" I said. "I almost killed the world. I murdered five people. I'm an unnatural magic-wielder—" I choked off.

"Seriously. At least just think about it."

"Right now," I said, "I need *structure*. This job is exactly what I need. A purpose. I can quit any time."

"Right." He didn't look convinced. "Try and get a bit more sleep, anyway."

He left the room, and I grabbed my communicator instead, checking through the various files for new Alliance members. The nerves kicked in again as I scanned the list of things I was supposed to know if I ever wanted to be promoted to an Ambassador. Okay, Nell had brought me up on awareness of the worlds beyond Earth, but looking at the list of worlds logged into the newsfeed, what I knew felt like a drop in the ocean. Every single world had its own laws, customs, outlook, and political alliances both within and without the Alliance itself. It made my head spin trying to make sense of it all.

You're just nervous, I told myself. Nervous. Yeah. I wasn't broken. I was fine. Relatively.

3

KAY

There really was nothing quite as alarming as the sight of angry centaurs first thing in the morning. Even more so when they were yelling at each other in Aglaian, which sounded unfriendly at the best of times. I couldn't make out all the words, but I got the gist. They were *not* happy to be dragged into the Alliance's Headquarters.

There were only four of them, but they made enough noise for an entire herd. People had gathered in the entrance hall and on the balconies above to see what all the fuss was about. In the centre of the chaos was Markos, who made more of a racket than the rest of them put together. All four wore poncho-like coats that looked like leaves knitted together, and horned crowns—as if they didn't look intimidating enough already—and no one else dared step within a metre of them.

"What the hell is going on?" I asked Raj, the other Ambassador, who overlooked the chaos from a safe distance. "Who brought them to Earth?"

"Markos's idea," he said. "They need to speak to a council member before we let our people go to Aglaia. It's not stable."

"Neither is that noise," I pointed out. "And I wouldn't mention stables. Who are they, Aglaia's council representatives?"

"Unfortunately," said Raj. "There was a misunderstanding about who the king's heir is, and they got into an argument in the Passages. Scared the hell out of the night guards, and you know those guys don't scare easy."

"They don't know who the heir is?" I said. "Really?"

"Well, they do, but he's not being very cooperative." Raj pointed to Markos.

"You're joking. *Markos* is the heir?"

"He seems to have kept a few things quiet. Doesn't get on with his family."

I stared at the centaur. Well, damn.

"Wait—what are you doing?" said Raj, as I approached the group. After all, it was generally considered inadvisable for a human to walk towards a group of angry centaurs as opposed to running for their life.

About normal for me, then.

"Markos," I shouted over the noise. He didn't even hear, so I shouted, in Aglaian, "Would you all *be quiet?*"

Thankfully, that got through. And four angry centaurs were now glaring at me.

"This is no concern of yours, human," said the one Markos had been yelling at, who I figured was some close relation to Markos. They looked almost identical. Might have been an inch different in height, but it wasn't easy to tell with seven-foot-high horse-men.

"You're causing a scene." I met Markos's eyes with a glare. "If you could all stop shouting for one second—"

"Let me talk to my colleague," said Markos, moving away from the group. In the sudden silence, his hoof-steps echoed on the glossy adamantine floor of the entrance hall.

"Let me get this straight," I said. "You're the heir. But you don't want to go back. Right?"

"Who told you that?" Markos sighed. "There I was, hoping I could keep the lot of you in happy ignorance. So inconvenient of my father to get himself killed."

So they hadn't parted on friendly terms. Markos must have exiled himself if he was royalty. He'd never talked about his homeworld. Couldn't say I blamed him.

"I know Aglaian laws don't leave much room for negotiation," I said. "But there's no reason that can't change. Screaming the place down will do nothing but annoy everyone at Central. Why did you bring them here?"

"I didn't have a choice. We were *supposed* to be meeting with the council, but they want to drag me back to Aglaia immediately. I am aware that reinstating an heir is the quickest way to resolve the conflict, but that won't solve the issue of the assassination—by the *gods*, I despise politics. That's why I left in the first place."

"I gathered." Unfortunately, 'abdication' wasn't a word centaurs were familiar with. Centaurs might live in tribes, but they all answered to the same king—all five million of them. They wouldn't want the Alliance getting involved if they could help it.

"Those are my delightful cousins. They're so friendly and accommodating." He indicated the three other centaurs, two of whom were circling each other in a threatening way.

"I don't think the council will be particularly happy if there's a centaur brawl in the middle of the hall," I said. Even I wasn't crazy enough to step in the middle of that one.

"You make a good point," said Markos. "Leonid! Petro! Tryfon! You forget yourselves."

"On the contrary," said the centaur who could have been Markos's twin. "It is you who is a disgrace to our kind, allying yourself with these humans."

"Yes, we've been through this already." He switched back to English. "By the gods, I never thought I'd wish for the straightforwardness of humans. Everything's a debate with Aglaians."

"I don't think this is the best place for family arguments. Are they the only other candidates for the throne?"

"There's my sister, but I haven't seen her in years," Markos said dismissively. "Haven't talked to anyone from Aglaia for over seven years until yesterday."

Well, damn, I thought again. If I'd had the option to leave Earth for good five years ago, then I might have taken it. But then, I'd been the only Walker remaining, and I'd had a second chance at the Academy. Aglaians were less forgiving of people who went against custom.

"They seem pleased to see you."

"Absolutely delighted. Frankly, I'm disappointed they weren't as enthralled by my tales of London as I expected. Even the trickiness of managing stairs and escalators, not to speak of the *climate*. Earth is much more varied than Aglaia. One grows weary of forests for miles on end."

"Why are you talking to that human?" One of the centaurs approached us, and I tensed instinctively, knowing how fast centaurs might lash out. They could easily outpace a human, and had hooves of steel. Hardly a fair match, without magic, at least. That was the only reason the violent—and more numerous—centaur population hadn't completely obliterated the humans on Aglaia.

"Because he's a more interesting conversationalist than you three," said Markos. "And because the council's on the way, and I'll thank you not to make a total embarrassment of yourselves."

The centaur tapped a hoof. But Markos only shrugged.

"If you would do your duty to Aglaia—" one of the other centaurs began.

"None of that," said Markos. "I distinctly remember you saying when I left never to darken your doorway again, or something along those lines."

The centaur advanced on him, tail swishing. Markos stepped forward, bristling.

"Whoa there," I said to Markos. "I am completely on your side in this one, but if you start a brawl, I'm putting in a call to the council." I pulled out my communicator for emphasis. "Feel free to start all the arguments you like back on Aglaia, but this is Alliance ground and you do *not* want to piss off Ms Weston."

Markos twisted to glare at me. "On my side, human?"

I shrugged. "I'll do what I can, if you try not to murder any of your cousins. Pretty sure that's punishable by execution, isn't it?"

"Damn you, human," said Markos. "I suppose you have our entire law scroll memorised."

"You're not the only one who hates politics," I said. "I'm supposed to oversee the council meetings and make sure the heir—you, I suppose—doesn't get himself killed, too. How you sort out your feud is *not* my problem."

"This feud will stop when they erase the word "duty" from their vocabulary."

I had a few choice things to say on *that* subject... none of which would be advisable in front of four pissed-off centaurs, and most of which wouldn't translate into Aglaian.

"One quick question," I said. "None of them understand English, do they?"

Markos shook his head. "Only a handful do on all of Aglaia."

"Right." I lowered my voice all the same. "Not to tread on any toes here... or hooves... but is there absolutely no chance the murderer wasn't a relation? I know," I added, as Markos's face darkened. "I know that's the worst crime. But I don't want to rule anything out. The title passes only within the family, doesn't it?"

"Yes, it does. But nobody within would have dared. For a centaur to kill another, it would demand an ambition most of us simply don't have. We aren't like humans, Kay."

"Not all humans are ambitious," I said. "Can you really say all centaurs aren't?"

Markos narrowed his eyes. "Alliance law demands all close relations are questioned. That's the other reason we were arguing. That idiot Tryfon—" He jerked his head in the direction of the centaur who might have been his twin—"is flat-out refusing to go through with it. Says it goes against our customs."

"Well, I can't imagine any centaur would want to be subjected to questioning by the Alliance," I said. "For one thing, I'd wager no one from offworld has ever got close enough to centaur royalty to know the first thing about what might motivate a murder. I sure don't. Aside from the obvious."

"Yes, there is that," said Markos. "Well, if we do manage to get to the stage of appointing a new monarch, it's customary to have Alliance representatives present, especially with our treaty coming up for renewal next week."

"Blasted customs," I muttered. "So, is there anything I need to look out for? People, centaurs or humans, who might see the Alliance as a threat?"

"There are a few, but they're unlikely to make trouble at the meeting."

"And could *they* have killed the king?"

"I wouldn't have thought so," said Markos, tapping a hoof. "The title is purely ceremonial, and the advisors make most of the decisions in any case. If they wanted power, they'd have targeted our own council."

"So the king must have had an enemy."

"Perhaps. The cause of death hasn't been determined, but it wasn't magic. That's why there's so much conflict. Nothing to prove humans did it, but it's the natural assumption to make."

"Not magic?" I said. "I see the problem."

Magic would point the finger right at the humans. Either a centaur had done it, or a human with the foresight to deflect attention from themselves. Either was equally likely.

"The humans had no motive. There haven't been any territorial disputes in over ten years, not since we joined the Alliance."

"Right. I'll think of the alternatives, but it looks like the council's ready," I said, seeing the three figures approaching out of the corner of my eye. Mr Sanders, Mr Shean, and Mrs Grey were, at the moment, the only council members present on Earth. The rest spent most of their time offworld, engaged in various meetings and debates alongside council members from the other branches of Earth's Alliance. I'd say they *tolerated* me more than that we got along, because I was the one who'd talked them out of arresting the people who'd helped the refugees on Earth. But if it stopped them looking at me like they saw only my father, I wasn't about to complain.

Markos turned to them, the defiance vanishing from his expression. Kind of odd, considering he towered over everyone and if they wanted, he and his brothers could pound us into the polished floor in a heartbeat.

"What is the problem?" Mr Sanders asked.

"Merely a family misunderstanding," said Markos. "It seems my presence is required on Aglaia."

"Then we should go."

As we left Central, the few passersby on the street stopped to stare or just moved as far away as possible.

Sensible thinking. At least they couldn't understand the centaurs talking about how filthy and hideous London was.

But soon enough, we turned into the side street leading into the Passages. No one lived there anymore, thanks to the damage caused by a rampaging wyvern. Though the torn up cars had been taken away, several houses were little more than crumbled brick and there were deep gouges in the road where the wyvern's tail had slammed down.

The place where Ada's attack on the Campbells had burned a small crater into the pavement drew my eyes before I had the sense to look away. Third level magic left permanent marks where it struck. Just outside the Passage entrance, a plaque on the wall had been engraved with the names of the people who'd sacrificed their lives defending Central. Mr Sanders paused by the memorial, head bowed for an instant, then continued into the Passages.

As Earth was back in its low-magic state, it made the impact of magic in the blue-lit corridors even more noticeable. Like an electric surge, and a faint red tint to the air, like through a coloured glass pane. With magic at my fingertips, it was difficult to forget how close I'd come to being another name on the list of the dead.

On Earth, I couldn't use magic at all, which was why I hadn't known I was a magic-wielder until I'd first broken into the Passages as a third-year Academy student. After I'd accidentally zapped Aric with second-level magic and nearly killed him, I'd never trusted magic. But in a hostile world like Aglaia, it would be a stupid move to ignore it.

The buzzing grew stronger as we went deeper through the wide, high-ceilinged corridors, past doors which led to various points on other worlds, starting with the Earth's close neighbours, the original five worlds of the Alliance. Aglaia, as a recent member, was a fair distance from London, almost at the second level, which was reserved for dangerous, non-cooperative worlds like the Enzarian Empire. Almost all were high-magic. On Aglaia itself, third level magic was highly illegal, but if it turned out a human had killed the centaurs' leader, that was the quickest, deadliest weapon. As easy as hitting a button... except for the backlash, of course. I'd been lucky not to get hit by the recoil when I'd used it, and even then, it had burned the skin off my hands. The aftereffects had gone on for weeks, like an electric shock through my fingers every other minute.

Cut that out, I thought, as magic tugged at me again. Like I'd fall for that now. I glanced at Raj, but he didn't appear bothered. I'd wondered before if having an internal source made magic react to me differently. Made it feel too damn good to resist.

But I did, though I half expected an ambush when we stepped through the door to Aglaia. The heat struck first, a marked contrast to London, which was fairly cold for early autumn. Aglaia's climate felt more Mediterranean. We'd crossed several time zones when moving through the Passages, and it was afternoon here judging by the position of Aglaia's burnished red sun above the trees. The doorway appeared to have been cut into a large tree, leading into a clearing in the midst of the forest.

Centaur territory. We were in a sunny, forested glade, and centaurs occupied the areas of the world untouched by humans. Several centaurs waited around a prepared wooden table with seats for the humans—at least, it seemed a thoughtful gesture, but the low seats gave the centaurs even more of a height advantage. I scanned the surroundings and more centaurs lurked behind the trees, armed with crossbows and spears. Not taking any chances, then.

Magic lurked here, too, but not like the wildness in the Passages. More like Valeria, where I could sense I could use it, but not the constant pressure. In Valeria, it was an aftereffect, like smoke from the vehicles that used it as a power source. Here, however, the smoky-red clouds visible through the branches above showed the altered climate from mages constantly adapting the weather conditions to suit what they needed. Like a gigantic ash cloud over the atmosphere. It wasn't harmful, as far as anyone could tell, but it was yet another point of conflict with the centaurs, who didn't appreciate the sky turning purple-red on a regular basis.

A string of introductions swiftly descended into another centaur verbal battle, while the council watched helplessly. *Bloody argumentative centaurs.* I'd have thrown Markos an exasperated look, except he was the one doing most of the shouting. Several of the council had their communicators out in case they had to call for backup, and I was acutely aware of being unarmed, except for magic. Raj appeared equally uneasy. He could only use magic up to second level and preferred to avoid it, like every magic-wielder from a non-magic world with a shred of common sense.

In the end, all we gleaned from the meeting was that the centaur king had been killed by a falling tree, not magic (naturally, the first argument was that magic could have been used to knock the tree down, which was undoubtedly true). No one wanted to make any commitments. Markos refused to stay in Aglaia. His siblings weren't even at the meeting, as they had some kind of mourning phase for close relatives, which Markos hadn't been invited into. He didn't seem particularly fussed.

"He wouldn't have wanted me there," he told me, when we finally extricated ourselves from the meeting and made our way back through the Passages, leaving the other centaurs behind. "In fact, it wouldn't surprise me if he rose from the grave to tell me never to come back to Aglaia again."

"That so?" I'd never asked the centaur about his homeworld before, primarily because a centaur living in London, Earth, of all places, had either been banished by his tribe or exiled himself. Going against family was the worst crime a centaur could commit. And that went double for royalty.

"My sister will not be pleased I've come here, either. Hopefully, I've avoided that pesky title ceremony and offloaded it onto her," Markos said, his hoofbeats echoing through the corridor. "She's a year older than me, and she'd do a far better job."

"Well, that's something," I said. "If you can convince them to let you leave."

"Worry not, for I am awesome," said Markos, with the air of a show master addressing a crowd.

I rolled my eyes. "Just don't go getting yourself into trouble."

"Yes, I think our office has rather an appalling track record for accidental deaths, doesn't it?" said Markos, manoeuvring himself around the corner at a Passage junction.

"It does," I said, habitually checking behind us before following him. "And I'll thank you not to remind Ada of that." She'd be at Central right now. If the universe played nice for once, I might actually get to see her before being called offworld again to chase invisible goblins…

"The infamous Ada? Is she working at Central now?"

"If she passes training," I said. "So, yes."

"Wow. Someone's certain." He looked at me slantwise. "You like this girl?"

Guess I hadn't exactly been subtle about it. I shrugged.

"Humans." He snorted.

We emerged through the doorway in London. Ada would either be at Central or at the training complex, but I didn't see her when I reported to Ms Weston.

"I'm glad you managed to avoid traffic accidents this

time," she said, stacking the papers I'd handed her on the desk.

"Considering centaurs travel on foot, I'd be worried if I didn't," I said. "I have to go back there tomorrow, right?"

"I'll update you once the council makes its decision. There's little the Alliance can do in this case other than stand on the side-lines. You're dismissed for now."

I nodded. "All right."

"Am I correct in thinking you intend to return to Valeria?"

Hell, yes. With the rest of the day free, I sure as hell wasn't staying on Earth. This was the real advantage to being an Ambassador—the total freedom to travel offworld, even off-duty. Each world and each door was only open certain hours and under guard, but Valeria had twenty-four-hour access.

"Thought I might," I said. "If it's goblin-free."

"I was going to ask that you keep an eye out for trouble, but I'm guessing you planned to."

She had a point. Even off-duty, Ambassadors never did get away from their jobs. Hardly a cause for complaint. I'd waited too many years for this, and up until I'd been handed my Ambassador's permit, part of me had still thought the Multiverse would snatch it away last-minute. I'd come close to fucking everything up enough times that now I had what I'd always wanted, the freedom was almost too much.

Not that anyone could know that.

"Got it," I said. "If there's any trouble, you'll be the first to know."

Aside from Aglaia's ridiculous debates, I almost dared to think the Multiverse was finally on my side. Until I got back to Central. Ada's older brother waited just inside the entrance hall, and glared at me when I stopped by the entrance, too. "You."

"What?"

"Where's Ada?"

I blinked. "I've no idea. I've been offworld."

"Of course you have," he muttered. "You were desperate to get her to work for you, but now she's here, you're nowhere to be found."

Someone was pissed. "What did the tech team do to you? Did a rat get into the storeroom again?"

"Funny," he said. "One of *your* team almost started a fight in the office."

"I don't know who you're talking about," I said. "You mean the guards?"

"The blond dude with the attitude problem."

"That's Aric, and someone shoved a stick up his arse. Nothing to do with me."

"He was talking shit about Ada. Said you hit her with a stunner."

Crap. "When I arrested her? I thought she was a dangerous magic-wielder. Someone had just died. I tried not to hurt her."

His eyes narrowed further. "You should stay away from her." He took a step towards me.

"Says who?" Great. Just what I needed. A fight with her overprotective older brother. I ignored the instinct to strike first and shifted, ready to block if he did throw a punch at me.

"I don't know what you said to her, but she's not herself. What happened messed her up. She wasn't in her right mind when she told you she'd join. And she'd kill me for telling you this," he added. "I'm not stupid. I know what's happening here. She's always had a thing for your type. And she always gets hurt."

I returned his glare with one of my own. "None of that is your business," I said, through clenched teeth. He took a step back. I shook my head, and stalked outside before I did something I'd regret. I hadn't asked Ada how she was dealing with what happened. I'd assumed she didn't want to talk about it. I *should* have asked what she expected from me, after she'd kissed me, but to be perfectly honest, I'd been in a state of shock that she hadn't hit me instead. Even when her defences had been down, I'd never in a million years have guessed she might see me as someone other than the person who'd ruined her life.

She's not herself.

I pressed my clenched fist to my forehead, berating myself for being such a selfish idiot. She'd survived trauma, for crying out loud. And I was the person least likely to be able to offer any kind of help. If that's what she expected…

"Kay?"

I spun around as someone else came out of Central. Not Ada. I stared for a moment in total shock. What in god's name was *Tara* doing here?

First Ada's overprotective older brother, now my ex-girl-friend. Right now, I'd take the former all over again.

Tara looked me up and down. "You're alive," she said.

I raised an eyebrow. "Really? I must have missed that notice."

Tara sighed. "I figured it was a joke. Dammit, Aric."

"Aric said I was dead?" That was a new one. "You can't really have believed it."

"Yeah. I told him he was bullshitting, but I thought I'd come here and see what happened. Seeing as I started working in admin at West Office yesterday." That explained it. As far as I knew, she'd gone travelling after we'd gradu-ated, though like everyone else in our class, she'd planned to join the Alliance. Which meant she was most likely here to fish for information on the attack on Central. Like I needed a conversation with someone who'd made it pretty clear two freaking *years* ago that she wanted nothing more to do with me.

I glanced at Central, hoping she'd get the message that I was waiting for someone else. I needed to talk to Ada. Screw her brother being there—she didn't need a freaking body-guard watching her all the time.

"Aric also said you killed two magic-wielders," she added. "Is that part true?"

Oh, shit. There was no point in hiding it, even though I figured from her expression she'd guessed already. *You didn't have a choice,* I told myself as I had countless times over the past few weeks. The shocked disgust on her face might be deserved, but she hadn't been there, and had no way of knowing what it actually felt like to be inches from death at the hands of a magic-wielder.

"I thought so," she said quietly.

I had no defence against that, because she knew what had really gone down with Aric and me two years ago. Just when I thought I'd buried it all, the past came clawing back.

"Are you done?" I said. "Because I'm waiting for someone."

She blinked. "Just wondered if it's true that you saved Central."

"If I was dead, it'd be a bit difficult," I said.

"Oh, for god's sake." She stepped in front of me, barring the doors to Central. "I'm not going to shout it from the rooftops, you know."

Yeah, but things have a habit of getting out. The last thing I wanted was to go through the whole story again. She could have asked anyone else. But after what happened two years ago, I knew she wouldn't take anything less than the truth from me. Dammit.

"Well? Did you?" she asked, hands on hips in that *give me answers or shit's going down* pose I once knew so well.

"No, whoever told you that is a liar," I said, having had about enough. "The details are classified. Read the papers."

Tara flushed a furious red. "Don't talk to me like that."

"It's true. Not my story to tell."

"Who the hell's is it, then?"

"Mine," said a voice from behind us.

Oh, damn. I knew before I turned around that it would be Ada, approaching Central with a scowl on her face.

4

ADA

I've got this, I thought that morning, as I waited in the corridor outside Office Fifteen. I fidgeted, stepping from one foot to another. I'd already spoken to Ms Weston, head of admin, aka my new boss, yesterday. Though she might be seriously intimidating, she wasn't interrogating me anymore. I had no reason to fear I'd be locked away in the Alliance's prison cells for eternity or sent back to what was left of my homeworld. Instead, if I played my cards right, I'd have a job by the end of the week.

The jet-black skyscraper in the middle of London had always drawn my attention even when it had been a place I wanted to avoid—at least, when I wasn't stealing from the stores. I'd never imagined in my wildest dreams I'd actually be getting to work here. Not that it was anywhere near as impressive up on the first floor, just a corridor lined with cubicle-like offices. Plain white paint, grey carpets. Totally mundane compared to the glossy entrance hall.

"Come in."

I drew in a breath, and went into the tidiest office I'd ever seen, with only a single piece of paper on the desk and everything else put away in cabinets. The sharply-dressed woman standing at the desk was just as impeccable. She rarely blinked, which made her a world-class expert at the kind of stare that intimidated almost everyone.

I met her gaze until my own eyes started watering.

"Ada Fletcher," said Ms Weston. "It's a pleasure to have you here."

"I'm glad to be here," I lied.

"If you're ready, of course."

"Why wouldn't I be?" Oops, that sounded too defensive. Better hold my tongue.

"After the excitement a few weeks ago..."

Yeah. So exciting, nearly destroying the world. The deaths were just the icing on the cake.

I clenched my teeth together. Apparently, self-restraint needed to be out in full force. I couldn't forget how this woman had torn my life apart in only a few words. I'd always thought it odd that I could use magic even though I wasn't mageblood, the magic-wielders of Enzar. It turned out the ruling nonmages had injected magic in its purest form into me, turning me into human adamantine, antimagic. If I channelled any amount of magic, I'd absorb the backlash myself. The power in my blood had literally destroyed worlds. And Ms Weston knew it—yet I sure didn't feel like a powerful magic-wielder when impaled on the end of her glare.

"I'm absolutely sure," I said. "I want to help people. Offworlders. It's what I've always wanted. I'll do anything."

"Good." She took a handful of papers from a cabinet and handed them to me. "Fill out these. There'll be more tests throughout the next couple of days. The timetable's there. And you'll be at the training complex later so we can evaluate your fighting skills, though as a witness to your astonishing skill battling that wyvern, I doubt it will be an issue."

I frowned. So she was praising me now? Whatever next?

What was it about Central and people being unpredictable? Kay had been the same.

Leaving the office and heading to the booth Ms Weston pointed out to me, I looked around for any sign of Kay. The other desks in the office were clean and no one seemed to be about. Several people in the department had recently been killed—by Skyla. *Don't think about that!*

Too late.

I hurried back to Ms Weston's office to return the papers to her, then stood for a few uncomfortable minutes while she scrutinised them. I'd been honest, but if she wanted to pry more details about my magic out of me, she'd have to take it up with Nell. She'd made no secret of the fact that she and the council were interested in employing new magic-wielders. True, the Alliance's mandate emphasised free will and they hadn't forced me to cooperate even as their prisoner, but Nell's paranoia wasn't unfounded. The Campbell family had strapped a bomb to my back to blow up Central, and though everyone connected with them had been locked up, I still couldn't walk down the street without glancing over my shoulder in case someone else jumped me. I'd always been cautious, but now I was almost at Nell's level. At least alertness was a valued trait in an Alliance guard.

"There's something important we haven't done," she said, looking up at last. "We need a more in-depth statement on the events of the attack on Central. Start from the beginning, from your capture at the Alliance's hands, and we'll progress from there. I'll need you to submit it in written form, of course, but I'm interested to hear your account now."

My heart sank. I didn't want to relive the whole experience again. But I'd been a fool not to expect it. Of course the Alliance wanted my take on events, especially as Kay and I were the only witnesses, and only I knew some things. Ms Weston knew I was Royal, the reason for my unusual magic, but my blood chilled at the idea of word getting around Central. Not to mention the antimagic inside me. How to explain how I'd survived the attack without mentioning exactly what I'd done?

Had *Kay* mentioned it?

I swallowed. "All right," I said. "But I'll have to start with my family. Did Kay tell you what—what we used to do?"

"Used to?"

Her sharp question jabbed at the raw wound. "Before—before everything happened, Nell and I used to help refugees from other worlds come through the Passages and make new lives here on Earth. It's what she did for me, so I started doing the same. When I was caught, we were—"

"We? This Nell is your guardian, isn't she?"

As if you didn't already know that. "Yes. And Alber and Jeth are my brothers. We were making a delivery in the Passages when a wyvern attacked us, and we ran into a patrol from Central. Kay arrested me. You know what happened after."

"There are several pieces missing. How, exactly, did you escape from Central?"

"I thought Kay would have told you. I wore an invisible earpiece my brother Jeth designed. He's working here now. Your tech team has one of them. I talked to Jeth through the earpiece, and he arranged for Nell and Skyla to meet me." Damn. I bit my lip. Shouldn't have said Skyla's name.

"Skyla," she said, not missing a thing. "She was the one who infiltrated Central, I believe?"

I nodded. "She fooled all of us. Anyway, they got in, and we escaped."

"Through attacking our guards." Her tone was even, not accusatory, but I fidgeted all the same.

"Uh… Skyla used magic, and it must have been amplified because the Balance was tipping."

Ms Weston reshuffled the papers. "Yes, I gathered. Skyla,

or Ellen as she called herself, has caused us the most trouble of all, because she did the apparently impossible. Never has the Alliance been fooled in such a way. You might have noticed when you were checked on entry that we now include a scan for illegal magical materials. Even bloodrock solution would not fool the test. Nor your... devices."

Of course they knew about Jeth's earpieces and Chameleon devices now. I'd been stripped down for weapons already and they'd used some scanning device. They knew me as a magic-wielder, of course, but bloodrock was a substance used externally and was nigh on impossible to spot even if you spent a lot of time in close proximity to people using it. Some offworlders used the bloodrock solution to appear like they were from Earth. Some wanted to blend in, some were afraid of being caught, and others just wanted a new face to go with their new life. But Nell had never ordered my brothers and me to do that. It had never really bothered me that I didn't look like I was from anywhere on Earth, and only my eyes were covered out of necessity.

"Naturally, we've scanned all our staffs' backgrounds following the incident. If you become our employee, then you will be subject to the same. Your guardian will have to register as an offworlder, that would of course have already been taken care of if not for the circumstances—don't look so alarmed, Ada. She is under our protection, as are you."

Somehow, I doubted Nell would be particularly thrilled to hear that.

"We see it as our duty to helpless victims of violence."

I had to fight to keep my face straight. Had she even seen Nell? Helpless was *not* a word anyone would use to describe her if they wanted to keep all their teeth. As a survivor of the Empire, she was the bravest person I knew. And she hadn't told me all the details, what she'd really sacrificed for me.

As she'd told me over and over, some things were better forgotten.

"We will not, however, entitle you to special circumstances."

Huh?

"It goes without saying that you'll have to follow our rules. You've signed several confidentiality agreements. That means what you used to do—travel through the Passages at will, talk openly about dangerous magic sources like bloodrock in public—will have to stop."

"Of course." I gripped one hand with the other to hide the fact that they were shaking with sudden anger. Did she think we'd go gallivanting off through the hidden Passage again after we'd nearly died there? As for the bloodrock, I could count the people who actually knew the name on one hand. Nell and I were careful, always. "Skyla's dead," I said, the slightest tremble in my voice. "No one else here would... would they?"

Ms Weston's eyes flashed. "Central is secure, but I'd advise you to be incredibly careful discussing anything related to magic sources outside of the Alliance, especially amongst offworlders."

Anger flared, and I had to bite my tongue to keep from saying something stupid. Of course I knew the Alliance was, for all its good intentions, neck-deep in old prejudices, but could she really forget so easily the person who'd murdered people here had been from *Earth?*

"You are twenty-one, aren't you?"

I nodded.

"That's our minimum age requirement, but age doesn't matter to the Alliance as much as your ability to do the job. Most novices go through at least a year of training first, but your experience gives you an advantage. Not as much as an

Academy graduate, of course. They tend to skip the first two years and climb the ranks quicker."

I'd figured that much, since Kay had got promoted within only a few weeks of joining, but then again, he was a Walker. Related to the organisation's founders and one of the council members. Not to mention he'd helped save Central.

"You know Kay Walker, don't you?" she asked, like she'd read my mind.

"He helped me. And my family." Well, that was the simplest way of putting it.

"I know." Her stare cut right into me. "Given what the two of you experienced, it's only natural that you'd form an attachment. But I want to make it clear that in this office, you will conduct yourself as a professional. It's none of my business, of course, what happens outside. And there is no preferential treatment here, regardless of what you may have accomplished."

Anger flooded me. If she thought I could quietly forget about how we'd survived hell, then she was sadly mistaken. And "preferential treatment"? I hadn't expected to be treated as a celebrity. I just wanted a freaking job.

I forced out the words. "I understand."

"Good."

More paperwork later and she handed me over to a young woman who smiled at me, to my astonishment. First friendly face I'd seen in Central.

"I'm Amanda," she said, tucking a blond strand behind her ear. "I'll be overseeing your training here. You've met my sister Danica already—Ms Weston."

They were related? I'd never have guessed. "I'm Ada," I said.

The training complex was two streets down from Central. From the outside, it might have been any generic building, but the high fence surrounding it kept out curious onlookers, and had the Alliance's logo imprinted on the gate. Unlike Central, it succeeded in averting the attention of the tourists, though I'd spotted a group of rainbow-haired, camera-carrying individuals hanging about near the road alongside Central. Possibly trying to snap a picture of the trail of devastation a wyvern had left there when it had attacked Kay and me.

"So what'll I be doing?" Behind the translucent glass doors to the training complex, I couldn't make out a whole lot. "This place is for Alliance members only, right?"

"Yes, it's essentially a gymnasium with free entry for Alliance members only, with a few enhancements. We'll be testing you in the simulation chambers." Amanda swiped her key card in the door to gain entry.

"Simulations?"

Amanda nodded. "Klathican technology, custom-made, and it costs the Alliance a small fortune to maintain. Come with me."

She led me through the reception area into a corridor, turning left to descend down a set of stairs. Muffled shouts and crashes came from below, but when we reached the lower corridor, nothing but doors lay on either side.

"Here's a free booth." She pushed open one of the doors. A windowless room greeted me, and claustrophobia kicked in without warning as the image of an empty warehouse flashed before my eyes. I swallowed back the panic clawing my throat. *You're not there. You're safe.*

I followed Amanda into the room. The walls were made of an odd reflective material, as was the floor, which was soft under my feet. I poked it with a foot, experimentally.

"That's so you don't injure yourself when you're caught in the simulation. Try to keep the room's dimensions in mind. I can't count the number of times someone's run right into one of those walls and freaked themselves out. It won't hurt, especially with your guard uniform on, but it can be a little jarring. The simulation's meant to be all-encompassing. The technology's sensitive to the material of your uniform, so you just need to clip this over your head to get the full experience. If you want to fight with weapons, wear these gloves."

She handed me a pair of gloves made of a thin material, and the smallest, most lightweight helmet I'd ever seen. I took it hesitantly, flipping it over to examine the shiny panelling on the back. Jeth would have a field day here. *Holy hell, this is awesome.* "Wow. So this is used for training?"

She nodded. "I'm told you have extensive hand-to-hand combat training already? You can fight non-humans as well as human opponents, right?"

"Yeah, I took martial art classes, but I learned most of it from my guardian in practise. She taught me how to take down most of the monsters in the Passages. And I can kill a person with my bare hands," I added. "But I've not actually done that..." *No. Magic took care of it for me.*

"Well, you're far ahead of most new recruits, aside from the Academy graduates, of course. Though the lesson even people with training often fail to grasp is that as an Alliance guard, the majority of your opponents are going to be much bigger and stronger than you are and have external protection. The best way to win is to outwit them rather than relying on brute force alone, though this is a case where your size and speed is also an advantage. You're small and fast, and the larger monsters would have no chance of catching you, as long as you don't let them drive you into a corner. Use the enclosed space to your advantage."

"Okay. So it's the same in simulation as it'd be in real life? The monsters seem... real?"

"Crude Earth terminology would call them holograms, except they're solid and mimic the behaviour of their real-life counterparts. Essentially, it works like an advanced version of a touch-sensitive video game, except it also mimics sensations as well as sight. The room itself is made of an extra-sensitive material that adds to the realism of the experience. Pretty impressive, am I right?"

"Yeah, absolutely," I said, and meant it.

"Want to give it a go, then? I should warn you, it might feel a little uncomfortable if you get hit, but it isn't real, however it might seem. If you're killed in a simulation, it'll restart itself. Happens to everyone at some point. It's important not to panic."

"I'm good," I said, with more certainty than I really felt. You could *die*? Even if it wasn't real, the idea gave me chills.

Drawing a breath, I put on the gloves and then the helmet. Darkness flooded my vision, blanking out my surroundings, except for my own body, and it was seriously weird to see my hand floating in front of me in empty space. Except the space wasn't empty anymore. I stood on the edge of a cliff, mist rising in front of me and obscuring what was on the other side. Nothing else but hardened ground beneath my feet and cloudless blue sky above. Kind of spooky. In fact... I took a step forward, unnerved when my foot kicked a loose stone and I felt the movement, heard it clatter on the ground.

Jesus. This is all an illusion?

"Oh, it's stuck again," said Amanda's voice in my ear, startling me. "Stupid loading screen—hang on."

Scenes flicked on and off before my eyes, like changing television channels. Fields, mountains, cities. And then a gleaming square, like a computer screen, appeared in front of me. Menu screen. When I lifted my hand, it was like operating a touch screen, scrolling through a list.

Holy wow. Alber would love this.

Following Amanda's instructions, I navigated my way through various menus and screens, and set up a basic combat scenario. You could customise according to what kind of opponent you wanted to fight, whether you had weapons or not, even change the setting.

My heart drummed in anticipation as the wide corridors of the Passages unfolded around me.

"Pick your opponent," said the overhead voice.

They must have every possible opponent from every universe logged in here, from humans to semi-humans to monsters. Rated according to difficulty level. It came as no surprise to find wyverns amongst the top level.

"Don't overestimate yourself. Remember, this simulates a real-life scenario. It *feels* real, and it'll take as much a toll on you as a real battle with one of those creatures would."

I'd beaten a wyvern, but I'd fought alongside two other people and it had already been injured. I didn't want to die, even in virtual reality.

"That's not to say it's impossible, but you want to get the most out of the experience. Don't do anything you aren't ready for."

"I've fought these things most of my life," I said. "I reckon I can handle this." And I selected a certain pain-tripping concrete monster.

The Passages shifted, warping before my eyes. And there... was a monster.

A chalder vox towered over me, seven feet of concrete-like skin, four tree-trunk legs, and five brutish arms. Drool dripped from a mouth of curved tusks, and manic pain-crazed eyes spun, resting on me. A familiar scenario. I relaxed into the fighting stance that came naturally from years of practise. A dagger appeared in my hand, and although I knew it wasn't real, I could actually feel its shape in my hand. But there was one thing I'd expected to feel even though rationally, I'd known I wouldn't. Magic.

I missed it almost more than I missed my old life. But I

couldn't use it again, not after it had taken me hostage, used me, almost destroyed the Earth. I'd been learning to defend myself ever since I was old enough to throw a punch, magic or no magic. Besides, killing this particular monster was easy. Just get to the weak point.

"Remember it's not real," said Amanda, through the headset. "The simulation's made for ground fighting. Jumping too high tends to confuse the system."

Oh, crap. I couldn't try my usual manoeuvre, not that I could jump six feet in the air without a magic boost anyway. Still, I had all the tools at the ready. As the monster lunged, teeth snapping, I ducked to avoid it. The sound and sensation of teeth just missing my feet was disarmingly lifelike. I crawled between its legs, forcing it to lumber around to find me. As its head bowed, I seized my chance to throw my dagger at the neck, but missed.

"Don't throw away your weapon!"

Damn. I'd relied on magic to get around that obvious error. Stupid mistake to make.

A new weapon appeared in my hand, and we danced around each other, me mostly crawling, as forcing it to keep low was the only way to reach the weak point.

The chalder vox lunged again, and I dodged, backflipping to land on its head. Quickly, I drove the point of the dagger in before gravity caught up and I fell to the ground. At least I landed on my feet.

"Nicely done," said Amanda. "Kay was right. You're a natural."

I grinned. *That's more like it.* I was where I belonged.

Also: Kay had said that? I hoped Amanda would think my flushed cheeks were a result of the exertion.

"Let's try again, okay?"

Simple, I thought, and then my heart started beating faster when I reached a certain name on the menu.

Dreyverns. Goblin-like monsters which had almost killed Nell. They worked in packs to overwhelm you, but as long as you disarmed them fast, a human could take on several of them at once. Three five-foot-high, scaly creatures wielding wicked knives appeared before my eyes. Grasping my own weapon, I faced them down, delivering a kick that sent the knife spinning out of the leader's hand. I grinned as it pierced the foot of another dreyvern. *Ha.*

The other one waved its knife at me, and I feinted a strike and then went for its weapon. Not quite fast enough. The blade grazed the top of my hand, and the sudden flare of pain jarred me so much I froze—*it's not supposed to be real!* And the second dreyvern stabbed its dagger into my shoulder.

Blunt agony tore through my body. I struck back with my knife, but my arm felt limp, heavy. Shallow breaths came too fast, and instinct warred with what my senses were telling me. *It's not real.* But it *felt* real. Every stab of pain.

A voice echoed through my head, barely restraining a laugh: *You're gonna kill worlds, Ada.*

The thud of a body hitting the wall of a warehouse. Sobbing. The world caving in—

Gasping, I ripped off the helmet, dropping to my knees. Lucky the floor was padded. My hand jumped to my shoulder, but the pain had disappeared when I'd taken off the helmet. Though the echo remained, as though my mind needed a minute to grasp that I hadn't actually been stabbed.

"Holy shit," I whispered. *Breathe.* I had to remind my lungs taking in air was kind of necessary. My pulse raced, and light-headedness swept through me.

"Ada! Are you all right?" Amanda's voice came from nearby.

"Oh. Sorry, I freaked out when I got hit. I'm okay." Somehow, I kept my voice even. My heart still beat too fast.

"Happens to the best of us. You did well for your first time."

No. I didn't. I shouldn't still be freaking out. It was weeks since that day. I was safe. Delta and the others were gone.

Thanks to me.

Every muscle ached when I left the complex later. When caught up in virtual reality, I lived in the moment, and the sudden energy drain came as a shock. At least I didn't have any bruises from getting hit. Which was more than I could say from Nell's over-enthusiastic combat lessons. Still, Alliance guards weren't supposed to panic when faced with monsters. I'd *never* panicked before, not even the first time Nell had taken me to the Passages and we'd run into a couple of dreyverns. I'd kicked one of them in the head, and Nell had had to drag me away.

Eight-year-old me was more hard-core than twenty-one-year-old me, apparently.

I headed back to Central to meet Jeth. But there was someone else I wanted to see, too. I didn't know if he'd be there, and god knew it'd be all kinds of awkward if my brother saw us together, but after the shit day I'd had, I wanted to. Though I hoped he wouldn't find out about how I'd screwed up in the simulations. I gave myself a mental shake, hoping to displace the lingering shame and anxiety. I didn't quite succeed.

Pull yourself together.

The gates were open as people were driving home, so I crossed the car park, heartbeat kicking up. Someone stood just outside—a dark-haired guy I recognised instantly.

I stopped. He was talking to a tall girl dressed in Alliance guard gear, her long auburn hair tied back, and her pretty face twisted in a scowl.

"Just wondered if it's true that you saved Central," she was asking.

"If I was dead, it'd be a bit difficult," said Kay, in the offhandedly sarcastic manner that had irritated me so much when we'd first met.

"Oh, for god's sake." Her scowl deepened. Common sense told me I should back away and not get involved, but curiosity won. "I'm not going to shout it from the rooftops, you know." Now she moved between him and the front doors to Central. "Well? Did you?" she asked him, hands on hips.

"No, whoever told you that is a liar," said Kay, in icy tones. "That information's classified. Read the papers."

The girl flushed, eyes bright with anger. "Don't talk to me like that."

Kay just shrugged. "It's true. Not my story to tell."

"Who the hell's is it, then?"

"Mine," I said. And then wanted to bury myself in a hole as Kay turned to look at me. The expression on his face suggested he wanted to do the same thing.

"And you are?" From her tone, I might have been one of Cethrax's ten-foot long worm-creatures.

"A friend." Or something. "What the hell is your problem?"

"My problem's with him." She jerked her head at Kay, whose eyes narrowed. "Not you. So you had something to do with the business at Central?"

"What's it to you?" I folded my arms and gave her my best Death Stare. "You keep looking at me like that and I'll give you a real problem."

Out of the corner of my eye, I saw Kay completely failing to hide his amusement. Damn him.

"I'll do whatever I like," she said. "Word of advice: don't trust anything he says. I'm done here."

She stalked off. I glanced at Kay, who was no longer smiling.

"Angry ex-girlfriend?" I queried.

"Something like that."

We looked at each other. Awkward, not at all how I'd pictured our—reunion? It had only been a couple of days, but today alone felt like it had lasted a lifetime.

"So is this likely to be a common thing?" I asked, breaking the silence. "Did you leave a trail of broken hearts behind you at the Academy?"

He raised his eyebrows in incredulity. "That's what you think?"

"Well, what did you do to upset her so much? Wait, I don't think I want to know."

"We broke up *two years ago,*" he said, the slightest edge to his voice. "Apparently, Aric's been spreading rumours that I'm dead. If you weren't so quick to jump to conclusions, I'd have told you."

I folded my arms. "Oh, that's right, try to make *me* feel bad. Hang on. No way." I laughed, more in surprise than anything. "*She* ditched *you?* Oh, my god."

I pressed my hand to my mouth, sorry for laughing already. Because I might not be an authority on the subject, but I knew enough to know being dumped hurt like a bitch even if the relationship was casual. I'd been on the receiving end of *that* conversation more than once. *Idiot.* It wasn't the first time I'd got completely the wrong end of the stick.

Kay shook his head, and started to walk past me, towards the gates.

"Hang on." I spun around, hurrying after him. "Sorry, that was tactless. I'm just... Ms Weston's been tormenting me all day."

"I did tell you what to expect, didn't I?"

Ouch. "Yeah, I know. She thinks I'm going to cause trouble."

No response. Kay turned left out the gates and I hurried to keep pace. We passed the bright-haired tourists again, who were now arguing with one of the guards. It sounded like my guess that they'd been trying to snap a photo of monster claw marks on the road around the back of Central had been spot on.

"Yes, I know I did end up causing trouble," I muttered, after we'd crossed the road and he still hadn't responded to me. "But—come on. I said I was sorry."

"It's becoming a habit."

Ouch. Again. "For crying out loud, slow down!" Gritting my teeth, I marched after him across the road.

"Don't you have to meet your brother?"

Damn. "I just thought... wait." I dodged another group of tourists, who appeared to be angling for a close look at Central. "Where are you going?" We'd turned into the street to the Alliance's training complex.

"To beat the crap out of virtual monsters," he said, without stopping. "And not think about bloody centaur politics."

"Centaurs?"

"You don't want to know."

"That's becoming a habit, too," I retaliated. "Quit deflecting my questions. I don't want to argue with you."

"Well, there's a simple solution, isn't there?"

I stopped, speared by the genuine anger in his voice. Without looking at me, he used his key card to open the gate. And went inside.

The fury drained out of me, making me feel even more tired than before.

And that's how you ruin everything, Ada.

5

KAY

s opposed to beating up monsters, I felt more like beating my own head against the wall. *Dammit, Kay.*

Instead, I fired up the highest setting on the virtual training menu, and an eight-foot-high, winged lizard exploded into life in front of me. The wyvern slammed its tail down with a noise that never failed to surprise me at how lifelike it sounded. Its fangs were bared and wicked-sharp claws gleamed white. One dagger versus twelve claws. Seemed a fair match.

I'd killed dozens of these things in simulation—as opposed to reality—since the real-life version had nearly killed me. The sure-fire way to deal with fear was to face it head-on, and kick the crap out of it. Worked for me.

Except I wasn't dealing with it, really, I couldn't help thinking as I dodged the wyvern's claws, spun and kicked and stabbed the dagger point through the weaker joints in its thick armour. I was running away. I'd completely panicked when Tara had brought up how I'd killed those magic-wielders—one of whom had been Ada's friend. Ada had used magic against others in self-defence, not with the intent to kill like I had, and she most likely wanted to forget the whole experience. But I couldn't afford to, not if I wanted to stop it happening again. Just the thought of her looking at me like Tara had made me feel sickened and angry with myself, even though I was jumping to conclusions as easily as she had. I didn't know Ada well at all, but maybe it was for the best she didn't know *me*. She'd suffered more grief than anyone should have to at the hands of the Alliance already.

Damn Tara. And Aric. Of all versions of the story about the attack on Central, I hadn't heard that one before... obviously. It was a pretty stupid lie. Probably, he'd just wanted to wind both of us up. As for what the hell he'd even been doing over at the West London Alliance branch, I had no idea. Let alone the tech office. I was pretty sure the moron could barely operate a communicator.

The wyvern lunged for me, I drove the dagger into the roof of its mouth. Right into the brain. Red blood drenched me, and I staggered back as the illusion disappeared in an instant. Breathing heavily, I let the loading screen fade so I could reassure myself I was still here in the booth, not in a simulation anymore. I wondered how Ada had dealt with her first experience here.

Why the hell did you say that to her?

Just when things might actually have been going my way for once, I had to wreck everything, with more efficiency than the way I'd crashed that blasted hover bike. Thanks to the Aglaian crisis, I'd be lucky to run into her again anytime soon, and if I did, she'd turn the other way. And her dick of a brother hadn't helped. *She's always had a thing for your type. And she always gets hurt.*

"Goddammit," I said to no one in particular, fiddling with the helmet so I could wipe the sweat off my forehead. Pity this simulator didn't come with custom settings so I couldn't make a virtual copy of Aric appear and punch it in the face.

I launched another battle sequence before the adrenaline wore off. The Academy's training had prepared me to fight human opponents, and I'd learned how to break a person long before I'd needed to use it in real life. Striking first was second nature. But magic was a different story. I wanted to go up against a magic-wielder, but there was no option for that here. Not even advanced Klathican tech could simulate something so exact and yet so unpredictable. But now I was going to be spending time on Aglaia, I needed every advantage I could get. Even after what happened. If I'd made an effort to research magic rather than avoiding it, maybe I'd have been able to stop the Campbells before they'd tried to use Ada to blow up Central.

No. I couldn't afford to be blindsided like that again.

Aglaia was going to drive me freaking insane.

The inaugural meeting had been going on for three hours, and so far there'd been five threats of bodily harm and seven high-volume centaur arguments. I expected someone to flip the table over next. There was little the Alliance could do, so we'd been stuck in the role of spectators for the past two days. The council told Raj and me we had to be there because if we left the centaurs to it and they solved the leadership issue, the first thing they'd do was complain that the Alliance hadn't deigned to show up. And if the situation went bad, we had to be the first to know. I got the impression we Ambassadors were there to act as bodyguards to the council if the centaurs *did* decide to flip the table over.

Nothing quite so interesting happened the first two days. Once I'd memorised the names and titles of the council members from the various worlds, I joined Raj in playing solitaire on my communicator under the table. By the look of it, half the new Ambassadors had the same idea. But by the second day, I had the distinct impression one of the Aglaian mages was watching me.

The mages sat in a line, serious-faced and robed according to status. At first, I figured the guy was staring at me in disapproval for screwing around on my communicator instead of at least looking like I was paying attention. He was probably twenty years older than me, and had the tanned skin and sharp ears of an Aglaian. His pale grey eyes were ringed with black, noticeable even across the room, because he was definitely staring at me. Like the other council members, he wore a ceremonial robe, blue, which represented a lower rank. I'd never seen the mages use magic, of course—no one would risk it in front of the centaurs.

Still, curiosity got the better of me after two days sitting in the wood-panelled room with a bunch of stuffy old council members and argumentative centaurs. I hung back after the meeting, watching the mage out of the corner of my eye. Sure enough, he approached me, skirting the wooden table. The council hall lay on the brink of centaur territory, so its simple features were in keeping with the centaurs' liking for everything to be close to natural as possible—in contrast to the humans, whose technologies and magical enhancements dominated everything.

"Is there something I can help you with?" I asked, in Aglaian.

"Perhaps. You're a magic-wielder, aren't you? It's in the eyes."

It is? I'd never thought about it that way before. The image of Ada rose in the forefront of my mind—specifically, her blinding white eyes with dark circles around the pupils as she'd unleashed her final attack. They'd taken her lenses out for a reason. Perhaps it *was* linked to her power.

Perhaps that explained why I hadn't been able to bring myself to look in the mirror for months after the experiment. I'd put it down to the fear of seeing another person entirely staring back. Someone who wasn't quite human anymore.

Ignoring the chill creeping up my spine, I said, "Yes, I am. Is there a reason you wanted to talk to me?"

Raj stood just behind me. The council were in earshot, but I'd guessed they'd inferred from my being on this mission that I was a magic-wielder, anyway. That didn't particularly bother me now. No Walker had ever been a magic-wielder, as far as I knew.

"Your name?"

"Kay Walker." His face betrayed no recognition of the name, which made a change.

"I am Ikor, and I merely wanted to ask if you are aware of how magic functions on Aglaia, and to offer to show you... if you are willing."

"That would depend," I said, "on what you're offering, exactly."

Why would an Aglaian mage be interested in someone from Earth? It wasn't illegal to *talk* about magic, and certainly, mages on Aglaia stuck religiously to the no-harm rule—even using a level one shot on a person was a crime— but I wasn't taking any chances. Mages didn't just offer help to offworlders.

"I am curious to meet an Earth magic-wielder. That is all."

Yeah. Sure it is. Did he know I wasn't a conventional magic-wielder?

"Right," I said. "Well, I'm here as Ambassador, and this is definitely not something that fits in with our purpose here. Academic interest aside, I've no desire to be drawn into mage politics. Given the circumstances, I'm sure you can understand why."

"Yes… it's unfortunate. Let me assure you I have no ill intentions towards the Alliance. But the fact remains…" He lowered his voice. "There is something wrong with magic on Aglaia. There has been for some time. As I'm sure you know, the Balance recently shifted, and for us, magic's power lessened as it was pulled towards Earth. Now it should be back to normal. But it is not. And, as much as it pains me to admit, the mage council is unable to determine why. Aglaia has few connections offworld, and none with offworld magic-wielders. It's possible that a non-Aglaian magic-wielder would be able to do what we cannot."

"I don't think so. As I said, my interest is purely a theoretical one. Earth is low-magic, so my experience is limited."

"We will see," said the mage. "I am sure we'll meet again."

And he strode away, robes sweeping behind him.

I turned to Raj, eyebrows raised. "That was dramatic."

"That was *suspicious*," he said, as we followed the rest of the council down the wood-panelled corridor. "Don't trust him."

"I'm not an imbecile."

Still. Was there really something wrong with the magic on Aglaia? The disturbance to Earth's magic levels the Campbells had pulled off was bound to have a ripple effect.

"I know that, Kay. Just be careful with these mages. They're not out for the Alliance's best interests. Or ours."

"Yeah, I got that much," I said, opening the door outside. It led onto a walkway linking the island to the forested mainland. Humans on Aglaia primarily lived on island-states, while the forests were the centaurs' home. No signs of habitation, but as far as I knew, the centaur tribes lived in camps hidden from sight. Though few humans dared to venture anywhere near their territory, old paranoia ran rampant.

Thick oaks closed in around us, the forest swallowing us in an instant. Five million hostile horse-men were out there, which didn't help the feeling of being boxed in. The council walked in close formation, and it was suffocatingly warm in our magicproof gear, but at least we wouldn't be caught off guard if the mages turned hostile. Though it was more likely to be the centaurs. Frankly, I was amazed they hadn't struck back against the Alliance already for interfering in their debates. It was pretty clear Aglaia's membership renewal in the Alliance would be postponed on the centaurs' side until they'd resolved the dilemma.

But Aglaia's mages intrigued me. An entire world where every human was on more or less equal standing as far as magic went didn't seem possible in my own experience, which I knew was limited. I shouldn't even have magic, after all.

"You've talked to the mages before?" I asked Raj.

"Not in person," said Raj. "Just in cross-world meetings. They aren't deep enough in the Alliance to stir up offworld trouble, but this is exactly the kind of situation we want to avoid. Now the Alliance is involved in their business, like it or not."

"Par for the course," I said. The Alliance's policies stopped anyone directly intervening in offworld affairs without prior permission, a necessity after so many worlds had suffered permanent damage as a result of exploitation of their resources. Like Valeria. For all the sophisticated technologies they had, half their main continent was a wasteland. Aglaia had only two doorways, so opportunities for interaction with other worlds had been limited, but that didn't mean there weren't people in the Alliance with a vested interest in their territories.

"At least they're one degree friendlier than the centaurs," I added.

"True," said Raj. "I think they just enjoy disagreeing with every comment made by a human. I'm sure most of them don't actually want a war. If all five million centaurs hated the Alliance, there'd never have been a majority vote to join."

"Yeah, I thought about bringing that up at the meeting, but I didn't like to use the word 'naysayers'."

Raj laughed, then abruptly scanned the trees either side of the path like he expected a horse-man to appear and throw a spear at us. I'd already checked we were too far away to be overheard, of course.

"Save it till we're back at Central," he said, crouching to pick up a loose stone. "This isn't a world we can trust. Certainly not as far as magic goes. Sure, they aren't overtly hostile with it, but if it gives an advantage…"

"Same can be said of most worlds," I said. "Humans, even. Hell, all species to some extent. It's that or die out. Survival."

"Hmm." He gave me a sideways look, tossing the stone into the air and catching it in one hand. "I have an inkling you have more than a theoretical interest in Aglaian magic, Kay. Doesn't have anything to do with the reason you're being so uptight about what really happened in the attack on Central, does it?"

Great. I'd thought I'd got away with being vague. Raj wasn't one for probing questions, because it was a common agreement that the best way to survive as an Ambassador was not to ask unnecessary questions.

"Maybe I just want to be prepared in case it happens again," I said. "It's pretty clear Earth's under-prepared as far as magical assaults go. And what are you doing with that?" I indicated the stone, following the motion as he caught it again.

He shrugged. "I collect tokens from other worlds. Might as well get something out of the experience apart from a national record at solitaire." He tossed the stone into the air once more. It looked no different from an Earth one, but I didn't question it.

"Where'd you learn Aglaian, anyway?" he asked.

I should have seen that one coming, too.

"Tutoring." Of the offworld languages I spoke, it was probably the most obscure, but in hindsight, I'd figured out that most of the tutors I'd had over the first sixteen years of my life had concentrated on new Alliance worlds, or soon to be members. "You don't speak it?"

"Nah. I speak six others, but I never figured I'd be watching centaurs argue. Most of my other missions have been a little closer to home." He pocketed the stone. "Earth doesn't normally have so many representatives involved in these kinds of missions. It's a sign, I think. Offworlders across the Multiverse have their eyes on us now, and it's not a good thing."

"Never is, in my experience," I said. "So they're watching in case Earth screws up again and waiting to make a move? Where'd you hear that?" I hadn't, and I always kept on top of the Alliance's latest. But then, I'd never have pegged Aglaia as a threat.

"I was on Valeria not long after the attack happened. Power shifted there, after the Campbell family got taken out. They didn't just trade with the Alliance, there were other Earth people involved. Rich tycoons, mostly. And there were some odd rumours about volatile offworld substances going missing."

"Yeah, I saw some of that," I said. "Those ravegens last week got hold of some. Turned themselves invisible."

"Damn."

"I know," I said. "See, that's what we ought to be dealing with."

"You want to be where the action is," said Raj. "I get it. There were other rumours on Valeria, too... kind of got lost in the ruckus around the Campbells, but someone mentioned witnessing questionable stunts and traffic violations on that day. Might you have had anything to do with it? Just out of curiosity, mind."

Hardly a subtle way of probing for information, but he wasn't the first. In the modified version of the story I'd been forced to relate a hundred times over the past few weeks, I'd glossed over the race through Valeria's capital to find Ada and the Campbells, and people were more interested to know about the final standoff at Central. I'd had to report to Ms Weston with the understanding that nothing I'd done on Neo Greyle would be used against me. The Balance had been at stake. No one was going to arrest me for hijacking a hover car, jumping onto a moving train, breaking into private property... even killing people in cold blood.

Cold blood. Inhuman. I was far from the only Alliance guard to commit murder that day, I knew that, but crossing that line, and with magic at that... it was like I'd taken the last, or first, step away from what I'd been before I'd been turned into a magic-wielder.

I slammed a lid on the thoughts. The past was a closed book, for a damn good reason.

"Depends what the rumours said, exactly." I kept my tone neutral, but I couldn't say I liked the idea of rumours of any kind about what had happened on Valeria—especially with Ada.

"Nothing specific. Does it matter?"

It did, if Ada was concerned. On Valeria, the Campbells had forced her to demonstrate her abilities as a magic-wielder on others who the Alliance had used as experiments. I only hoped the few people who'd known were all dead. It was a good thing her family was registered under the Alliance's protection now. But the collective offworld council had their eyes on both me *and* her, and I suspected they didn't buy into my claim that she'd just used regular magic to take out the Campbells. I'd never have offered her the job if I thought anyone in the Alliance would hurt her, but there was more than one way to harm someone.

Like the others who'd helped her and her guardian, and the Enzarian refugees. At least the London Alliance was on the way to setting up a proper shelter network of its own, helped by an anonymous donation. Now all I needed to do was convince them to give Ada's guardian, and the others her family had worked with, Alliance approval to carry on helping offworlders like they had before. I knew her family must be in financial trouble, but they'd never accept charity. Least of all from me. I still got the feeling she'd joined the Alliance from a lack of other options—a choice we'd forced on her.

I hadn't seen Ada in two days, because I'd been stuck in these blasted meetings and she'd been in evaluation. The last thing she needed was more complications, and god only knew anything that happened between us would fall into the category of "complicated". I hadn't thought ahead. It wasn't like we could just hook up and walk away, and no doubt that was the last thing on Ada's mind now I'd been a total dick to her. Yet it was still a feeble excuse not to at least apologise.

We reached the clearing, where the centaur contingent awaited us. Markos cantered over to me and said, in English, "Please kill me."

"Family reunion went well, then?"

"I would prefer to gouge out my eyeballs with a stick," said Markos. "Speaking of which, I am certain I've managed to offend most of my relatives. I forget they don't understand the concept of sarcasm."

"Now that's a tragedy," I said, and Markos laughed. Naturally, several centaurs glared at us and Raj backed slowly away.

"What's the latest from the council?" asked the centaur.

"Same as usual," I said. "Except someone seems to think magic is wrong in Aglaia. Since what happened to the Balance. I wouldn't know, but have the centaurs noticed anything odd?"

"Funny you should say that." Markos gave a sharp glance towards the other centaurs. "When they haven't been eviscerating me, they've been complaining that the mages are tampering with the weather conditions. It hasn't rained in a month."

"Hmm. That's not exactly uncommon here, is it?"

"True, but any excuse to blame humans…"

On cue, a female voice shouted in Aglaian, "Why are you talking to that human?"

How many times are we going to have to go through this? I turned to the interrupter, inferring at a glance she must be Markos's sister. They had the same long, dark hair and sharply angled features.

"Hello, Eidora," said Markos. "My sister," he added, for my benefit, switching to Aglaian. "Eidora, meet Kay. My colleague from Central, and Ambassador for the Alliance."

"Pleasure to meet you," I said.

"I cannot say the feeling is mutual," said Eidora, stony-faced.

Yeah, centaurs definitely didn't get sarcasm.

"My charming sister is, surprisingly, on board with my plan to get the hell out of here… that is, to respectfully withdraw from my role as the king."

"That's something," I said.

"Now we just need to convince… everyone else. We're working on it."

"And the king's death?" *Tread carefully,* I thought, as Eidora's gaze snapped onto me.

"No new developments," said Markos. "Yet. If we are to

determine whether magic was indeed the cause, we would need to convince the council to allow Alliance members from offworld in to check for traces. Central, for one, has the technology, does it not?"

"On Earth, our trackers can pinpoint an individual magic-wielder. I doubt it could be that specific here on Aglaia, but it would certainly help. Is there no chance the council would allow the Alliance to check? It seems an obvious solution."

"It does. But no human has set foot in our royal grounds since the last war. There would be backlash."

"That figures," I muttered. "No offence to you, but you aren't making this any easier for yourselves."

"It's none of your concern, *Ambassador*," Eidora cut in, her eyes narrowing.

"On the contrary," I said, "if magic is involved, it concerns the Balance. That affects the Alliance by default."

Eidora kicked her back hoof up, and Markos moved towards her.

"Watch it…" he said. "The human is right. You know it."

Eidora's expression could have frozen a river, but I crossed my arms and met her stare. "I'm sure the council will have come to the same conclusion."

"You'd better go," Markos said in a low voice. His sister appeared on the brink of lashing out with those hooves. I was fairly sure I could get away, but starting another argument wouldn't make negotiations any easier.

"I meant no offence," I repeated to Eidora. "The choice is yours."

"Get out," snapped the centaur.

Shrugging, I turned to find Raj staring at me across the clearing, near the doorway.

"What was that?" he said. "You're playing a dangerous game, Kay."

"I'm aware of that," I said. "Someone had to tell them."

We stepped through the doorway, and the temperature dropped about thirty degrees. Magic changed too, from a subtle presence to a persistent buzz. I didn't know the specifics of level difference between worlds. But suddenly, I *wanted* to know. Everything.

If anything would make this tedious mission worthwhile, it would be that.

Yeah. I was playing a dangerous game, all right. Next time we came here, it looked like I'd have to talk to the mage again. True, some people distrusted magic-wielders. Looked at them differently, warily. But I was used to that already.

Magic-wielder. Maybe it was about time I owned the title.

6

ADA

"**Y**ou passed," said Ms Weston.

As she spoke the two words I'd most needed to hear, the knot in my chest loosened.

"I did?" I tried not to sound too surprised. Aside from my freak-out in the simulation chamber, my grades from school were laughable and I'd almost accidentally mentioned that time I'd illegally taken Delta for a tour of London.

Note to self: don't mention illegal excursions in front of the boss.

"Yes, you did. You'll start work properly on Monday, and report to me. I'll contact you if anything changes—you might hear from Carl, too. He's the head of the guards, and it's him you'll have to speak to if you lose or break your communicator."

Excuse me? Did she really think me that careless? It wasn't as though fancy electronics fell into my lap every week.

Apparently reading my expression, she said, "It happens more often than you might think, especially when guards run into trouble in the Passages."

"Insurance against monster damage?" I tried a smile, but she didn't return it.

"Meanwhile, all communication devices are fitted with a tracker for emergencies so they can be found anywhere within the neighbouring worlds."

She went through the Alliance's rules again, and handed me a proper key card. It even had my name on it—Ada, not Adamantine, thankfully, though I knew she was well aware of my real name.

"As for patrols, we're putting you on the rota... with conditions. You'll be supervised, of course. Though the odds of running into trouble are low at the current time, we want to make sure you're ready."

Ready to go back into the Passages. My chest knotted again at the thought. *Stop it, Ada.* I'd walked those Passages most of my life. I could play my new role as guard. It was the key to seeing the worlds I'd always dreamed of.

The smile on my face was genuine as I flew downstairs to the entrance hall. Jeth was already there, and before he had the chance to ask, I said, "Good news. I'm in."

"You go, Ada," he said, and we high fived.

"I start on Monday." As we approached the doors, I couldn't help scanning the car park in case Kay showed up, but I wasn't holding out much hope. I hadn't seen him since I'd made such a spectacular idiot of myself the other day, and I gathered from overhearing Ms Weston's conversations with others in the office that he'd been roped into some kind of offworld crisis involving centaurs. It sounded a million times more exciting than paperwork, but I was one step closer to the Multiverse. I practically skipped out the door—just as Kay walked in.

I managed not to stop, but it was close. Kay now wore a different black jacket to the guard uniform, one with silver edges to the sleeves and a badge marking him as an Ambassador. I turned my eyes away before my gaze wandered further. To my own annoyance, my face heated up.

"I got the job," I said lamely, as he walked by without stopping.

His blank expression didn't change. "Knew you would."

No "congratulations", then? Though it didn't help that Jeth still hovered at my side.

"Um, I guess I'll see you next week?" I said over my shoulder.

"Yeah, maybe."

Please. Kill me. Now.

"Wow," said Jeth as we left him behind. "Friendly, isn't he?"

"He's just... I have no idea." I shook my head. "Never mind. We have to celebrate, right?"

"Actually, the tech team invited me out tonight," said Jeth. "You can come if you like."

I pulled a face. "Your tech talk goes way over my head."

"Okay, just a thought. You don't really know anyone at the Alliance yet, right? Aside from Sunshine over there?"

I laughed. "I guess not. And please don't call him that to his face."

"Oh, come on... no, you're right, it'd probably be the last thing I ever said." He ruffled my hair. "Ada, you deserve some fun in your life."

"I guess I do. Sure thing. I'll come."

Maybe it would make me feel a little less deflated. My social life up until now had consisted of sneaking around the Passages and the occasional ever-awkward work social in which I'd had to pretend to have things in common with people who'd never believe me if I told them how I spent most of my spare time. I'd barely thought about my old job recently.

"My life's so weird," I said, aloud, as we passed by a group of tourists. The ordinary street, red-brick buildings and thick traffic, smothered in the smell of car fumes, couldn't be more different to the almost-otherworldly atmosphere of Central.

And I knew which world I belonged in more.

"You only just figured that out?"

"Very funny. How're things in Technoland, anyway?"

"Technoland? Pretty awesome, actually. These guys are the real deal. And it's nice to be hero-worshiped a little."

"They're impressed with the Chameleon, then?" We stopped at the crossing opposite the tube station.

"Hell, yes. The head of tech had to lock them away because people keep trying to steal them to prank each other. I've created a monster."

"Hey, could be handy for the Alliance. Spying and so on... though it's a bit creepy." I pushed back the image of identical twins appearing from thin air in a warehouse, and concentrated on the ever-present roar of traffic and not getting hit by a maniac taxi driver as we crossed the road to the station.

"Yeah," he said. "They'd need authorisation to take them offworld, of course. There's enough trouble with invisible goblins..."

"Um... what? Did you just say invisible goblins?"

"Trouble in Valeria," he said. "Cethrax got hold of some bloodrock solution, apparently, and without the Campbells to keep them in check, they're running amok with it."

"Damn."

"I know. Hope they can deal with it."

"Sure they can," I said. The Alliance coped just fine with regular monster attacks from the beasts of Cethrax in the lower Passages. But the idea of them getting hold of blood-rock solution didn't exactly fill me with confidence. Skyla had used that to fool the entire Alliance. Then again, Central had new defences in place now.

But Nell had been the one to make the bloodrock solution. Nobody else knew how to do it. We'd given it to the Knights, who'd had it confiscated by the Alliance... so how had Cethrax got hold of it?

That's not part of your job, I told myself.

After all, I had a bigger worry: breaking the news to Nell. I'd barely seen her all week, because she'd been running errands and dealing with the Alliance representatives in charge of getting us proper Earth citizenship. Since we were technically illegal offworlders, it had taken a lot of time for the Alliance to sort out our situation, and I had a feeling Kay must have been behind some of it. And I'd repaid him by, once again, acting like a crazy person. I guess I'd never pictured an evil ex-girlfriend appearing at Central and throwing insults at me. My track record for screwing up relationships was pretty pathetic, but up until now, it had been because I couldn't afford to care too much. If I opened my heart, I opened myself up to the wrong kind of questions. As for the guys I'd been with, most had either fled from Nell's wrath or got freaked that I kept knives in my boots in case of an impromptu monster attack. My last boyfriend had ditched me when I'd showed up at his house covered in slime that wouldn't clean off, thanks to a close encounter with a swamp monster in the Passages.

Hmm. Maybe this wasn't the worst way I'd screwed up a potential relationship. It hurt a lot more, though.

Our house door was open, and Nell waited in the hallway, wearing her stoniest expression. My heart sank.

"Um," I said. "I got the job."

I didn't expect a congratulations, and I didn't get one. Nell merely made a "huh" sound and moved aside to let us pass.

"Hey, Ada!" Alber came out of his room. "Good news?"

"Yeah." I forced a smile. "I got the job."

Snap. I jumped, but it was only Nell shutting the front door. She turned around, and I felt like I was ten years old again, in trouble for climbing on the roof.

"Epic," said Alber. "When're you taking me to Valeria, then?"

"Patience," I said, impersonating Yoda. "I don't get to go offworld until I get my permit. Just help out in the office and run patrols."

"Holy hell, Ada. You're a legit Alliance guard now."

"I know, right?"

"Criminals the world over should cower in fear." Jeth grinned at me.

"Awesome," said Alber. "What're you doing now?"

I shrugged. "Jeth and I are going out later, with some of the Alliance guys, right?"

"Yeah," said Jeth, "but it's over-eighteens only."

"Not fair." Alber had turned seventeen four months ago.

"You're going with *them*?" said Nell, who had been watching me throughout our exchange.

"Yes," I said, warily. "I work there now. I want to."

"Nell," Jeth began, and Nell glared at him.

"I'm gonna back out of here," said Alber, literally backing into his room again. Jeth, too, made for his room, giving me an encouraging nod which said, *talk to her.*

I folded my arms, turning to Nell. "I know how you feel about the Alliance, but this—it's a good thing. Honestly."

"Adamantine," said Nell, all but spitting out the word.

I flinched. "Yes?"

"I named you so you wouldn't forget who you really are. Earth is not your real homeworld, and the Alliance have nothing to do with Enzar."

"You're the one who always goes on about putting it all behind us!" I snapped. "You wouldn't teach me my own language. You say we have to pretend it never happened. We live here now. This is the only life I've ever known. How can I remember a world I left when I was a baby?"

"I don't expect you to remember Enzar, but every time you put yourself at risk, there's far more at stake than your own life. The Royals would have used you as a warrior. As soon as the Alliance found you, what almost happened?"

A vice clamped over my heart. She was right. As long as we'd stayed under the radar, we'd been safe. Soon as the Alliance had caught me, word had got out and Earth had almost paid the price.

"Adamantine has another meaning: it was meant to be unbreakable. *You* were meant to be unbreakable. But the Alliance has the power to break you. And they will. They have no mercy."

I shook my head. "No…"

"They can and they will, whether they intend to or not. The reason they want you is because you're valuable to them. A commodity. Like those poor kids they experimented on."

The sharp sensation in my chest dug deeper. "That wasn't everyone in the Alliance."

"It was a *council member*," said Nell. "I spoke to Skyla's last adoptive family. They didn't believe her when she told them what the Alliance did. It was one of the reasons she left home. The Alliance injected human beings with pure magic they didn't even understand themselves."

Kay. I swallowed hard.

"And," Nell went on, "this council member—Walker—was the same as the man who issued the noninterference directive against Enzar. Odd coincidence, isn't it?"

Ice flooded my veins. I couldn't tell her Walker had also put his own son, Kay, through the same experiment. Nell despised the whole family, and nothing I said would ever change her mind. And I didn't know all the details. Someone who would experiment on children—it seemed incongruous to compare him to Kay, who'd refused to hurt me even when the Alliance thought I was a dangerous criminal, and who'd ensured the refugees from Enzar could get to a shelter even when the Alliance had shut down ours.

"You saw what the Alliance did to those children, turned them into monsters—"

The words burst out. "Stop it."

Nell's eyebrows lifted as I stepped towards her, fists clenched.

"You just called *me* a monster," I said. "Because what the Royals did to me—it's exactly the same thing."

Nell's stern composure cracked. "Wait. Ada—"

But I was already heading for the back door, before the tears choking me escaped.

"Ada?" Jeth's face peered up from just outside the door. "What in the world are you doing up there?"

I sat on the edge of the shed roof, like I was a kid again.

"Sulking," I said, as flippantly as I could manage.

"Come down," he said. "You must be freezing."

I shrugged. Now he mentioned it, the early September evening was chilly, and the sun had sunk below the rooftops, turning the sky to a fiery red.

"I made pasta."

"Oh, all right." I leaped from the roof, landing on my feet.

"I shouted at Nell, by the way. We're both in the doghouse now."

"I don't want to be in *this* house," I said. "I hate it. I hate her being so hostile all the time. It's like living with a tiger, only less fluffy."

"Pretty accurate." He paused, glancing over his shoulder

at the house. "I can afford my own place soon on the Alliance's salary, actually."

"Wait, you're thinking of moving out?"

"You know I've been planning to for a while, but my old job didn't pay that well. I couldn't save enough for a deposit. But a couple of the tech guys might have an opening for another flatmate soon. Less costly than living alone."

"That's the issue I'm having," I said. "I have zero savings. Blew them all replacing my combat boots."

"Priorities, Ada."

"Ha. Come on, the boots are an essential purchase. But really. I can't deal with being in this house much longer, especially now I'm working all the way over in Southwark. Except I don't think anyone outside the Alliance would be all that thrilled to have me as a flatmate. Can you imagine me replying to a housing ad? Warning: I keep antisocial hours and throwing-knives."

Jeth laughed, then shook his head at me. "You never know. You might make friends at Central."

"My office is full of invisible people," I said. "And I'm pretty sure my boss hates me already."

"Nah, that can't be true," said Jeth.

I shrugged. "At least she didn't call me a monster."

Jeth winced. "I wish I could say she'll get over it, but it seems to be one problem after another lately. Still up for coming out later?"

"Honestly? I kind of want to get out of here."

"I thought so."

Half of me did, anyway. The other half just wanted to bury myself under my bedcovers. But I wasn't going to let Nell know how much she'd hurt me. I knew she was looking out for my best interests, though she hadn't always gone about it in the kindest way, but there was a world of difference between *that* and calling me a monster.

I returned to my room to find my communicator on the bed, with the background image changed to a cartoonish scribble.

"Jeth, what in the world is this?"

"I upped the security settings for you, just in case," he said from outside the door.

I turned the communicator upside-down. "Seriously? What's this supposed to be?"

"A goblin. Sorry, I guess it's in bad taste—I'll get rid of it."

"Nah, it's all right," I said, "but for the love of Cethrax, never go into graphic design. Stick to hacking the Alliance's tech."

"I'll keep that in mind."

Brothers. Honestly.

I changed into a fancy top, jeans and heeled boots, not so high-heeled that I wouldn't still be able to deliver a well-placed kick if need be. Hey, this was London after all.

The city came to life at night, tower-block lights glittering like a constellation of stars. Turned out the place we were going was pretty close to Central, where the building's gleaming black shape obscured the lights and stood out against the deep-blue sky. The Alliance's headquarters always appeared to be part of another world entirely. Which was why it was downright bizarre to find what seemed like half the employees of Central, out of uniform, in a local pub... called the Blind Wyvern. *Very funny.*

Jeth and I squeezed past crowded tables and found the tech team at the back.

"This is my sister, Ada," Jeth had to shout over the noise.

"Holy hell, it's the prisoner," said one of the tech guys.

Brilliant.

"Employee now, actually," I said, but in a jokey way.

"Don't you start interrogating her," Jeth added. "No one's to say a word about you-know-what."

I felt infinitely grateful to my brother right then. He introduced me to everyone and I did my best to remember names. But soon as he left to go and get us drinks, everyone stared at me. I sighed inwardly.

"So, you're working in… what? Offworld defence?" asked one of the guys, Andy.

"No, I'm just in admin at the moment. I'll get to patrol the Passages, too."

"Ugh." Andy shuddered. "I'd rather be in the labs than risk my neck in that place."

"I like it there." Of course, that earned me a few raised eyebrows.

"You *like* being threatened by monsters?" said Andy.

"There was a secret Passage, right?" asked one of the others. Vic.

Oh, crap. "Yeah."

"And you used to go in there all the time? Alone?" asked Andy, eyebrows raised.

"Not always alone," I said. "I met—others. We helped people escape back to London."

"Holy shit," said Andy. "I thought that was just a rumour."

"Which part?"

"I can't believe anyone would ever go in that place alone. I'm well shot of it. The last week at the Academy still gives me nightmares."

"Oh, right," said Vic. "They made you guys patrol in there and set monsters loose at you, didn't they?"

"Yeah." Andy shuddered. "Mental. Imagine giant effing swamp rats trying to eat your feet."

"Do I really want to join this conversation?" asked Jeth from behind me, handing me my vodka and coke.

"Thanks," I said. "And probably not. We're talking about the Academy's crazy idea for a final exam."

"Oh, that place," said Jeth, sitting down next to me. "Did I hear something about monsters?"

"Yeah," said Andy. "I can think of exactly one person who seemed to enjoy the insanity, and he's right over there." He jerked his head towards the bar.

I turned, and my heart flipped over. Kay was there, with a bunch of people I didn't know, and in the act of throwing a dart at the wall—as I watched, the dart hit the board dead-centre. He didn't see me, but that was because he'd put a blindfold over his eyes. It was the first time I'd seen him out of uniform, in jeans and a casual black shirt rolled to the elbows, exposing the jagged scars on his left forearm from a close encounter with a wyvern. Left-handedly, he scored another bulls-eye. *Wow.*

As he took the blindfold off to general applause, I made myself turn back to the others, hoping no one had seen me gawking at him.

"Walker's son?" asked another of the tech guys.

"That's him," said Andy. "You know, he broke into the Passages two years before we were allowed to go in there."

I glanced over at Kay again, and I wasn't the only one. Everyone at the table over by the bar seemed to be laughing at something he'd said. I'd never seen him like this, totally at ease. He'd never been that way around me. The opposite, if anything.

A pretty, raven-haired girl leaned over to whisper something in his ear. From the smirk on his face, I could hazard a guess that it was complimentary.

I wanted to hit something.

"Seriously? Who the hell'd do that?" I said, louder than I intended.

"A thrill-seeking lunatic," said Andy.

"Heard he saved Central, though," said one of the others. "Unless that was…?"

Now everyone was looking at *me.* My throat went dry, so I sipped vodka and coke to compensate and ended up choking.

"I said don't mention you-know-what," said Jeth, patting me on the back. "Go pester him, instead."

"I tried," said Andy. "Wouldn't tell me a thing. You'd think we hadn't been in the same class for five years."

I said, "There's a good reason. Both of us would get into trouble with the council for talking about it. It's dangerous information."

"Yes, it is," said Jeth, nodding. "We aren't trying to screw you guys over."

"It's cool," said one of the others. "Just, you know, curiosity. Never been an attack on Central before. Thirty-odd years it's been here, right near the Passages, and there has *never* been anything like that."

"Yeah, it's totally crazy," said another guy, Vic. "Did you see the papers? Scare stories all around."

"Like alien-abduction stories," said Jeth, shaking his head. "Nothing new, really. Whenever something weird happens, it's pinned on offworld. As an actual alien, technically, I take it as an insult." He grinned. Jeth didn't look conspicuously like he wasn't from Earth. In fact, more than a few people thought he, Alber and I were actual siblings and Nell was our real mother, and we never bothered to correct them. It was only my real eyes, hidden, that marked me as dangerous.

"Heh," said Vic. "I guess you'd know about the Multiverse if you're from offworld, though, right? Hey, don't look at me like that. Everyone knows you're from a mysterious, top-secret other world. Come on, you can't expect us not to be a little curious."

"All right," I said, relenting. "How would you like being stared at all the time?"

"Wouldn't mind it, actually." He grinned. "Just messing with you. You can't blame us for being curious."

I looked at Jeth, who shrugged. "I spent an hour answering questions on my first day. Problem solved."

"If you say so." I turned back to Vic, and gave a brief account, omitting the truth about my magic, of course. And the experiments. But the rest was dramatic enough. At least the guys were friendly, and the alcohol relaxed me for the first time in what felt like forever. But with that came a new vulnerability I hadn't expected. As my limbs loosened, my first thought was that I'd be too slow to intercept an attacker, I wouldn't be able to strike back in time. *Relax. You're not in the Passages.*

The growing fuzziness in my head made shadows creep in the corners of my vision, and when someone knocked into the back of my chair, I spun around, heart hammering, and my gaze fell on Kay. Our eyes met...

I turned back to the table, ducked my head. Tried to ignore the sensation like my chest was caving in, like the walls were too close. People kept bumping into my shoulders. I hunched over, each breath harder than the last. *Calm down!*

I muttered something about getting some air and shoved my way past tables to the door, feeling more and more like a vice had clamped around my lungs, like I was in a tight space shrinking smaller by the second. I stumbled against a wall, spots crowding my vision, trapped between one breath and the next.

The walls of the warehouse closed in. Light flashed, red and purple, sparking in the air like fireworks. Alluring. Deadly. Sparking from my own hands.

The thud of a body striking a wall, falling, falling.

Silence. Apart from a soft, quiet, heartbroken sobbing.

"Ada. Breathe."

Breathe, Ada. Another day, another world, a fast-moving train, a hand holding mine—

The world was out of focus, slanted the wrong way, but when I stumbled forwards, I didn't hit the wall, but a person. Hands rested on my shoulders, steadied me, and I leaned in, close enough that I could hear their breathing. I tried to match each breath.

"Ada. It's okay. Breathe."

I knew that voice. I sucked in air, sharp and cold, and the world came back into focus.

Holy crap. I wasn't dreaming.

"Kay?" I tilted my head up, and he moved. His dark eyes were bright under the lamplight. Concerned.

"Ada." His voice was quiet, so quiet. "You're all right." Goosebumps sprang up on my arms.

"The hell are you doing to my sister?" demanded another, louder voice.

Oh. Shit.

I looked up to see Jeth glaring at Kay.

"She's having a panic attack."

"Get the hell out the way, then!"

"I'm fine." I moved, shakily, and Kay drew back, without taking his eyes off me. "It's true," I said to Jeth, who glared at Kay.

"Let go of her."

"Only when I'm sure she's all right."

Maybe I was dreaming after all.

"I can take care of her," snapped Jeth. "I'm her brother."

I shook my head, willing my limbs to unfreeze and the blank panic in my mind to turn to coherent thought. "Stop it, Jeth. He helped me." Kay let go of me, fully, as I turned to face my brother. The ground stayed steady. Jeth, however, quickly stepped in.

"I'm *fine*." I turned back to Kay. The concern in his

expression sharpened to annoyance as Jeth pulled on my arm. "Uh. Thanks. Again." Could this possibly get any more embarrassing?

"No problem. You should go home." He nodded to Jeth, who still eyed him distrustfully.

I tugged my arm free. "Jeth, I'm fine."

"Right. Good. Come on, let's go home."

I looked back at Kay. "Sorry about that," I said, swallowing. I wished Jeth wasn't here. I wished *I* wasn't here.

"You don't need to apologise." He paused. "You stay safe, okay?"

"Yeah. Thanks."

My communicator buzzed as Jeth unlocked the front door. I debated a minute then made for the shed roof again. The cold night air helped. I used to lie up here all the time, regardless of the lectures I'd got from Nell. Watching the stars just visible under the city's light pollution used to be as close as I got to the Multiverse here on Earth. I flicked on my communicator screen to find a message: *"Does it happen a lot?"* It was listed under Kay's name. He must have a new communicator code, then.

I swallowed. It was pretty obvious what he was talking about. He'd recognised my panic attack right off. I'd half thought he was with that girl who'd been checking him out at the bar. But he'd ditched her to come and help me. And now—what the hell was this?

"I guess. Sometimes." I hit reply before I lost my nerve.

This was stupid. I should know how to *breathe*, for Christ's sake. It was a fairly important part of *staying alive*. Most of the time I was fine. But when it hit me, it hit hard. Harder than any monster.

"If you're worried about patrolling, try the simulators. You're in control of the environment there."

Simulators? Walking *into* an enclosed space might not be the best idea right now. And was taking advice from Kay Walker ever a good idea? The guy didn't seem to know the meaning of fear. But unless I'd imagined it, I was sure I'd seen something when he'd looked at me in the dark. More than concern. Understanding.

It wasn't your fault, he'd said to me, that awful day. Once again, Kay Walker had taken me completely off guard. I couldn't recall anyone outside my family ever checking up on me before. Even Delta.

The pain sank in like the point of a knife. *He betrayed you.* And if I was being horribly honest, the betrayal hurt more than the fact that I'd killed him. And his family. My skin crawled all over at the idea that they'd been watching me. That they'd kept magic-wielders as *pets.* I could see why Nell kept even her friends at a distance. Did you ever really know someone's motives? Even magic-wielders couldn't read minds.

I wouldn't be that helpless again. Not ever.

I clicked off my communicator. I had to get a handle on things if I wanted to be a real Alliance guard—that much was clear. Somehow, I had to believe it would get easier. Like we always told the refugees we helped: however frightening and unfamiliar it might be to adapt after your entire life shifted, it did get easier. After I'd woken from the coma, I'd been terrified even to leave the house. But staying in was as much a trap as the nightmares. And I still knew what I wanted. What I'd always wanted. The Multiverse.

Nothing would take that away, not even fear.

7

ADA

Decked out in my new guard uniform, I discovered it was possible to feel both badass *and* scared shit-less. Carl, the patrol leader I recognised from when I was captured by the claw mark-like scar on his face, gave our small group what I assumed was a routine safety lecture. Another patroller, a big guy with buzzed-short blond hair and a pierced ear, kept giving me filthy looks for some reason. I ignored him and paid attention to the instructions on how we were to *never* use our weapons to harm another person—he seemed to be directing this at Blond Dude.

As the guy shifted, I recognised the scowl on his face. He was the bastard who'd tried to choke me when I'd been arrested, when Kay had stopped him. Aric.

That explained the glaring. I gave him one of my own.

"Use the knives only in an emergency. The stunners will incapacitate any attacker, armoured or not. They contain only three shots, however, and work only when applied directly. If you fire it into the air, there's a chance it will rebound on you. We don't want any more accidents, do we, Aric?"

Aric's expression said, *Screw you,* but he just nodded.

I wasn't overly comfortable with the stunner, but I accepted it without hesitation. It looked like a flat remote control, with a switch on the back, and the tingle of whatever magic they'd put inside it brushed against my fingers. I quickly pocketed it, hoping I'd not have to use it. Or the knife, for that matter, which was made of reinforced adamantine and could cut through virtually any armour. Kay had sliced the claws off a wyvern with one.

I tried not to think about how the flat, sharp-edged blade was made of the same material the Royals had implanted inside me. Though the knife weighed virtually nothing, its presence pressed against my arm in the sheath, ready to slide into my hand. I'd fought more monsters than I could count with my own daggers bought from Nell's offworld traders, but I'd never replaced the daggers I'd lost in the attack, and hadn't even touched a weapon since, except in virtual reality. For the first time in my life, the idea of a real-life fight didn't appeal at all. I hadn't had the chance to try out the simulators again since my disastrous first attempt. But fighting was second nature to me. I'd been raised by a woman whose response to the postman knocking the door was to get the poor man in a headlock. Instinct didn't disappear overnight, whatever happened. I just needed to calm down, get on with the job. Keep an eye out for trouble. Do what I had to. If anyone thought my mental health was in question, I'd struck off the rota. That couldn't happen. It was just a routine. No reason to assume anything would happen.

But it wasn't Cethraxian monsters I was afraid of. Nell had called *me* a monster.

Soon as we left the building, however, Carl told us to hold back. Three other guards approached, talking urgently amongst themselves, and Carl went to join them. Before I could follow, Aric moved to block my path.

"I can't believe you had the nerve to show your face here," he said. "You nearly destroyed the place."

"Want to see what else I can do?" I folded my arms with my hand resting over my dagger. Judging by the way Carl had spoken to him, he was clearly on shaky ground already.

"Keep your empty threats to yourself, magic-wielder," he said. "You're almost as bad as Walker. Trouble-making arrogant bastard."

"You're kidding me. Pot calling the kettle black, much?"

"Very funny." He took a step towards me, like he was trying to intimidate me. Okay, so he was three times my size and basically a wall of muscle, but size and strength didn't mean anything when you knew what you were doing. And I'd learned from the best—a five-foot-two woman with a killer right hook.

His fist flew, and I caught his arm before it reached my throat, twisting. Hard. As his other hand curled into a fist, I brought my knee up, and slammed it into his groin. He let out a yell, doubling over. Even through the protective uniform, that had to hurt like a bitch.

"Fuck you," he spat through clenched teeth. "You really are a psycho. Just like Walker."

Despite myself, my grip faltered, and he wrenched his arm free.

"You're off your head," I said. "You're the one who threatened *me*. And Kay isn't a psycho."

"You think you know him, do you?" said Aric, breathing heavily. "You know what happened at the Academy? That bastard tried to kill me." He straightened up, face still twisted in pain.

"I—what?" *Don't listen to him.* I glanced at Carl, but he wasn't looking in our direction.

"It's true. He used magic, and almost killed me. All because I found out he's a criminal and a raging psychopath.

And he got away with it because of the Walker family's reputation."

I took a step back, then another. *No way.* Kay might have killed people, but he wasn't a psychopath. There had to be more to this story.

"A criminal?" I repeated, clenching my fists so he couldn't see my hands shaking.

"Hell, yeah. He's like a serial arsonist or something. He'd have been in jail if the Academy hadn't found out and wiped his record clean because he's a Walker. Moment he stepped in the door I knew there was something off about him. He was *too* perfect. Top of the class in everything, and everyone worshiped the ground he walked on. It made me sick."

Some of the tension eased out of me. "Jealousy is an ugly thing," I said. "I reckon you're lying."

"Believe whatever you want. He's a criminal and he tried to kill me. He'll tell you himself, if you ask. Everyone in our class knew. Only reason they still talked to him was 'cause he ran into a wyvern right after."

I took another step back from him, wobbling like I stood on the edge of a bottomless pit.

He *must* be lying. Or mistaken. But Kay *had* almost been killed by a wyvern. I knew that already...

The clamour of voices rose, like someone had turned off the mute button on the world. And Carl beckoned us over, urgency etched on his face.

"There's been an incident in the Passages," he said. "We had to intercept several dreyverns trying to get through a door—some trouble on Valeria again. We *think* it's taken care of, but some of the guards are still back there making sure there aren't any more of them."

"I can deal with goblins." Aric straightened upright, glaring daggers at me. "Why the hell aren't we going, then?"

"There's a complication," said Carl. "Seems some got hold

of a dangerous magical substance and turned themselves invisible."

Hell. Bloodrock. It had to be. A shiver went through my whole body.

"We should head for the Passages anyway. The more of us, the better. We need to make sure they don't get through any of the other doors."

"Sure," said Aric. "Let me at 'em."

"Do I need to warn you about arrogance?" Carl shook his head. "Come on."

So the four—now seven—of us headed out of the car park, via the same back gate I'd broken in through, a lifetime ago. To the street where Kay and I had battled a wyvern, past houses now abandoned, past a massive crater in the road where I'd almost died. Where I'd taken four lives. And to a metal door set in a blank factory wall, barely distinguishable from its surroundings unless you knew what you were looking for. The static tingle of magic filled the air even before it slid open.

A door to the Passages.

Wide, high-ceilinged corridors. A maze. Ice-cold with a constant breeze, lit only by a faint blue from the walls and ceiling, like nothing on Earth. I shivered, the chill wind cutting through my new faux-leather coat. Magicproof. *It's waterproof and hides bloodstains, too,* Carl had added when he'd given it to me. Reassuring.

Magic waited for me. A static tingle ran up my arms. A constant presence like a buzzing in the ears, a breath on the back of my neck. Tempting and terrifying because now I knew just how much damage it could do.

That thought made me shiver harder, but I held my head high. Nobody spoke. It was too quiet. Even our footsteps made no sound, though my new Alliance guard boots were made for stealth. Memories crowded the edges of my mind. So many times I'd been here, listened for a whisper of another world behind a door, used magic to boost myself to strike at a monster. Guided terrified, broken war survivors through these corridors, hushed crying children. Wished that just once, I could step through one of those doors.

Now I felt like I was playing a part. Alliance guard on patrol to face monsters. *Invisible* monsters. I pushed away the memory of two identical faces appearing from nowhere in a warehouse—*for god's sake, Ada!*—and concentrated instead on the unmistakable sounds of fighting coming from ahead. Adrenaline surged through my veins, and I wished it could wash away the doubt.

"Let's go," said Carl, and we picked up the pace. We rounded a corner to find several other guards running amongst blurred shapes of small figures. Several somethings, by the look of things, and four, maybe five feet high. Sparks flew from stunners, fists hit out at nothing, and curses echoed around the corridor.

"Fast little buggers," said Carl. "Go easy, guys, and watch your backs!"

I kept on the defensive, my dagger already in hand. As we drew closer, Carl shouted out, "Use your stunners. It'll make them visible for a short time!"

Crap. So much for not using magic. I transferred my dagger to my left hand and pulled out the stunner with my right, doing my best to ignore the tiny sparks jump from the end though I hadn't activated it yet. The device was intended to subdue, but I didn't trust magic not to explode out of me again, hitting everyone nearby.

My chest tightened with every step. The stunner trembled in my hand.

The guard at the front struck out without warning, the stunner colliding with a solid target. The tingle of magic resounded as the charge hit the target, and a short figure momentarily appeared in front of us. And vanished again.

Hell. They could be anywhere.

Invisible hands closed around my throat. I hit out, my elbow striking with a *crack*. I spun around, dagger at the ready, and almost dropped it as it connected with something rock-hard.

Their weapons were invisible, too. *Crap.* I had no choice but to activate the stunner. My finger hovered over the switch. Sparks flew out, flickering around me like tiny bolts of white lightning.

I let my grip slide on the stunner, and it fell from my hand.

The goblin appeared in front of me, wide mouth stretched in a smile, and slashed with its dagger.

8

KAY

You've actually lost it, said a voice in the back of my head. As per usual, I ignored it.

After two tedious hours of more arguments, it was an unbelievable relief to finally get outside. Even if 'outside' was a deserted cliff-top, in the company of a mage who could kill me in a heartbeat.

Waves lashed against the cliff, a hundred feet below. No surviving that drop. The only way down was the steep path we'd climbed, which led back to the island where the council meeting had been held. No barrier between me and the ocean.

But then, I was a magic-wielder, too.

The mage, Ikor, wore a ceremonial coat, which for higher mages was dark blue. Aglaian fashion wasn't made for practicality or combat—with magic, it didn't need to be. I was glad the Alliance's policy was to wear magicproof gear at all times. No way was I standing near a magic-wielder, alone, without some kind of protection.

Dangerous games.

Ikor's pale eyes stared into mine. Classic intimidation tactic.

"So, what is it about magic that means we had to come up here?"

"Less chance of disturbing anyone."

"That so?"

I was pushing him. But I suspected he wanted me to.

"Very well. On Earth, you will only know magic in its crudest sense. Three levels, am I right?"

I gave a tight nod. If he wanted to pry me for Earth's secrets, he'd have to try harder.

"I was only confirming what is commonly known. Magic, in pure raw form, is energy, like in the between-world. Magic here is not like that. As a magic-wielder, I am sure you can tell."

"It feels restrained, almost." I was certain I could draw on it if need be, but none of the persistent electric buzz that followed me around the Passages existed here. In the Passages, magic was like an out-of-control forest fire. Here, it was contained. A heightened sense. Still potentially deadly— and all the more dangerous for being unobtrusive.

"That's a good way of putting it," said the mage. "It's part of the atmosphere here. That is how we can influence certain things—the weather, for instance. My role as Ambassador has made me aware that another kind of magic exists in different worlds, however. Valeria is one you're familiar with, are you not?"

"Of course." I watched him carefully. Though Aglaia and Valeria were both high-magic worlds, they had virtually no interaction, even on their councils. Aglaian mages simply weren't interested in other high-magic worlds. Perhaps they saw them as a threat.

"Magic is an energy source there, is it not?"

I weighed my chances. "Yes." He was a council member,

after all, and any other Ambassador would have answered the same. But if he pushed any further for other worlds' secrets, he'd be disappointed. No matter how curious I might be to see where he was going with this.

"In other words, it's Aglaia's opposite. Magic in distilled form is used to fuel high technology. Here, it can be used to affect the world, but cannot be *captured,* like on Valeria. It cannot, for example, exist inside a person."

Shit. He knows.

I met his gaze with careful blankness. "Your point being?"

"I hear things, magic-wielder. The business at Central didn't go unnoticed amongst the mages. Other worlds, too. There were rumours of a girl who could absorb the backlash of uncontrolled magic."

Damn. How much did he know? If it had reached a distant world like Aglaia, how far had word spread? I'd been the only witness, of course, but anyone who knew the three principles of magic could have come to that conclusion if they really thought about how things had gone down. The way Ada and I had both survived the fight with the Campbells suggested something was screwy, but the Alliance had been too preoccupied with the carnage left after the fight in the Passages. Until now, apparently.

"How odd," I said, with an indifferent shrug.

The mage's brow furrowed, like he was trying to figure out if I was lying. *Too bad magic can't give you the power to read minds, isn't it?*

"Of course," the mage said, "that would be largely irrelevant on a world where the use of such magic is illegal—it is, to use your word, restrained. I was merely interested in how such a thing worked. There are substances that can capture magic inside them, are they not?"

"I am not authorised to say anything of what may or may not have happened at Central," I said in my coldest tone.

"I would never ask you to. I only wondered at the possibilities."

Yeah, and I just wanted to learn magic for kicks.

"Right. If that's all, then I'm wasting my time here."

"Oh, I never said I have no knowledge that would be useful to a magic-wielder from a low-magic world. It's not illegal to do this, for example." He raised a hand, and the air shimmered. It wasn't as vibrant or dramatic as gathering magic energy in the Passages, but it was definitely magic.

The energy swirled around his hand, which he held in a relaxed position. How the hell did he do that, if internal magic didn't exist on Aglaia? Magic demanded to be released. If not, it would burn you from the inside out. At least, that's what I'd always believed. And it went double for people like me. Human lightning rods.

"It's a matter of control," said the mage. "The truth is, this world barely reaches the second level. Every human on Aglaia can use magic, but that doesn't mean it is *strong* magic. This world is weak in comparison to those who live on genuine high-level magic worlds."

No way. Why the hell had he just told me that? It had to be a trick. Council members wouldn't disclose information to an offworlder unless they had an ulterior motive.

"You wonder why I just told you that?"

"Anyone would," I said. "If this is a political manoeuvre, it's a poor one. Earth may be low-magic but there are people who would pay for that kind of information." Because while Aglaia was a member of the Alliance, there was no requirement that they forfeit all their secrets. One of the drawbacks of allying the worlds was the inevitable secret-exchanging and mind-games that happened behind the scenes. I wanted absolutely no part in it.

He'd just handed me a live bomb.

"Yes. Perhaps you're right."

I narrowed my eyes. *"Did* someone pay for that information?"

A pause. I'd got him.

"I did not come here to talk politics, Kay Walker. I merely wanted to give you some context. Information can be traded, fabricated. Magic is a force all on its own. To those of us it affects, it is both blessing and curse."

I said nothing. Aglaia was swimming in secrets, all right. And I was less inclined than ever to dive in.

"Try to do what I did, and control the magic. It might prove a valuable skill. I had best return to the council. We are discussing the possibility of extending our role in the Alliance—perhaps, for some of us, moving offworld. That is, in part, why I wished to know more of Earth. But the circumstances do not allow for friendly visits, as I am sure you can imagine."

That could just be an excuse, of course. I certainly didn't intend to take what he'd said at face value. I hadn't left *all* that remained of my common sense on Earth.

Still. I watched, to make sure he'd started climbing down the sloping path, before I held my own hand, palm-down, over the ground. It felt ridiculous. Yet I'd seen the evidence with my own eyes, and now I concentrated on the magic rather than pushing it away, the static charge responded to whatever magic lived in my skin, swirling around my outstretched hand. Controlled, not wild, but I couldn't help thinking of the third level lightning had flared out, striking Ellen, Skyla, dead, in a heartbeat.

Maybe I was deluding myself. But I didn't believe magic was simply a force of destruction. As the mage had shown, it wasn't even really a weapon, not in its natural state. Everyone had the tools to kill. It didn't mean they *had* to be used that way. Aglaia's mages had built an entire civilisation on magic. If a million mages could control it, then so could I.

I pulled magic into my hand, and my skin tingled instantly. I held onto it, held my hand steady though it tugged at me, an unseen force. I directed it downwards, like the mage had.

A small crack appeared in the ground. Far from the uncontrolled storm of sparks the same action would bring in the Passages.

Wait. Magic was a force, true, but I'd only ever used it in the Passages, where it was unstable at the best of times, and on Valeria and Earth when the Balance had been knocked off. That made it wild, inconsistent, barely controllable even to wielders. But in worlds like this, where it was calm, it *could* be channelled. If I worked *with* it, not against it, I'd be able to do more than strike people down and cause destruction.

I concentrated, not on the magic swirling around my hand but on the restrained presence in the atmosphere itself. And then I moved my hand, just a fraction. A nearby pebble clattered off the cliff, and the backlash wasn't even visible.

I glanced behind me and realised I'd come dangerously close to the cliff edge. My pulse kicked up, and I gave myself a mental shake. I'd spent enough time here. A steep stone path led down to the small island that hosted the between-territory council meeting building. No one was outside, though people moved on the other side of the windows. The rest of the Alliance's council had returned to the mainland via the walkway. I walked fast, alert for any danger. Hell, everything I'd just done was far from advisable. Not illegal, but reckless at best. I had the Alliance's protection, of course, but 'accidents' were easy to arrange.

I knew that all too well.

I picked up the pace, reaching the other side of the walkway. When a dark shape appeared from behind a tree, I struck first, without stopping to think.

"Damn, Kay." Raj staggered back, almost tripping over a tree root.

"Sorry."

Raj rubbed the side of his jaw where I'd hit him. "It's all right. I don't blame you being jumpy. Why in the name of all gods did you wander off alone?"

Good question. "The mage had something he only wanted to speak to a magic-wielder about." That much was true. And he didn't need to ask for specifics. Raj might be a magic-wielder, but he didn't need to be burdened with potentially dangerous information. He had no interest in politics and hadn't even commented on my name when we'd met.

Raj shook his head. "You're mental."

"Yeah, people have said that." I looked over my shoulder at the island we'd left behind. As though the mage was watching me. He might not have given any indication that he was up to no good, but blindly trusting magic-wielders was about as advisable as taking a solo mission into Cethrax's swamp.

"We have to go back, anyway," said Raj. "The council's probably done arguing with the centaurs by now."

"What's the issue this time?"

"The heir's cousins had a little disagreement. One of them thinks Markos should leave Aglaia and never come back. The other says it's his duty to take the throne. And the other's still insisting the king was murdered."

"Nothing new, then."

"One of them threw a chair."

I raised an eyebrow. "There's no hope left for the centaur race."

And right now, I wanted nothing more to do with this world. Should I should risk passing on what I'd learned to the council? I hadn't lied when I said people would pay for that information. But *which* people depended on who had political advantage at the moment, and right now, nobody knew who did. What had happened at Central had changed the playing field, brought Earth to the centre of offworld attention, and the Campbell family's imprisonment might mean others lining up to take their place.

Markos waited, but the other centaurs had gone.

"Thought you'd got lost," he said. "Is now really the time to explore Aglaia?"

I shrugged. "I was talking to someone from the council. I heard something about a chair?"

"Eidora wants the Alliance to leave us alone. My cousins want—well, at least Tryfon wants justice, while Petro just wants me gone. And Leonid is throwing the word "duty" around so much it's lost all meaning."

"Perfect harmony," I said. "Thought you wanted Eidora to take the throne."

"Yes, my uncle's in support of that. But he doesn't like me. And he believes Tryfon, he thinks the king's death wasn't an accident. Of course, there's the slight snag that only Alliance technology would be able to confirm what killed him. It goes without saying that *no* technology is allowed near royal ground. By the gods, it's like house-training a wyvern."

"And just as likely to be fatal, if this keeps up," I said, with an eye-roll. "Are you coming back to Central?"

"No. My family is probably looking for me right now, but I wanted to make sure one of the few humans I can stand didn't get himself trampled by a herd."

"Is that likely?" I asked.

"At the moment? I'd say there's a fifty-fifty chance of an attack on the Alliance. If someone doesn't find a solution soon, we might well be in open warfare by the end of the week. You two had better get out of here."

"Good advice." Raj glanced uneasily behind us. "I don't want to stay in this place another second, to be honest."

"Right. I'll see you later, then," I said over my shoulder to Markos, as we re-entered the Passages. "Watch your back."

All was silent, the others far ahead. We walked quickly even though we weren't offworld anymore. Leaving the dark corridors of the first level's furthest reach took us past the half concealed staircase to the forbidden second level. Only higher guards were trusted to patrol there. The worlds on the other side of *those* doors were at best unfriendly, at worst suicide, and Alliance interference simply wasn't feasible. I might have been an Ambassador only a few days, but I wasn't naïve enough to assume the Alliance could solve every issue. Ambassador missions failed. People got killed. Even arrangements like the one I'd instigated to help the Enzarians were always one disaster away from collapsing. They'd been desperate enough to place their trust in the Campbells, moral-free traders who'd only pretended to help the Enzarians to front their other illegal activities, like smuggling bloodrock. And when the Alliance had restricted offworld trade, they'd decided to claim something more dangerous— or some*one*.

A shout tore through my thoughts, from a corridor somewhere ahead. *Crap—there's trouble.* Raj nodded at me, and we moved into guard stance as the clamour of fighting reached us.

Shit. I had no weapon. Except magic, and I wouldn't use that here.

It was too late to turn back now. Raj shot me a grim look, and we turned the corner.

On the right, a door lay open. In the corridor, guards were grouped together, daggers swiping at empty air. No— something invisible. More than one of them. The formation broke, revealing other guards further behind—including one familiar redheaded figure.

Ada. Oh, shit.

The shadows moved. Raj swore, hitting out at a dark shadow that had crept up alongside us. Not invisible. Dreyverns—half-shadow goblins from Cethrax—had sneaked up from somewhere. Five feet high, armed with sharp knives, and sporting wicked grins. Three of them, and judging by the shadows moving behind, they weren't alone. A knife flew from the shadows and narrowly missed the guards.

They were aiming to kill.

Screw it. I made for the closest target and took out the dreyvern with a strike to the throat, bone breaking beneath the side of my palm. With my other hand I took its weapon, but it had already crumpled. Before it hit the ground, I put it out of its misery with a slash across the neck, then threw myself at the second. A third had driven Raj against the wall. I kicked it in the back of the leg, wrenched the weapon from its hand, breaking a couple of its fingers in the process, and handed him the dagger. He took it with a grateful nod, and I made for the others. And Ada, facing something invisible. She held a stunner, but as sparks flew from the tip, her eyes widened, and she dropped it.

She'd drawn the dreyverns' attention as a target, and before I broke through the clamour of guards fighting their invisible enemies, seven or more dreyverns surrounded her.

I ran through the thick of the fighting, stabbing at a shadow that tried to trail me. Another guard grappled with an invisible enemy, and the flash of a stunner's light revealed a small, hunched figure with wicked-sharp claws. Great. The ravegens, or invisible goblins, were back. And these ones wouldn't get any mercy.

The dreyverns were the most threatening right now, because they were armed. But Ada was, too, and several other guards had joined her. As I reached them, one spun around to intercept me, but too late. One strike, and it dropped its weapon. I slid the knife under its armour. Blood dripped down the short, ugly blade and glinted in the sparks from a blast of magic.

The air rippled and everyone ducked to avoid getting caught in the blast. I took advantage of the opportunity to knock down another dreyvern. As the magic rebounded, my knife found its neck.

"Aric, what did I tell you?" Carl's voice yelled from ahead. Damned idiot had fired his stunner into the air again, I guessed. No one else would be that thick-headed. Swearing, I trod on the arm of a dreyvern trying to claw its way over to me. *Get to Ada.*

She slashed with her dagger, but fear flickered behind her eyes, and she hadn't picked up her stunner again. I kicked at another goblin in the act of sneaking up on the guards from behind, and it crumpled. Ada, meanwhile, drove the blade of her dagger into her opponent's throat. She swayed a little as it fell, but stood her ground. I glanced behind, and it looked like most of the dreyverns were dead. Guards were standing up, checking injuries, moving the dreyverns' crumpled bodies.

"Ada. You okay?"

She took a step back, blinking in surprise. "Kay," she said. "I—yeah, I'm fine." She moved away from the dead dreyverns, biting her lip. Even spattered with blood, she was sexy as hell—that uniform left almost nothing to the imagination.

"This is yours." I picked up her stunner from where it had fallen on the floor.

She took it without looking at me. "Thanks. I shouldn't have dropped it."

Something was definitely up with her. But now wasn't the place to talk. We had to do something about these dreyverns.

"You're not hurt, are you?"

She shook her head. "I'm fine. Really. You're bleeding."

Huh? Oh. Dreyvern blood stained my knife arm to the elbow. "It's not mine." Wait. Blood dripped down my other arm, too. "Hmm. Might have run into one of their knives." I pushed up the left sleeve. No, it was just dreyvern blood.

"Might have? Do you not feel pain?" Ada stared at me.

"Hmm? I can't feel pain around the scars." Thanks to a certain wyvern's claws damaging the nerves in my left arm. I turned the dreyvern's ugly blade over in my hand. I didn't particularly want to hang onto it, but leaving it lying in the Passages wasn't an option. I glanced back at the others, and saw Carl in the process of crushing another of the dreyverns' weapons beneath the heel of his boot. Looked like the best idea to me, so I did the same. Ada wiped her own Alliance-issued dagger on her jacket, still wearing a slightly dazed expression.

"Are you two all right?" asked Carl. "I'm asking my team to clear this lot out, but you can go through to Central. Ada, you can go back if you like. Kay, I'm taking a wild guess that's your communicator on the floor over there."

Oh, crap. Must have fallen out of my pocket. "Tell me I didn't break it."

"Not this time. You should go."

"Right." I glanced at Ada, who still seemed out of it. My communicator lay a few feet away, but it was still in one piece.

And the door nearby was still open a crack. I frowned, stepping closer. It led to somewhere on Valeria. *Shit.* Some of the ravegens—or worse, the dreyverns—might have got through.

"Hey," I called to Carl. "We should check on this. The door was left open."

"Damn," he said. "Okay. Raj, Amanda, you two go with Kay. If they're invisible, tracking them will be difficult, but not impossible. They have a tendency to make a spectacle of themselves."

"Okay," said Raj. "Kay, you know Neo Greyle, right?"

Oh, for crying out loud. And Ada had disappeared.

"I've dealt with goblins here before," I said. "They took hover bikes last time."

Amanda, a tall blond woman I recognised as one of the staff at the training complex, joined Raj by the door, pushing it fully open.

"Looks like that's an accessible entrance, too."

He was right. Most of their Passages opened into the sky, but this one was in the back of an alleyway. Still, the hover cars and the soaring skyscrapers were familiar enough for there to be no doubt.

Damn it all to hell.

So, with the other two on my heels, I walked through the door to Valeria.

9

KAY

The alleyway dead-ended against a high fence, but the other way led out onto a road. I quickly fired up offworld maps on my communicator. A registered, unguarded doorway was unusual for Valeria, but not unheard of given that they freely let people come and go as they pleased. They weren't as open to offworlders, but the area of the Passages we'd been in was far away from anyone who might want to use the door.

Except those ravegens. This was getting out of hand.

"This is ridiculous," said Raj, staring out at the multi-layered skyways, which made the M25 look like a deserted country lane. "Place is a maze. What was Carl thinking?"

He had a point. Neo Greyle was a warren of almost-identical skyscrapers and four-lane roads, nigh on impossible to navigate without a map. While most locals were wired to the Valerian network via navigational eyeglasses—which I assumed also had a feature to stop users walking into one another, because no one seemed to actually be looking where they were going—the rest of us had to deal with wandering at random until we found something familiar. Even without the invisibility, the ravegens would have long since been swallowed up by the crowds in the time it took for us to wait to cross the road.

"If nothing else, we'll have to inform the guards at the main door." I checked the map as we reached an island in the middle of the road and the hover-traffic started moving again. "I know where that is. We can't risk them being taken unawares. Those ravegens were up to something."

"Like a diversion," said Amanda. "That might have been their plan, but they don't generally work together."

"Unless they have a common cause." I tapped a foot impatiently, waiting for the lights to change. "Like the ones I stopped last time. They were delivering contraband offworld technology parts." The unlucky ravegen I'd cornered had confessed to having business with someone, but apparently they hadn't deigned to share their name. The Campbells' headquarters had shut down and the surviving members were imprisoned, but they were bound to have other contacts. "Were you there at the start of the fight? I only came in at the end. I didn't see how it kicked off."

"We were ambushed," said Amanda. "Our patrol, and we called for backup, too. You weren't patrolling, right?"

"Raj and I were coming back from Aglaia," I said. "Got caught in the middle of it. Did you see the door open?"

"It was already open," said Amanda.

Damn. They'd got us, all right.

The lights changed. We crossed to the other side and were almost instantly swept up in a crowd. This was near the main city square, an area the size of a football pitch and surrounded by sculptures representative of the various worlds that had made their mark on Valeria's capital. Even Cethrax was represented in the shape of a vox-sized statue.

Raj stopped to stare at it. "They did check it wasn't moving before putting it in a public place, didn't they?"

"Hope so." Amanda shook her head. "Only Valeria would make a monument to a monster."

"No goblins," I pointed out. "Living or otherwise. But last time they took hover bikes—don't suppose either of you know how to operate one?"

I knew the theory now, as I'd actually read up on it this time. Plus, I'd replaced my own car, which had got clawed up by a wyvern, with an actual Earth motorcycle. Someone here in Neo Greyle had tried to sell me an enhancement to make it hover. As tempting as the idea was, I wasn't *that* interested in experimenting with gravity on Earth, where magi-tech tended to unpredictably explode.

Amanda shook her head. "I'm pretty sure that's illegal, isn't it?"

"Surprisingly not," I said. "We're authorised to be here, seeing as Carl's senior. That gives us leeway. We'll report first, though." I used my GPS to lead the way, cursing the crowds swarming the square for slowing us down.

"Right. Report first, steal transport later," Raj muttered. "If we get arrested, it's on you."

"Yeah, speaking of, where's an Enforcement Office when we need one?" I checked the map again. "Okay, we're gonna have to shortcut through here."

We headed into a busy shopping arcade, further slowed by the relentless crowd. Valeria was obsessed with shiny tech, obvious from the number of stores devoted to the latest gadgets. Valeria had been linked up to other universes for so much of its history that its native cultures were long gone, and the city-continent of Neo Greyle dominated half the globe. For centuries, it had sent people out to other worlds to bring back anything new to adapt for their own use. Since there were hundreds of doorways offworld in Neo Greyle alone, it had had far more success than other worlds which had tried to do the same, making it one of the most advanced worlds—by its own admission. Loud, discordant Valerian rock music pounded from loudspeakers overhead, with the general sound effect of a train crash.

And then came the sound of what, for a moment, I thought was an *actual* train crash. The glass front of the arcade, barely metres away, shattered, and I leaped back, arms raised to shield my face. Shards cut the back of my hands but I ignored the stinging pain and focused on the source of the explosion—a hover bike had driven right through the glass front doors.

"Shit!" Raj yelled, as the bike turned in our direction.

Cursing, I dropped to the ground, the others following suit, and the screams of shoppers and tourists mingled with the crashing music. The bike itself, being magic-driven, made no sound aside from a faint whirring, and there didn't appear to be anyone driving it, either.

"Damn." I pushed to my feet and picked splinters of glass out of each hand. "I think we have our ravegen."

The bike had already been swept up in the rush outside the doors.

"Son of a bitch," said Raj. "How are we supposed to catch that thing?" He picked slivers of glass from his own hands, wincing.

Law Enforcement Officers had arrived on the scene, clad in shell-like suits. *Crap.* We could either stay and explain the situation and risk our target getting away... or take off after the goblin.

A second hover bike made my decision. It shot through the crowd, and as it passed us by, I jumped for the tail end, pulling myself onto the back. Like the other, the bike had no driver—or so it appeared—and it shook and then swerved left without warning, as the driver obviously became aware of their unwanted passenger. Swearing, I inched along the bike, digging my fingers into the headrest to stop myself sliding off, and let go with one hand to grab my stunner.

"Let go, human," said a hissing voice.

"Not a chance in hell." I fired the stunner directly into the passenger seat.

The ravegen appeared in a tangle of limbs, screaming. I jumped into the seat and locked my stunner arm around its neck, just enough to incapacitate it while I took a handle with the other hand. Crowds stared as I steered the bike one-handed through a pedestrianized district, but it was too late to turn back and avoid the main road.

"Tell me where you were going!" I yelled into the squealing goblin's ear, voice muffled by the wind.

"No!" yelped the goblin, and I pushed the deceleration lever, steering around a corner into the main road. The bike slowed enough for me to give the goblin a warning squeeze around the neck. It choked out, arms spasming and making it even more difficult to one-handedly hold the wheel. The traffic stalled at Valeria's equivalent to a red light—which involved symbols flashing on a screen attached to a post suspended over the road.

I glared at the ravegen. "If you tell me where you were going, I might spare your life."

With Cethraxians, threats always got through. The goblin screamed several phrases in Cethraxian, and then, in garbled English, "The Campbells, by all the great under-gods, the Campbells!"

"The Campbell family's residence?" I asked, feeling a plunging sensation that had nothing to do with the hover bike. Ada had been held hostage there. Where I'd first killed. "They're gone. Jailed."

"Others are... argh!" His words cut off in a scream as the lights changed and I was forced to accelerate again.

"What do you mean, others?" I yelled over the raging

wind. I couldn't just keep driving, as much of an entertaining show it was proving for the spectators. Damn, they'd be taking photos next, and I had no intention of making Neo Greyle's Network headlines. As we hit another traffic jam, I twisted in the seat, looking for a stopping point. It was only a matter of time before patrolling Enforcement Squad saw me and demanded to know why I was strangling a goblin.

The goblin just wailed, a mix of Cethraxian and gibberish. I steered the bike off-road to a parking area, and hit the "stop" button. Naturally, the bike didn't just stop, it skidded to a halt, flipping over in the process. The goblin yowled louder as we slammed into the ground, rolling over in the dust. It wriggled from my grip and ran, but I dived after it. My arm locked around its neck again and I used the leverage to pin it to the ground.

"Nice try."

"I—beg—you!"

"Stop, there!" demanded an Enforcement Officer. Cursing the Multiverse, I gave the goblin a zap with the stunner, and then dug in my coat for my Alliance ID.

"What is this?" The officer strode over to me, sharp eyes taking in the overturned bike, the limp form of the goblin, my blood-stained hands.

By the time I'd explained the situation, Amanda and Raj had caught up to me. The Enforcement Officer nodded, not looking too pleased. Two others had joined him and one of them cuffed the now silent goblin. When it had started squealing again, I'd tightened my grip on its neck until it passed out.

"If that's the case, then I'll need you to report to our Alliance representative at the gate," said the officer.

"There are others," I said. "I'm certain of it. Another bike crashed, too. And this one said it was on the way to the Campbell residence."

"The Campbell residence is shut down. Cleared out," said the officer. "I will alert the team, of course."

The others eyed us with distrust, but the officer dismissed us with a brief "Thank you, Ambassador". With a glance at my bloody hands.

"Kay, you should get those bandaged," said Amanda.

"Most of it isn't my blood. I'll sort it later."

"And leave a bloody trail all over Neo Greyle?" Amanda shook her head.

"Hmm." I wiped some of the blood on my Ambassador's coat. Red stained the silver cuffs. *That figures*, I thought, resigning myself to taking the damn thing to the dry cleaner's and scaring the living daylights out of the staff.

"Is this a normal situation for Ambassadors?" asked Amanda. "I've never even been offworld aside from holidays before. Only started at the Alliance two years ago."

"It's been 'normal' ever since I met this guy." Raj jerked his head in my direction.

"Hey, I caught the bastard." And got a clue about their plan. The Campbells... it meant bad news, all right.

"What the hell were you thinking?" Raj said, shaking his head, as we made our way across the city—on foot again—to the official gate back to the Passages. "I thought the officers were gonna arrest all of us."

"I was thinking that I needed to catch the criminal. Also, the Campbells are involved somehow."

"But they're in jail," said Raj, with a significant glance at Amanda, who wasn't an Ambassador and technically shouldn't have been involved. Then again, the usual rules had gone out the window lately.

And yet I still felt as out of my depth as though I was stuck in quicksand.

"Yeah," I said wearily. "They are. God knows." I reached in my pocket for my communicator and found it had stuck on the loading screen. "Really?" I hit the screen again, tried the reset button, and nothing happened. Must have hit the ground when I fell off the bike.

"What?" asked Raj. "How many times has that happened now?"

"What's this?" asked Amanda. "Kay—hang on. I've seen you at the training complex. You're the one who keeps putting the simulators to the highest setting, aren't you?"

She was probably the first person at Central who hadn't commented on my name before anything else, or else the attack on headquarters. I'd seen her at the training complex before, but she was usually instructing newcomers. There were quite a few at the moment, as so many guards had died in the attack. And she looked vaguely familiar, too, though I was pretty sure we hadn't spoken before now.

"You work there, right?"

She nodded. "I help the novices who haven't already been through training. I tested that new girl, Ada. She's one of the best I've seen, took to it immediately. You know her?"

"Yeah." I hadn't even asked how training had gone. Really, I should have had the balls to talk to her face to face. *What did you think would happen?* It was clear being at Central wasn't helping her deal with what the Campbells had done to her. I'd been stupid to assume otherwise. But seeing Ada at the Blind Wyvern had done away with my brief resolution to avoid getting involved with her any more than I had to. Maybe I should just leave her alone, like her brother said. I'd been the one to wreck her life in the first place.

Luckily, we weren't detained for long at the exit.

"I'd get that blood off your hands before you report to my sister," said Amanda, as we approached Central.

"Your sister? Who…" I frowned at her. Why didn't I see the resemblance before? "Ms Weston."

Amanda nodded. "Yes, she's my older sister. And won't be happy about this."

"I think that's a given," I muttered.

Amanda ended up dragging me downstairs to the medical division while Raj went to report to Ms Weston.

Saki, the nurse, sighed over the state of my hands. "What in the Multiverse did you do?" she asked, wrapping bandages around my knuckles. "Put your hands through a window?"

"Pretty close," I said.

"He chased down a ravegen by hijacking the hover bike it stole," said Amanda.

Saki sighed again. "You Academy graduates think you're invincible." She pulled the bandage tight with more force than necessary. For some reason that had to do with my father, she'd never liked me.

"What was it carrying, anyway?" Amanda asked of no one in particular.

"I've no idea," I said. "Some kind of tech. Valeria's Alliance has it now."

"Hmm. I wonder who gave them the orders? They'd never dare trespass through a doorway on their own."

"Someone with dealings with the Campbells." I kept my expression neutral, but one eye on the others to see if anyone reacted to the name. Not that I thought the Alliance was involved this time, but old suspicions died hard.

"The Campbells?" Saki frowned. "Oh—that's odd. There were complaints at West Office about something going missing. This bloodrock solution?"

"I'm sure that's what they used to turn themselves invisible," I said. "Who the hell stole that stuff, anyway? I thought security was up."

"It is," said Amanda. "I think they confiscated it, and someone else stole it before they could lock it away. But Central's bloodrock supply's safe as anything."

Good. Sure, nobody aside from me had seen the file containing information on that particular substance, which could function as an energy supply in a high-magic world, but that didn't mean it wasn't dangerous in the wrong hands. Interesting how she knew so much about it. I guessed it was inevitable, with her and Ms Weston being related.

"Good news for the tech team, then," said Amanda.

"What do the tech team want with bloodrock?" I asked.

"New devices," said Saki. "Based on the one we took from that girl. Ada."

Of course. The Chameleon, as she'd called it, could turn anyone invisible for up to ten minutes—a level of magi-tech considered impossible on Earth. Magic-powered technology was too expensive to be cost-effective in Earth's atmosphere, and most simply didn't work. Ada's brother had somehow found a way around it. Using bloodrock.

"They're going to use them in the field, then?" I asked. I'd heard it mentioned here and there. The idea of being able to get into places unseen was pretty radical, considering the risks Alliance Ambassadors put themselves under in high-magic worlds.

Wait a minute... being invisible might give us a way around the centaurs' issue with humans investigating a murder in their territory.

"Possibly," said Saki. "Can't say I like it, though. Considering what it's been used for in the past—keep still!"

My hand had twitched as my pulse started racing. Only Ms Weston knew the significance of the experiment. As far as Saki and the others concerned, it was dead and buried with the other victims. Skyla, or Ellen. That other girl I'd killed. There'd been another, too, and I'd inferred that Ada had accidentally caused his death.

I was the only one left.

Teeth clenched, I willed my hand to stay steady as Saki applied another bandage.

"I heard about that," said Amanda. "I know I shouldn't be authorised to know, but the Westons have always been involved in med-tech even if Danica decided against it. She said it's common offworld, human enhancement. She told me… she was an intern at the time. Thirteen years ago?"

Saki looked up. I hoped she'd put my shaking hand down to the pain I barely felt. My heartbeat kicked up another notch, and it was all I could do to keep my expression blank. I remembered every fucking second of that day, but I didn't recall seeing Ms Weston. But it explained how she'd known.

"I don't know their reasons," said Saki. "I wasn't in this department when it happened. I'd just transferred over from the Tokyo branch to the Law Division. Clearly, it was a political move, a downright stupid one, in my opinion." She shook her head. "For the risks they took… it's surprising that the Alliance would have allowed it to go so far."

Yeah. It would be, to anyone who didn't know what Lawrence Walker was capable of. Who hadn't escaped by the skin of their teeth.

"It is." Amanda nodded grimly.

It was pretty clear Ms Weston hadn't mentioned my father's involvement to anyone. *Why not tell everyone?* She had nothing to do with the Walker family. I'd know about it if she did. Maybe she just didn't want to risk the backlash of challenging the most powerful name in Earth's Alliance. There'd doubtless be a cover up if the truth came to light, even if Lawrence Walker was cut off from the Alliance, on a distant world beyond reach.

More to the point, she hadn't mentioned *my* involvement, even though for all she'd known, I could have been as unhinged as the others and gone on a killing spree. But then, she was a master at reading people if I ever saw one. Even me. She'd inexplicably decided to trust me even after I'd majorly fucked up multiple times, letting me go after Ada and the Campbells instead of detaining me at Central once she had the file in her hand.

I'd never seen the contents of that file…

"You had the information from the experiment," I said to Saki, "Did you see which magic-based substance worked?"

"Honestly, I don't know a lot about magic-based substances," said Saki, with a glance at Amanda. "The only reason our division knows about them at all is because they're responsible for most magic-related injuries. Sounds like the old council hired Klathican scientists."

"I was with the guards who searched that Skyla girl's apartment," said Amanda. "She listed three substances in her diary that they used in the experiment: bloodrock, obsidiate and lustre. She was trying to find out which one worked. Ada's report said two of the teenagers could turn themselves invisible. It matches lustre's properties when it comes into contact with another source."

"Really?" I frowned. "You know about magic sources?" Ms Weston sure hadn't mentioned it.

Amanda tucked a strand of hair behind her ear. "My sister decided to put me through admin when I joined up two years ago and I spent a week updating the files on sources based on the most recent discoveries. I was the only person she trusted to do it. It's not the kind of information we want getting into the wrong hands."

Hmm.

"I meant non-Alliance members," she clarified. "The general policy is not to tell people any more than they *need* to know, especially on Earth."

"And bloodrock?" I said. "The file… I don't know if your sister told you, but people got killed over it."

"Yes, she told me." Amanda shook her head. "That's why I

volunteered as part of the search team. That information's normally reserved for higher-up Alliance members."

"Including this... lustre? You said that one worked?"

No way. I didn't know what it was. Hell, I *couldn't* have known.

"I asked around when I paid a visit to Valeria's Alliance's labs," said Amanda. "It's certainly not common knowledge even over there. Lustre... they must have got it from Klathica, that's where it was discovered. But I can't imagine—the dangers of injecting a pure source into a human are high enough that even there, it would be carefully monitored. This was... thirteen years ago? Before the rules changed?"

The rules changed? I made a mental note to check up on that. Obviously, I'd figured the experiments weren't a common occurrence. But it sounded like whoever my father had employed hadn't much cared if the subjects had survived or not.

It shouldn't have been a surprise. But a chill crept across the back of my neck all the same.

"Klathica. I thought so," said Saki. "They aren't averse to ridiculous experiments. I've been there, and half their Alliance guards have weapons growing out of their *hands.*"

Of course it had been Klathican scientists who'd done it. On Klathica itself, almost everyone was born with magic. The experiment would only have worked, if at all, on Earth. And there was only one person with the authority to allow something like that.

"Did anyone happen to mention whether those teenagers' abilities had a limit?" I asked, casually.

"Eh?" Saki blinked, as though only just aware of who she was talking to. "I have no idea. You fought one of them, didn't you?"

"Yes," I said. "Two of them. They didn't turn themselves invisible, though. I'm not overly familiar with the properties of lustre." Though I'd be researching it now. *Lustre.* I finally had the name.

"Most people aren't," said Amanda. "Half the difficulty with magic-based substances is that almost all of them *look* alike in their natural form."

My eyebrows lifted. "They do?"

"It's one of the reasons Earth's so reluctant to incorporate magic-based substances into their technology," said Amanda. "Obsidiate's a volatile explosive, and it appears identical to adamantine, which is an absorbent. Only magic-wielders can tell the difference."

They can? That explained... a lot. Adamantine was what gave the guard uniform its magical protection, and was built into Central's walls, too. And the daggers were made of the same thing.

"So... what *is* lustre?"

"Rare," said Amanda. "It's mined on Klathica, and they only properly classified it a few years ago because it looks so similar to other sources, no one realised it wasn't the same. It's an enhancer, and only works in conjunction with another source. It's even rarer than bloodrock, and no one actually knows where Central got *that* from. I hadn't even heard of it until a few weeks ago. It wasn't filed with the other information on sources."

Enzar. I glanced over my shoulder, unable to help myself. This was exactly the kind of knowledge that turned worlds against one another, and started wars.

Saki was looking at me suspiciously. Hell. "What about obsidiate?" I asked, half to distract her, half out of genuine curiosity. "You said it's an explosive?"

"A mild one," said Amanda. "It's in your stunners."

"Yeah..." I saw her point. The stunners' batteries were the same gleaming black as the magicproof walls of Central. *Only magic-wielders can tell the difference...*

"Did the file say anything about other side effects? Those kids seemed pretty unhinged," I added, in explanation, glad Saki had let go of my arm so I could clench my hand to stop it shaking.

"Unhinged? Skyla was angry, out for revenge, but no, there weren't any other side effects recorded."

I closed my eyes for a brief moment. Just having it confirmed lifted some of the weight off me. I wasn't endangering people by seeking out magic, not in the way the others had. Perhaps I wasn't the best judge of my own mental state, but at least I knew magic had nothing to do with it.

"And those twins?" asked Amanda. "They tortured Ada."

My other fist clenched. I wasn't sorry I'd killed that girl, nor that her twin was dead, either.

"I have no idea," said Saki. "Weren't they adopted by the family who wanted revenge on the Alliance? Brainwashing, I imagine. Or family loyalty."

I didn't doubt that. I could imagine all too clearly.

"We should report to Ms Weston," I said to Amanda. "Thanks," I added to Saki, whose eyebrows rose at the acknowledgment. My father must have made quite the impression on her.

I still had to face an extremely displeased Ms Weston. She wasn't at all happy about her sister's involvement, and barely listened as I told her my suspicions about the Campbells and the ravegens.

But her attention sharpened when I told her the idea that had occurred to me in the nurse's office.

"I know it's risky," I said. "But Markos told me a war's likely within the week. These are desperate times."

"That they are, Kay," she said, regarding me shrewdly. "And we certainly intended to test the Chameleons in the field. That was remarkable thinking, though I shouldn't be surprised."

I blinked. Was that meant to be a good thing or a bad thing? You never could tell with Ms Weston.

"I'll put your plan forward to the council," she said. "You're absolutely right—it's risky. But our options are limited. You're dismissed for now."

I left the office quickly. I needed to get hold of a new communicator if I wanted to research lustre. Unless I went to the archives...

A familiar figure waited at the bottom of the stairs, red head bowed.

"Ada," I said.

She spun around, and her eyes widened as she took in the bandages on my hands. She'd cleaned the blood off her face and changed into office gear rather than guard uniform, but she stood awkwardly, shuffling from one foot to the other.

"Oh. Hi. I was just waiting for my brother."

"I figured. Are you okay?"

She studied the floor rather than meeting my eyes. "Yes, I'm fine. Why do you keep asking?"

One eyebrow raised, I said, "Need you ask?"

"Yeah. Answer a question with a question. About right." But despite the savagery in her tone, she looked... miserable, really. Though she tried to hide it. Her shoulders were hunched, her shifting feet impatient. Someone had upset her.

"Ms Weston didn't say anything to you, did she?"

Tell me what's wrong. But if I asked, I'd get another snappish retort.

"No."

"She's skinned all of us alive at one point or other. It's just how she is. Amanda said you were one of the best she'd tested in the simulations."

"You talked to her?" She glanced up at me then, a slight flush spreading across her face.

"We tracked some more of those goblins on Valeria. I just

got back." I held up my broken communicator. "Reckon I should try and sue those goblins for breaking two of these?"

That got a faint smile out of her. "Goblins? And there I was thinking this'd be as dull as my last job. Which, for the record, was stacking shelves and serving ungrateful customers at a supermarket."

"I don't think 'dull' is a word the Alliance understand," I said, with a half smile. She'd worked at a supermarket? No wonder she'd been so astounded when I'd offered her a job here. "You're forgetting what happened in my first week."

"Oh, yeah," she said, some of the tension relaxing in her posture. "Okay, I haven't picked up any trespassers yet. Or arrested anyone."

"First time for everything."

"Yeah." She frowned, biting on her bottom lip. "I—Aric said something…" She stopped, looked away almost guiltily.

"That bastard," I said. "He didn't give you a hard time, did he?"

"I can take care of myself," she said, suddenly on the defensive again. "He won't be bothering me again."

Whoa. "Wait, what happened? What did he do?"

"Nothing."

"Right." Next time I saw him, I'd make him sorry. I should have guessed he wouldn't leave well enough alone.

"You don't have to do anything," she said, like she'd read my thoughts.

"I'm pretty sure he'll give me a reason to. Aric does nothing but stir up trouble. If that was him firing his stunner in the Passages earlier, he's probably off the rota. Hope he gets sacked next. God knows he most likely bribed his way in in the first place."

"Is that possible?" she asked.

I shrugged. "His family provides Alliance technology from Valeria. They own an empire across three universes, pretty sure the connections are there. He got in here before he even graduated, and his grades were shit."

"Hmm." She chewed on her bottom lip again. She had bruise-like shadows under her eyes that hadn't been there before. *Ah, crap.*

Before I could say anything, she blurted, "Did you really try to kill Aric?"

Whatever I'd expected, that sure as hell wasn't it. *Should have guessed,* a voice in my head berated me, as my heart beat loudly in my ears.

"He told you that?"

"Just answer." She turned away. "I just want to know."

"I'm guessing he only told you part of the story," I said, carefully. "In the Passages, after I first found out I could use magic, I lost control of it."

The colour drained from her face. "Why?"

"Because he's a dick, and he happened to be in the way." I could almost see her thoughts playing on a wheel—suddenly I had a good idea why she'd dropped her stunner. "I wasn't trying to kill him, but I didn't know what I was doing. It's not going to happen to you, you know that, right?"

"It's not about me," she said, a tremor in her voice. "It's—I have to get out of here."

"Wait." I moved towards her. Her entire body went rigid, as her gaze fell on my still-blood-stained sleeve.

"Go away, Kay," she said. "I don't want to talk to you right now."

I stopped. *Goddammit, Ada.* What could I say? That I hadn't meant to kill him? Because I still didn't know if I had. Besides, I'd crossed that bridge long ago. Magic couldn't rewind the clock.

"What're you doing?" a voice demanded. Her ever-grateful brother. *Next time you're thinking of doing someone a favour, Kay, don't bother.*

"Nothing," I said, icy-cold. "You should go talk to her."

"Hmm." He gave me a suspicious frown, then went to join his sister.

I watched them both leave in silence, my hands curling into fists. Muttering a curse at the Multiverse in general, I went to the guard office to get another effing communicator replacement, hoping I'd get to beat the crap out of Aric on the way.

10

ADA

"How'd it go?" Jeth asked. "First patrol, right?"

"Ugh. It was a disaster," I said, as we turned into a main road and the noise of London enveloped us in a cigarette smoke and exhaust fume-scented fog. I reluctantly summarised the fight, feeling another pang of helpless anger when I admitted to dropping my weapon. Out of fear of magic, fear of *myself*.

Aric had been telling the truth? Kay really had lost control of magic? It shouldn't have been a surprise. I'd seen him *kill* with magic before. I knew it was a force beyond human control, even magic-wielders. And yet it seemed every new piece of information hammered further home just how much of a danger I was. To others. Even to the Alliance.

My head hurt just to think about it.

"You did fine, Ada," said Jeth. "Don't worry about it. Honest. Everyone has moments like that. They won't blame you."

"It shouldn't have happened. I knew I'd have to use a stunner. It's not the same as the magic I used. I had no reason to freak out. I could have got people killed."

"Ada, I wouldn't stress too much. You're new. You're a step ahead of most of the new recruits who have barely any experience at all. Of course it's going to be intimidating at first, it's like any other job. Well, apart from the monsters."

"Yeah," I said. "There is that."

"Seriously," said Jeth. "I know you know your own mind, Ada. But you're not happy. You can't deny it. If you need a break, you should tell them."

"I am happy," I insisted, and Jeth raised his eyebrows. "I am, and I'm not. This is what I always wanted, always, but—I guess there's a price to pay for getting what you want most in the world."

"Ada, you're not allowed to get yourself down," he said, as we pushed through the crowd into the Tube station. "You should stay away from Nell until she apologises."

"Thought you'd tell me to talk to her. But I suppose that didn't work out so well last time."

"Exactly. You don't need to worry about her problems on top of your own, Ada."

But it didn't matter, because Nell wasn't there when we got home.

"Gone to the Knights' again," said Alber, leaning on the door frame to his room. "Dunno what the issue is this time, but they aren't happy with the Alliance."

My heart dipped. Like we needed anything else to worry about.

"Not our problem," said Jeth, with a significant glance at me. "Right. I'm the eldest here, and I'm hereby forbidding all moping in this house. Tonight, there will be no mention of you-know-who—of a certain paranoid guardian of ours. Got it?"

"Yes, sir," said Alber, with a military salute. "What's this about, anyway? She-who-must-not-be-named? Or did something else happen?"

"I completely freaked out today, is all," I said. "Jeth's over-reacting. But I vote no talking about it tonight, okay?"

"All right," said Alber doubtfully. "But I'm watching a film."

"Bring it into the living room." Jeth pushed open the door. "I'm gonna grab my laptop and order pizza, and you, Ada, are going to smile."

"Uh-huh." But I did feel a little better. My brothers were on my team, even if Nell wasn't.

"So, how's Technoland?" I asked Jeth later, as I curled up on the sofa. He frowned at me, and I added, "Come on, that's not talking about you-know-who. Or moping. I really want to know."

"Well, neither of you will understand most of it," said Jeth, typing on his laptop.

"I'm so sorry. I bow down to your technological awesomeness," said Alber. "What happened to the Chameleons?"

"That's actually what we're working on. Turns out Central's looking into using bloodrock with technology. Just like we did," he added to me. "It's like my inventions. To help. They can get into top-secret places on missions and not be seen. No world in the Multiverse has perfected total, cross-world invisibility before."

"Ooh, get you," said Alber. "You're gonna be famous?"

"Nah, but if this keeps up, I might get a promotion. Not right away, but they're seriously impressed."

"Help," said Alber. "Your ego is crushing me over here."

"Hey, just being honest. Ada, that reminds me. I was going to say earlier, but... the tech guys want a word with you. Nothing serious, don't worry. It's just you were the one to use the Chameleons the most, they want some pointers. Nothing to worry about."

"Oh," I said. "Okay."

Those days felt like a lifetime ago. Turning invisible to break into Central.

"Ironic, I know," said Jeth.

"Spying?" said Alber. "My sister's like James Bond. Awesome."

"You're a total dork," I said.

I didn't need to worry about Nell, not when I had my brothers. My family. Some things would never change.

"Ada Fletcher: report to my office at seven in guard uniform."

I stared at my communicator screen, totally disorientated. Why would Ms Weston message me at this ungodly hour to ask me to come into work? I checked the time, five a.m., and groaned.

"Thanks for that." I rubbed my forehead. Just for once, I wanted a decent night's sleep, but apparently something had come up at Central. *Please no more invisible goblins.*

To distract myself, I pulled out my old laptop. For once, the Internet connected. I launched the browser, idly wondering if I had access to anything confidential now I was a full-fledged Alliance member. I knew they didn't like any information on their staff being accessible online. I didn't have a problem with that, seeing as I'd lived in hiding all my life. No social networking for me. Or, I imagined, for people like Kay, who'd been born into instant access to information on other worlds…

"It's true. He used magic, and almost killed me. And he got away with it because of the Walker reputation. All because I found out he's a criminal and a raging psychopath."

I groaned again. This was going to drive me insane. And it was really none of my business. I'd hate if anyone had probed me for every detail of my life.

Except I couldn't sleep. I had Internet access. And before I quite knew what I was doing, I'd run a search on the name WALKER within INTER-WORLD ALLIANCE. I honestly didn't know why it hadn't occurred to me before.

"Maybe because you've reached a new low, Ada," I muttered to myself. But… wait, someone had set up a whole information page on the Walker family, starting with Robert Walker. Kay's grandfather had died five years before I was born, but he was listed as one of the founders of the Alliance on Earth. Wow. I'd known the name, but it had kind of escaped me until now just how deep in the Alliance the Walkers were. They'd been involved with other worlds long before most people on Earth even knew about them.

Lawrence Walker was listed as a council member and advisor to Earth's Alliance. Wife, Elizabeth Walker, deceased. She'd died thirteen years ago. Son, Kay… By the date of birth listed on the page, he was twenty-one, only a couple of weeks older than me. That was all. It didn't say whether his mother had worked for the Alliance, too. I scrolled down. It was just a list of Lawrence Walker's achievements, and half of it had been blacked-out. Probably the Alliance's doing. Kind of creepy how someone had set this page up.

I shouldn't be reading this. Yeah, it was there on the Internet for the world to see, but…

Well, I'd already dug myself into a hole. I scrolled further down, hit the bottom of the page. Walker family… *Currently believed to own properties across multiple universes, including Earth, though several in England were destroyed in a fire shortly after Lawrence Walker removed his tracker from the Alliance on Earth. His current location is unknown.*

Destroyed in a fire? I ran another search. Just one newspaper article showed up, and it said an arsonist had destroyed several properties belonging to the Walker family, in different locations, in a single night. Apparently they'd all been uninhabited at the time. No talk of the culprit either. It screamed, "cover-up". *He's like a serial arsonist or something.* Was that what Kay did? Set his family's properties on fire? It would make sense, given the little I knew of his family, and it was easy to believe the person who'd experimented on children would take off to another universe leaving his only child behind with no family or guardian. There were no other surviving Walkers, if I believed the article. I didn't know about his mother's family.

Maybe that was why he'd been arrested. In fact... I checked the dates. Five years ago. Same year he'd joined the Academy.

I rubbed my eyes, not sure what to think. Right now, I was glad I'd never said anything. *I'd* been a criminal up until recently, and I guessed now I understood why he'd tried so hard to persuade Ms Weston to let me go when I'd been locked in the cells.

Really, I only had *more* questions now. But I couldn't deny the tightness in my chest had lessened slightly.

The last thing I expected when I arrived at work was to find Kay in Ms Weston's office when I knocked—and a centaur. The seven-foot-tall horse-man seemed to fill half the office.

"There you are," said Ms Weston. "Ada, I don't believe you and Markos have met?"

"Um, no." *I think I'd remember meeting a centaur,* I wanted to add, but didn't. "Nice to meet you."

"The same." Markos inclined his head. Long dark hair framed his face, which was tanned, as was his horse-body. The human half wore a black coat similar to Kay's Ambassador jacket.

Kay himself barely glanced in my direction. He appeared

tense—not that that was particularly unusual—and his hands were bandaged, as they'd been yesterday after he came back from Valeria. I hadn't asked what happened, but it couldn't be serious if he was going offworld.

"Good. Well, we have ourselves a dilemma," said Ms Weston. "A situation has arisen offworld which the Alliance is badly placed to deal with, yet if action is not taken swiftly, there is the high risk of warfare."

My heart lurched. "I—how?"

"Aglaia's centaur leader is dead," said Ms Weston. "It appears to be an accident, but the centaurs are blaming the humans. The two have always been at odds, and unfortunately, humans aren't allowed to access the centaurs' royal grounds. Unless we find proof one way or another, a group of particularly vocal centaurs intend to directly challenge the mages." She fixed her gaze on me. "We have been exploring the possibilities, and we've concluded to employ the tech team's latest invention in order to solve this dilemma. I'm told you can operate one of these... Chameleons?"

So they are using them.

"Yeah, I can," I said. "So—you're going to use them to sneak into centaur territory or something?"

"Exactly," said Ms Weston. "Kay's idea, as it happens."

I glanced sideways at him, annoyed to feel myself flushing. *Dammit.* I'd totally freaked the last time we'd spoken. Was I really going to let what Aric had said bother me that much? Worse, Kay was doing his job, actually achieving things, while I struggled in a quagmire of self-created problems.

"Right. Uh, I should probably warn you they only last ten minutes tops," I said. "Low battery. You'd have to be fast."

"That shouldn't be a problem," said Ms Weston. "We were hoping for a demonstration, however." She held out the small piece of metal, just like the one I'd used to break into Central's stores.

"Sure." I took the device and showed them the clip on the underside. "Just clip it to your sleeve like this. You need skin contact for it to work." I demonstrated, clipping the Chameleon into place and flicking the switch. In an instant, my body turned invisible.

Kay's eyes widened a fraction, as did the centaur's. Ms Weston, who I swore was never startled, just gave a slight nod.

"That's enough."

I released the switch, and my hand reappeared, followed by the rest of me.

"We never found a way of making batteries that would last longer than ten minutes, not on Earth. Might be different offworld, though."

"We'll certainly have to look into that," said Ms Weston. "In any case, we need to act now to stop a war. If it turns out the centaur king's death was indeed murder, then we'll have another problem on our hands. If not, then the mages are absolved of all blame and we'll have to take action to stop the centaurs from declaring war. This isn't an ideal scenario either way. I'd rather not antagonise the centaurs further, but the fact is that a certain group of them blame humans and refuse to listen to reason. We need to find out how the centaur king was killed and take action accordingly, even if it ultimately alienates us from them."

Damn. I glanced at Markos, whose face was still.

"I have good reason to take Alliance technology within my territory," he said quietly. "If it turns out the mages aren't responsible, then I'll have to tell my sister that I was the one to use the tracker. I'm already outcast, there's nothing else she can do to me. She doesn't want a war." He tapped one hoof on the floor. "But the boss insists I don't antagonise my sister further unless we know for sure how our father died. Instead, the two of you get the dubious honour of risking your lives."

"The… two of us?" Though I'd suspected from the instant I'd walked into the room.

Awkward, I thought, as the three of us walked through the blue-lit Passage, Chameleons at the ready. I wore my guard uniform, too, and had one of Jeth's invisible earpieces clipped to my ear, which functioned as part of a three-way communication device. Kay and Markos had the other two. Apparently, there wasn't time to get council permission for anyone else to remove the devices from the tech office, and Kay and I were already authorised because we'd used them before. Supposedly, the Alliance wanted to limit the number of people who knew about magic-sourced technology, though by the way the tech team was gossiping about the Chameleons, every world this side of Cethrax would know about them by the end of the week. Personally, I was slightly less freaked out about the fact that our deaths would require less paperwork than letting someone else in on the plan, than the fact that the last "mission" we'd used the earpieces on was when I'd been *kidnapped.*

"Death by bureaucracy," Kay muttered as we passed by a stretch of sealed Passage doors. "I won't ask Simon to put that on my grave."

Markos the centaur snorted with laughter. I was less amused, though I could hardly believe I was actually going offworld. The situation must be desperate, because there was usually a crap-ton of paperwork before taking a non-Ambassador to a world as far out there as Aglaia. The door was literally miles into the Passages.

Considering what had happened last time I was in here, to say I was tense would be an understatement. Ms Weston had said if we were caught armed on centaur territory it would mean a death sentence. But we had magic, even if Ambassadors were usually forbidden to use it in front of the centaurs because they hated it. She knew what I could do. And Kay, of course. I had a sneaking suspicion that was the real reason we'd been picked for this mission.

Just the thought made my limbs shake and my lungs threaten to close up again. If we were attacked, if I freaked out like yesterday, we might die.

Not gonna happen.

"Oh, lighten up, the pair of you," the centaur burst out, after almost half an hour of silent walking. "It's not like we're going to our deaths."

"You were the one who said there's a sixty percent chance we're going to die," said Kay, irritably fiddling with the back of the bandage on his right hand.

"That depends on the reliability of your technology, doesn't it?"

"Oh, it's reliable," said Kay. "I've no intention of getting trampled by a herd of centaurs."

"Tell me that's not likely to happen."

Markos turned to me. It was kind of intimidating. Those hooves looked like they could deliver a painful kick. Let alone getting trampled under them. I suppressed a shudder.

"Not if I have anything to do with it," said Kay. He hadn't mentioned our conversation yesterday at all, as if it had never happened. As if I hadn't asked him if he'd tried to murder someone. If I'd known we might die today…

"Well," I said, talking to stop myself thinking. "We just need to get into the capital. Activate the Chameleons, go to the place the king died, and use the tracker to check for magic traces. And then get out."

"Simple," said Markos. "There won't be anyone there now. It's unguarded. Doesn't need to be, since most centaurs are naturally respectful of royalty. That's probably the only reason I'm still alive."

"Why?" I asked.

Markos threw Kay an exasperated look. Kay shrugged. "You'll have to tell her sooner or later."

"Tell me what?"

"Markos is the heir to the centaur leadership," said Kay. "In theory. He's trying to get the position passed to his sister instead, but the others aren't being very accommodating. And one of his cousins won't let the king's death drop. How much do you know about it, anyway?" he asked.

"Uh," I said. "No more than what Ms Weston told me, really. It doesn't have strong links with Earth, does it?"

"If most centaurs had their way, it'd have no links at all," said Markos. "We're required by law to have representatives in the Alliance since the council voted to join, but the mages don't like to share their secrets with offworlders. And centaurs don't like magic. That's putting it mildly, anyway."

"Or humans, generally," Kay added. "Strictly speaking, we aren't allowed on their territory at all. Even Ambassadors."

"Why did you come to Earth, then?" I asked Markos. "I mean, you're the only centaur at Central, right?"

"Yes," said Markos, "and I'll thank you not to ask nosy questions, human."

"Sorry. Just wondered, that's all. I used to help people from other worlds migrate to Earth and settle in. I was curious."

"It's true, then?" asked Markos. "Curse this political fiasco for keeping me from meeting the most interesting human I've ever heard of. You helped offworlders behind the Alliance's back?"

"Yeah—well, they were from worlds the Alliance wouldn't help, for one reason or another," I said. "Like Enzar. There was this network set up to help them escape to worlds like Earth. I helped them through the Passages."

"Unbelievable." Markos shook his head. "Never, in ten years at Central, have I heard of anything so audacious. I would have said Kay was exaggerating, if the dragon lady hadn't confirmed it."

"Dragon lady?" I said blankly.

"Ms Weston," said Kay. "You didn't actually call her that to her face, did you?"

"No, but she likes me," said Markos. "Says I'm the most efficient admin she's met, not that it means a blasted thing on Aglaia."

"Why—" I stopped at a warning look from the centaur. "Come on, you must get asked a lot."

"Strangely, no. Most people would rather run a mile than ask me a question. Except this idiot," he said, indicating Kay.

"I don't recall asking you anything. He likes to wind people up," he added to me. "Whatever you do, don't mention stairs, and if you want to live to see tomorrow, never ask for a ride on a centaur's back."

"You just had to bring that up," Markos muttered.

"Huh? Why would I even ask that?"

"No reason," said Markos firmly. "We are *not* horses, human."

"I gathered," I said. "So, we're literally just going to sneak into the royal grounds? We aren't going to see any more of Aglaia?"

"This isn't a field trip, human," said Markos.

"I know," I said. "It's the first time I've been offworld, though, apart from Valeria, and I don't know much about it, except humans and centaurs hate each other, and aren't keen on the Alliance."

"That's about as much as you need to know," said Kay.

"Centaurs and humans stick to their own territories, and don't talk to one another if they can help it."

"And that's unlikely to change?" I asked. "I mean, some of you've joined the Alliance now. *You* don't mind humans, right?"

"I find you entertaining," said Markos. "To answer your earlier question, human, I chose Earth because it's low-magic. I don't hate humans, but magic is unpredictable at best and destructive at worst. It has no place in centaur life. And if magic *did* cause my father's death, then the chaos it would cause is unparallelled. There hasn't been open warfare for over a hundred years, by Earth measurements, and certainly not involving magic. Even the mages know its capacity for destruction."

"We can't rule out the possibility of magic being involved," said Kay. "Not yet, anyway. If it *is* true… what will you do?"

"Come back to Earth," the centaur said, his tone bleak. "And try not to get killed. Aglaia will be at war, sooner or later."

"Unless we find out who did it," said Kay. "I know these trackers can't pinpoint an individual, but surely there are only certain mages who would have a motive? And sneaking into royal grounds isn't something just anyone could do. Even magic-wielders." He stopped, but I'd got the sense he'd been about to say something else. Or something had occurred to him, maybe.

I was liking this mission less and less by the second.

"Is there nothing anyone can do to stop it?" I asked.

"No," said Kay. "You know the Alliance has limited power to interfere in magical warfare. Earth least of all."

That was precisely the reason the council had withdrawn involvement in the Enzarian Empire's war. Only now did I really appreciate how hopeless the situation seemed from *their* side, too. Ms Weston had said there were five million centaurs and close to a million mages with full magical abilities. How could anyone stop a war on that scale? Even the Inter-World Alliance?

Kay looked at me. "All we can do is keep a Passage open for evacuation, if necessary. The Law Division are working with the transition points, searching out volunteers to expand them under the Alliance. Including some of the people who worked with you."

"They are?" I asked. This was one of the other things my arrest had caused by chain-reaction. Not only had our family's details got out, but the details of all of our contacts including the offworld transition points where the refugees were evacuated to. The transition points were behind doors in the Passages that were supposed to be out of use. Between-world safe-houses. They were technically illegal, and I'd assumed they'd been shut. Not that the Alliance would actually work with the volunteers there.

"Of course," said Kay. "I explained what they do to the council, and they've been working to reach an agreement. It's been tricky, but they should be open again soon."

Wait, what? There I was again, expecting the worst, and he'd proven me wrong. I didn't even know what to say.

Aric's voice drifted into my head again. *A murdering psychopath... he tried to kill me.* Of all the things to believe, why had I chosen that? What Aric had said seemed incongruous with the man who'd stood up against the council on behalf of people who'd been doing something illegal, just to help Enzar and the other worlds caught up in conflict. And he'd just come back from Aglaia, where he was powerless to help in *their* conflict, when the first thing I'd asked was if he'd tried to kill someone who quite honestly deserved it.

I swallowed, unable to bring myself to speak. I bloody

hoped we weren't going to die. Like *hell* was that going to be the last one-to-one conversation we ever had.

After an eternity of walking, Markos and Kay finally stopped by a door.

"Do you learn all these when you become Ambassador?" I asked, breaking the silence. "The doors, I mean. How do you remember where they lead?" Honestly, all the doors were identical. Even I only knew where a few of them led.

"Mostly by rote," said Markos. "I can't say I know all of them. Aglaia's, of course, I learned first. And this one knows the entire Passages inside out," he added, indicating Kay.

"You do?" I asked.

"I have a copy of one of the original maps," he said. "But it doesn't have the new Passages on it. Guess it needs updating."

"Oh, yeah," I said, thinking of the old lower level Passages I'd used from the door near home. "Wow, though. How many doors *are* there in here? There must be millions."

"Probably," said Kay. "A fair few are closed, or lead to dead ends or the bottom of the ocean—that's one reason we're not allowed to go around opening unknown doors. And new ones are logged in whenever they're discovered, I imagine. Only the higher-ups know for certain. This one leads to the boundary of centaur territory," he added. "Markos is going to lead us up to the royal grounds. He says he knows how to avoid any other centaurs. Then we'll acti-vate the Chameleons and head right for the murder site. Either way, we need to get out of their territory as fast as possible. You used the earpieces to communicate when you were invisible, right?"

"Yeah. But we can't do that if there are centaurs around."

"That's what I thought," said Kay. "All right. I think if we stick close together we shouldn't need them, but they work as a backup. You'll have to speak quietly, but if you see or hear anything, let me know."

"You humans and your contraptions," said Markos. "You turned Central's technology against them?"

"Um, my brother did," I said.

Markos shook his head. "You have nerve, human. Let's hope you've plenty of that today."

I tried to conjure up the old excitement, the thrill when I'd thwarted the Alliance and stole from under their noses.

I didn't even know who that person was anymore.

11

ADA

My first impression of Aglaia was the heat. Even though the faux-leather uniform wasn't thick, I was sweating within seconds. I'd never been abroad to warm places—we'd never been able to afford holidays—but Aglaia had a kind of classical sense about it, like pictures I'd seen of Greece. Trees with wide, autumn-coloured leaves surrounded a clearing with a wooden table and at least a couple of dozen chairs, but no one was there, human or otherwise.

"This is our usual meeting point." Markos indicated the table.

We appeared to have walked out of a tree, inset with a metal door which looked oddly out of place in the forest. Paths branched off the clearing, recognisable because the undergrowth had been trampled flat. Fallen leaves in all shades, combined with the sun, gave a deceptively peaceful picture.

Underneath, magic brushed against my skin, but soft, like warmth rather than electricity. Markos hadn't said whether centaurs couldn't use it or if they just chose not to, and poking further would probably run me up against a wall. No wonder he and Kay got along.

Kay was still acting like I was just another colleague, like he didn't know me at all. After what I'd said yesterday, it came as no surprise. I just really didn't want to mess this mission up, and not just because I didn't like the idea of getting trampled by centaurs.

Markos motioned for silence and led the way into the forest proper, down one of the paths. *We're in enemy territory now.*

We walked in total silence, the centaur leading the way. *I'm not cut out for a career as a spy.* The silence, heat and monotony were starting to get to me. Kay didn't seem particularly bothered, but at every noise, he tensed slightly, ready to react at a second's notice. Lucky I was well-practised at sneaking around, and our Alliance-issued shoes were designed for stealth, making no sound even on a carpet of fallen leaves.

We halted at a junction in the paths, and Kay glanced back at me and waited for me to catch up. The Chameleon made no sound as it activated and he vanished—a second later, I'd activated mine, too, where it was clipped to the inside of my sleeve. And then almost jumped out of my skin when his hand brushed against mine.

"Stay close."

Ten minutes until the Chameleon effect wore off.

"Ninja skills, activate," I whispered, more to bolster my own confidence than anything. I heard a quiet laugh from Kay.

We barely made a sound, though we walked close enough that I was sure he'd be able to hear my heart drumming. Were it not for the shiver of tension in the air, I might have been alone.

The forest path opened up into another clearing, one blocked by a fallen tree. There, Ms Weston had said the centaur king had been crushed by a falling branch. But the tree itself was at least a metre thick. No human could have knocked it down, right? I took a step towards it, squinting to see if I could spot any obvious signs of magical damage. The tree's trunk was reddish brown, but there didn't appear to be any burn marks, and magic didn't feel noticeably stronger here.

I heard the slightest of beeping sounds as Kay activated whatever piece of Alliance tech he was using to check for traces of magic. It took only a second, then his hand brushed against mine again. No indication of the answer. With one last glance at the tree, I turned around, and we headed back down the path, without speaking a word.

A prickling sensation crawled up my spine. The trees were tall enough to completely block out the sky in a web of orange-brown leaves. The sunlight didn't shine on this path, and dark shadows crowded the undergrowth. Rustling sounded amongst the trees, and I stopped dead as Kay rested his hand lightly on top of mine.

Centaurs had gathered on the path ahead, too many to count. Towering horse-people armed with spears and crossbows like a scene from mythology come to life. All wore the same style of crown, made from interwoven leaves and branches twisted into a certain pattern, and all carried weapons. *Oh, hell.*

Kay swore in an undertone, too quiet for anyone else to hear.

We had maybe five minutes left before we'd be fully visible. I glanced over my shoulder, and my heart sank when I saw centaurs gathered in the clearing behind us, too. They'd covered every possible path, sharp spear-points aimed forward, ready to attack. The suspicion and anger in their eyes told us they knew there was something out of place. My heart beat frantically.

"Climb a tree." Kay's voice was barely a breath, but I caught it.

Hell. I needed to pick out one tall enough that if I climbed high, I'd be out of sight of the centaurs. If we bypassed the centaurs directly in front, then we could get back to Markos, assuming nothing had happened to him. These centaurs sure looked unfriendly.

Ignoring the voice in the back of my head telling me we were totally screwed, I picked out a tree and pulled myself onto the nearest branch within reach. Then climbed higher, higher, thanking all the stars for my sense of balance. Falling now would be fatal even if I didn't break my neck. And I had no idea where Kay was. For all I knew, I was alone, surrounded by armed centaurs. But I kept climbing, until I was above the centaurs, above the leafy canopy. I scanned the forest. Nothing but trees in either direction, extending for miles.

A hand on my arm startled me. Lucky I had a tight grip on the branch.

"You're going to reappear in a minute," Kay said, dead-quiet. "We've got to get back to the clearing. Keep moving that way." He moved my hand to point in the right direction. "And stay off the ground. If any of them spots you, I'll cause a diversion."

I shook my head, even though of course he couldn't see me. "Don't be—"

"Trust me," he said. "That way. Keep moving. Don't let them see you. We'll get out."

The hand moved from my arm, and I breathed in, out, in, out. There was the quietest rustling in the leaves, and the slightest movement of the branch behind me. He'd jumped for the neighbouring tree.

This is completely freaking insane. But it was impersonate an invisible ninja or get speared by a hundred centaurs. So I shimmied along a branch, and jumped to the next tree, grasping the branches and pulling myself higher.

Then my body reappeared, balanced in an awkward crouch on the branch.

My heart slammed into my ribs. *Don't panic.* I was too high up to see, a good fifteen feet off the ground, hidden by the thick, wide leaves. I just had to keep moving. I was quick and light on my feet, and knew how to move so I barely disturbed the branches thanks to a childhood spent climbing into high places. But heaven help us if the centaur wasn't waiting for us, or if the others had blocked the Passage...

Move!

I jumped, feet scrambling for purchase on the bark. Jumped again. Again. I hung suspended in the air, heart beating wildly. A centaur stood directly below me, palomino-patterned and armed with a crossbow bigger than me.

Keep moving, Ada.

Another jump, another tree. On the horizon, a promising streak of blue sea told me I was heading in the right direction, towards the coast. I kept one eye on the horizon as I climbed from one tree to the next, a heart-stopping dance of death fifteen feet above the earth.

Nothing to worry about... unless I fell.

I recognised the junction in the trees where we'd left Markos but there was no sign of the centaur, nor any clue as to where he'd gone. Given the proximity of three other, more hostile-looking horse-men, it was clear why. And I hadn't heard another word from Kay. With lack of any direction, I carried on above the path we'd come by, climbing from one tree to the next. The trees grew close enough together that I never had to jump, but I cringed whenever I accidentally knocked the branches and sent autumn-coloured leaves spiralling to the ground. *This wasn't in Alliance training.*

Then I stopped short. I'd almost passed right over a small gathering of centaurs, five in total, and if any of them had glanced up, I'd have been spotted in an instant. My shaking hands held onto the branch of the tree behind a curtain of leaves, and I hung on grimly, hoping they'd go away. They were talking, in their own language—Aglaian. I couldn't understand a word, but the tone made the skin prickle on the back of my neck.

A hand clamped over my mouth. Very good job it did, otherwise I'd have screamed when a second hand grabbed both my wrists to stop me panicking and knocking the branches. Kay's voice was barely a breath—"It's me."

He's still invisible?

"Fifty metres to the left. There's a cave below a cliff. Markos is there."

I nodded. Kay let go of me. A branch from a nearby tree had shifted enough for me to climb onto it. I mouthed *thanks*, even though I had no idea if Kay could see me.

Talk about communication issues, I thought wryly, heading west. Fifty metres. Totally do-able. Ignore the centaurs...

KAY

Somehow, impossibly, I was *still* invisible.

From high up, I saw at least fifty centaurs scattered amongst the trees. All wore leaf-crowns I recognised from Markos's description of a disparate group wanting the throne for themselves. These centaurs wanted Markos dead, so he must be hiding.

I kept one level lower than Ada, one eye on her progress as she kept moving as I'd told her. She was pretty damn good at keeping her balance above the canopy, barely disturbing the leaves around her. But if any of the centaurs looked up at the wrong moment, she'd be in trouble. Which meant I needed to be ready to cause a distraction.

Being invisible gave me a few options, at least. I'd told Markos I'd draw their attention somewhere else. Naturally, he'd objected, but if they saw him, they could shoot him down and claim it an accident.

I did have one option, though. I *could* use magic, in such a way that wouldn't draw attention to myself. I'd not had too many opportunities to practise, but here, it was possible to achieve that level of control. Guess I had the mage to thank for that. But I'd have to time it right, and get the centaurs as far away from Ada as possible.

Ada had managed to pass the centaurs, but we were still too far from the clearing for my liking. And their restless movements indicated they'd sensed a disturbance.

The scanner had picked up traces of magic, all right. Faint traces, but something *magi-tech* in origin had knocked down the tree. Not pure magic. It couldn't have come from Aglaia, where the technology style was totally different. Which meant it came from offworld. Someone from another *universe* had killed the centaur king.

And the scanner couldn't detect which world, of course. It only worked on individuals, and even that wouldn't work here, where magic was a constant presence. What could an offworlder possibly have to gain by murdering Markos's father? The mage had said magic was lower than it seemed. Aglaia didn't have any resources the Alliance needed, or anyone else, for that matter. It was barely acknowledged by most worlds, and the migration rate was negligible. Nobody ever moved there, and few left, especially the centaurs.

It was needle-in-a-haystack impossible to tell who might have killed the king. No, there might be up to fifty worlds with a motive, and that was only within my limited awareness. For all I knew, every goddamned universe had a potential reason to ignite conflict on Aglaia.

Five of the centaurs had moved closer together, and Ada was near enough to reach with those crossbows no matter how fast she climbed. I had to cause a diversion. But centaurs moved quicker than any human even though they couldn't climb.

I kept just below the canopy, moving as quickly as I dared without drawing attention. The group of five had moved close enough to talk to one another. Despite myself, I paused to listen.

"Tryfon said there'd be more."

"This is just a sample. Be careful handling it."

They were passing something around, but I couldn't move further down without putting myself in range of an attack. I dropped to a lower branch, and saw Ada.

Shit. I climbed back to the top, searching out a likely target. Swiftly, I pulled on the magic in the atmosphere and released it just as quickly. A stream of purple-red, thankfully too high for the centaurs to see, aiming for a tree a mile or so out.

The tree fell with a crash that shook the whole canopy. The centaurs turned in that direction, exclaiming curses, talking about intruders. When they started to move down the path towards it, I went the opposite way, pausing when I knew they were out of sight.

How to turn off this invisibility? I wasn't sure how I'd even done it. There were only two ways I'd used magic before—the normal way, and…

When I'd killed, I'd shot pure magic into the target... from me. Had I somehow self-directed that power when I'd switched on the Chameleon? The device was dead, the light was out. The power was coming from me, not the atmosphere, buzzing in my skin, the way it always had.

Lustre.

I concentrated on the magic buzzing in my skin. *Turn off.* But willpower did nothing. Magic—external magic, at least— did as it pleased. And I'd only ever used magic for destruction. To kill. I didn't know how I'd done *this*.

Still, it wasn't permanent. I had to get to Ada and Markos. I'd figure this out later. We had bigger problems to deal with now.

~

ADA

I reached the spot Kay had pointed out. The trees sloped downhill. At the bottom of the hill was a tree-free area, like a quarry, of some kind of bronze-coloured rock. The cave must be that way.

I hoped so, because to get there, I'd have to climb down to the ground.

I twisted around, making sure there were no centaurs nearby. Nothing but trees, by the look of things, but instinct wanted me to stay off the ground. Pulling myself above the canopy again, I surveyed the whole forest. We were still a fair ways from the coast, and the door to the Passages.

Crash. I gripped the branch harder as the whole canopy shook. The source of the shaking was somewhere further back, deep in the forest. The centaurs? Or something else?

Either way, my hands were slipping. I slid down the tree and dropped the last few feet, running for the cliff edge. Now the trees had thinned out, the sun's glare hit my eyes from a dazzling blue sky, overlaid by an odd purplish tint that I realised must be the high-magic level in the atmosphere. Yet I hadn't felt it nagging at me as I did in the Passages. Probably for the best.

I climbed slowly, testing for footholds with my toes. As my feet touched stone, the sound of a hoofbeat made me jump a foot in the air.

"Only me." Markos stuck his head out from beneath an overhang of rock. "Good. You're alive."

"Kay…"

"…is busy knocking half the forest down, by the sound of it," said Markos. "He insisted on being the one to distract the Anthos tribe."

"He *what?*" I said. "And… the Anthos tribe?"

"They're trying to get onto royal territory. I'll deal with *them* later, once I've got you two out of Aglaia."

"Did you know this would happen?" I asked.

"Of course not!" The centaur bristled in a way that made me take a step back. "They were breaking our laws, as it happens, but I wouldn't have been able to report it if they were there to arrange my death. They didn't know we were here, if it's any consolation."

"Not much," said a voice from above.

"Kay?" I said, half uncertain, half relieved. "Why are you still invisible?"

"Because I can't turn it off. Get out of the way."

"You what?" I yelped as pain shot through my foot. "Ouch! I think you just broke my toes."

"Sorry. I did tell you to move."

I leaned on the wall to massage my foot. "You can't turn it off? It was only supposed to be ten minutes."

"I realise that," said Kay. "It's not the device that's doing it, it's me."

"You're invisible," I said stupidly.

"I think we all know that, human." Markos stared at the spot Kay's voice had come from. "What in the name of all the gods did you do?"

"I didn't do it on purpose!" said Kay. "I think I amplified it or something."

"Magic-wielder," said Markos coldly, and a shiver went down my spine. The centaur *hated* magic. Yet he must have had some idea what Kay could do.

Like those two teenagers in the warehouse.

"Is there no 'off' switch?" I said. "How'd you even do it in the first place?"

"I have no idea, and this isn't the worst of it," said Kay. "Magic knocked the tree that killed the king down, all right. But not Aglaian. An offworlder killed him."

Markos's expression changed from incredulous to aghast. "No."

"It's true. The scanner couldn't get a reading, but it sure isn't local. It's offworld, for sure."

Markos cursed loudly in Aglaian. "We can't tell Eidora or the others. They'd have me flayed for bringing you here in the first place. We can tell the council, though. They'll take action... but it might not stop the war."

"Do you have a record of every offworlder who's come here?" Kay asked. "I'm sure it's pretty limited. It'll have to have been within a recent time frame, and with access to the centaurs' territory... this just doesn't add up, though."

It was kind of disconcerting to hear an invisible person talking to himself.

"Wait," Kay said. "Damn. *Damn.*"

"What is it, human?" said Markos. "We can't see you."

"That's the bloody point, isn't it? *How* many invisible

people are running around at any one time? Don't you think any of them could have got through the doorway to Aglaia—to any world? Like the ravegens on Valeria."

"Bloodrock," I said. "Oh. *Shit.*" If that bloodrock solution had got out, literally anyone could have got hold of it and used it to sneak onto Aglaia and murder the centaur leader. Anyone, from any world.

"Yeah," said Kay. "Of course, Cethrax is the obvious choice, given all the trouble they've been causing recently, but we can't count on that. We can look into which worlds might have a motive to cause a war on Aglaia. Let's face it, that's the most likely reason—on the surface, anyway. We'll have to get more people involved. The council will know more details about the precise machinations…"

"You're making my head spin, human," said Markos. "Tell your council, but I would wait before speaking to any Aglaian. Tryfon was dead right about the murder, but I doubt he would have considered the possibility of another world being involved. If anything, this would prove to most Aglaians that our becoming involved with other universes was a terrible error on our part."

"Maybe it's that distrust the killer is counting on," said Kay. "Why target Aglaia? It's naturally contentious *and* anti-Alliance for the most part—no offence," he added.

"None taken," said the centaur. "I'm as aware of the shortcomings of my own world as you are of Earth's, human… though I never will see the appeal in *flying.*"

"Wish we could do that right now," said Kay. "How do we get out of here?"

"Now the others are occupied, I think we can safely cross the plains this way. There's a path back to the forest east-way… nobody ever comes here, but it goes without saying that humans are banned."

"Figures," said Kay.

"You really can't turn it off?" I asked, as Markos moved out of the cave, glancing up at the forest bordering the cliff top.

"Never mind that. We need to move first. What even is this place?"

"A quarry of sorts, but we don't use it," said Markos. "This is a blasted nuisance. If any of my family knew I'd brought humans here… but it can't be helped."

He led the way over the rocky ground. Without the canopy above, I felt exposed, and not just because the invisibility had worn off. I concentrated on not tripping over the cracks in the paving-stone-sized rocks, stopping to squint when I saw something glittering in a gap between two smooth, bronze-coloured stones. Ahead, Markos didn't look back, but I heard a sharp intake of breath from beside me.

"That's… wait." Kay paused. "I know what that is." He went very silent.

Markos muttered something in Aglaian. "By the gods, human, if you mention this to *anyone,* I'll kill you myself."

I stopped, staring at him. His expression was stony. He couldn't possibly be serious? Despite myself, I crouched, peering between the rocks. A black substance gleamed beneath. *No way.*

"That's intense," said Kay, in a low, angry tone. "What the hell do you take me for?"

"Sorry, human," said Markos, "but not even the mages here on Aglaia know anything of centaur territory. We can barely keep them from cutting down the whole forest. If they get the slightest idea of the resources hidden here, especially *that,* then we'd effectively undo a hundred years of peace."

"I gathered as much," said Kay. "I have no intention of mentioning any of this to the council, as it happens. Nor that I saw those Anthos centaurs exchanging something, and they mentioned your cousin's name. Tryfon."

"They *what?*"

"I didn't see what they were exchanging. I tried to listen in, but they were too close to us, I had to distract them."

"Tryfon… and them? That explains a lot." A shadow passed over the centaur's face.

I edged away from him, and jumped as I backed into something solid.

"Sorry," I said, turning around. "I didn't see… obviously. You're so quiet."

"You're standing on my foot," said Kay.

"Ah—sorry!" I stumbled back. And now Markos was looking at me, eyes narrowed. "I won't tell anyone about… whatever that is, either," I said quickly. "Never. I've been keeping secrets most of my life, remember? I know things I'd never tell the council, even though I work for the Alliance now."

"Sensible thinking, human," said Markos. "I would never have allowed this if I'd ever thought there was the possibility… no matter. I'll take you home."

He'd believed me. And it was true. Some of the things the refugees had told me, I'd never repeat in a million years. Yet I was only now appreciating the value of information. I wasn't sure what to think, really, only that I definitely hadn't planned to get involved in Alliance politics.

But it might be too late already.

12

ADA

Our path took us over rocky ground. God only knew how Kay could possibly tell where he was going, being invisible. When I'd first used the Chameleon, it had taken a ton of practise not to accidentally hit obstacles or trip over my own shoes, and even visible, navigating the gaps between the rocks was precarious in places. At least we could actually see the sky here, the red sun a disc shape above the trees. It struck me then that I'd never been so far away from human habitation, unless you counted the Passages. I'd been in London my whole life. Even with the faint sounds of birds calling amongst the trees, the silence was as unnerving as the presence of a hostile species which would happily shoot us all dead. I kept glancing over my shoulder, hoping it was just paranoia that made the hairs stand up on the back of my neck. That, or Kay being simultaneously present and absent.

"Are you even still there?" I asked Kay, as we reached the forest on the other side of the rocky plains. Markos had said the clearing was only a short path away. Although I couldn't see it, some of the tension seeped out of me. We were in a safe zone now, Alliance ground.

The voice came from on my left. "Yes. Why?"

"I can't hear you at all. I was starting to think you'd learned to teleport."

"Yeah, right. If I could, I'd have used it to circumvent the public transport system."

"Ha," I said. "Good one. To be fair, you'd think the Passages would be used for that."

"Strangely, no," said Kay. "You've never been on the main Passage at peak time, have you? Worse than the bloody train."

"Humans." Markos shook his head.

"What? We can't all get by on four hooves."

Markos sighed. "Aren't you going to try and undo that spell, human?"

"I *am* trying," said Kay. "Maybe it'll wear off when I get into the Passages, or back to Earth."

"And if not?"

"Then I'll have to fall back on a career as a spy."

I grinned despite the urgent silence wrapping around the forest. Joking kept the fear at bay. "You do move quiet enough."

"Hmm. I'll think about that one."

We'd reached the clearing now. *Thank goodness.* But the tension didn't relax out of my body even as we crossed over the threshold of the Passages.

"You should come back to Earth," said Kay, as Markos paused, tapping a hoof on the ground.

"And leave the Anthos tribe to cause trouble?"

"You said they might be there to arrange your death."

"They wouldn't dare attack me. Eidora will see to it."

"Right," said Kay. "Where *is* Tryfon at the moment, anyway? We can't report him if he's vanished."

"Yes, I'm aware of that slight hitch," said Markos. "The good news is, I think it'll make my sister come around and accept the leadership. She'll believe I overheard him. She never liked him."

"So, where are you going?" Kay asked. "I'd rather you didn't go out into the forest and get yourself killed."

A sudden *neigh* echoed through the trees. Markos's expression sharpened. "Go. I'll send word to you later, when I know what's happening."

Kay muttered a curse. "You're joking."

"Get out of here, humans!"

Good advice. I hurried down the Passage, glancing back at the still-open door.

"Kay?" I said. "Dammit. We have to go. You can't stay here."

The door slid closed, seemingly of its own accord.

"Good," I said. "Come on. We have to get back to Earth."

"Yeah," said Kay. "I just hope the damned idiot knows what he's doing. We're up to our necks in it now."

I nodded. "We sure are. Whereabouts are you?"

"Here." The voice came closer than I expected, and I shivered.

"Wow. This is… weird."

"You don't say." Kay sounded annoyed now. "Bloody magic doesn't come with a guidebook."

The Passages here were quiet, because this area was rarely frequented by anyone from the Alliance. These worlds were recent additions, some still relatively unstable. I wanted to ask Kay about it, but the silence unnerved me. True, my own footsteps made no sound either, but that only added to the sense of being watched.

"I can't tell if you're ahead of me or behind me," I said into the quiet. "Wait. I don't know where we are."

No reply.

EMMA L. ADAMS

"Kay?" I asked, heart sinking. He hadn't gone out of range, had he? No way to tell.

"Uh… Kay? Seriously?"

Great. I carried on walking, hoping I'd catch up sooner or later. Unless he'd gone back to help Markos.

"Dammit, Kay," I said. "Tell me whether you're there or not."

Silence, apart from my own heartbeat.

"Brilliant." Nothing to do but keep on walking and hope I didn't run into any monsters. *They ought to issue maps.* The one thing my communicator didn't have, even if it was hooked up to offworld GPS for the five neighbouring worlds. Which were literally miles away from here. It wasn't like I could call home either, not until I got within at least a mile of Earth. God only knew where *that* was. All these Passages looked the same.

I tried to recall which way we'd come as I walked down the corridor. This one had a lot of doors on either side, marked only with numbers—seriously, did *every* Alliance member from *every* world have to learn where they led? Now I saw up close, though, there were symbols carved along the edges, invisible until they caught the light. I examined the nearest, curiosity getting the better of me.

Someone grabbed my arm suddenly, and I jumped a foot in the air. If there'd been a target to see, I'd have hit them.

"Jesus Christ!"

Kay appeared—literally appeared—right in front of me, grinning. "Hey, Ada."

"You—you nearly gave me a heart attack."

"I'm sure you'll live."

I glared. "That wasn't funny."

"It was. Admit it."

"Well, I hope you're entertained. If you do it again, I'll

break your face." My heart was still beating like it was trying to escape.

Kay tilted his head to one side. "Not even one per cent entertaining?"

"Were you planning that the whole time? When did you figure out how to turn it off?"

"About a minute ago."

"And your first thought was, I'm going to scare Ada half to death."

"Who wouldn't?"

I moved to hit him, and he vanished again.

"That's not playing fair." I groaned. "I want out of these Passages, Kay. You know I don't know the way."

"Oh, what a pity. I'll send a patrol to come and get you."

"You aren't serious." What the hell was he up to?

"Bye, Ada."

"Kay, you complete dick—" I yelped as he grabbed me from behind. I twisted around, but he'd apparently moved again. "Should we really be messing around in here?"

"We're on the first level." He still hadn't reappeared.

"So?" I spun on the spot, and I could hear him laughing at me. "Kay Walker, if you don't appear *right now*, I'm going to break into your apartment and steal your limited edition *Lord of the Rings.*"

Kay appeared, a metre in front of me, wearing an expression of absolute incredulity. "You wouldn't."

"Don't underestimate me. I know how to pick a lock." I folded my arms. "Quit it. I want to get out of here."

"Yeah, I got that." The corner of his mouth quirked. "You remember where I live?"

Uh... no. But he didn't have to know. "Either lead us out of here or give me a map. Won't Ms Weston think we got killed on Aglaia?"

"Don't mention the dragon lady," he said. "She'll string us

up from the ceiling, actually." And he strode off. At least he wasn't invisible this time.

"Great." I hurried after him. "Question. How in the world are she and Amanda related? Amanda's really nice, but she's... uh. Not."

"I have no idea," said Kay. "She'll want our report... dammit. Don't say a word about that quarry, okay? Even to her. She'd tell the council for sure. Of course it's confidential, but if the Aglaians find out, they'd take it as a threat either way."

And we were back on that topic again, the brief levity fading. We hurried through the Passages, though I had the sense Kay was holding back to make sure I didn't fall behind. A sharp, unexpected pang shook me, reminding me of all the ways I'd screwed up lately. The whole thing with his ex— what did it matter, anyway? And as for Aric, it was like Kay had said, magic didn't give you a choice. I *was* a freaking hypocrite. The things I'd accused him of, I'd done myself, and worse. Maybe after everything that had happened, I'd sabotaged a good thing out of some bizarre impulse to self-destruction, because deep down, I still didn't believe it could be real. I'd kissed him, I'd actually felt something... and it scared me to death.

And had he even felt the same?

Before I could think of anything intelligent to say, we reached a corridor I recognised. Central's door was opposite one of Valeria's, the one Delta had dragged me through. Kay paused outside the door, testing it with his hands as if expecting to find it open.

"What're you doing?"

"Keeping an eye out for ravegens," he said. "I'd say it was those bastards who got into Aglaia, but they aren't intelligent enough. It wouldn't surprise me if this was all interrelated, but I don't have enough information to figure it out yet."

"You—is that your mission? Figure out what they're doing? I thought it was up to the council."

"Technically. But now we know things they don't. Things we can't tell them. Damn. I didn't want you dragged into this, Ada. Offworld politics are dangerous as hell on a good day."

"What?" Was he actually worried about me? Was that why he'd been so distant? Not that I'd given him reason to be otherwise, considering. "You don't have to figure it out, Kay. If it's that dangerous—"

"Like I said. I know things I damn well don't *want* to, but I'm not leaving this alone now."

I tried to wrap my head around that logic. "Right. Just don't get yourself killed."

"Wasn't planning to." He moved away from the Valerian door, crossing to the one that led to Central.

"What're you doing now, anyway?" I asked.

"Dealing with the dragon lady." He glanced at his communicator. "Then beating the crap out of virtual monsters."

"Is that your default response to a crisis?"

"Huh?" This time, he did meet my eyes.

"Just trying to figure you out, is all." I'd have better luck with Aglaian politics. Kay Walker was an enigma.

"Yeah?" He raised an eyebrow. "Good luck with that."

Was that a dismissal? For all his teasing just now, we were virtually strangers.

"What're you staring at?"

Busted. "Uh. Zoned out for a moment there."

"You... all right?"

I bit down on the instinct to retaliate. I'd never liked being asked that question. Especially now. "I guess. Apart from the near-brush with death back there. Which, to be honest, I'm starting to think is a side effect of hanging out with you."

"Hanging out?"

Great one, Ada. At least I hadn't insulted him this time. That was a step forward.

"It sounds better than 'risking our lives'," I said.

"You may have a point there."

I swallowed. *Say the freaking words, Ada.* "Thanks for the other night," I blurted.

He blinked. But I couldn't read his expression, as usual. "No problem."

"And… uh. Can we just disregard every stupid thing I've ever said up until now?"

"Starting from when? That wouldn't leave much."

"You—" I swatted at him, but his reflexes were too fast. He caught my hand in his own the instant it moved. "Dammit! Let go of me!"

"Only if you promise not to hit me."

"I can't make any promises. You're really annoying."

"Thanks. You're ridiculous."

I spluttered. "That's a pretty crappy insult." I swatted with my other hand, and ended up with both of them trapped. "Not fair." It was kind of hard to keep up my sulky expression with his face inches from mine. My traitorous heart beat faster.

Kay, however, was totally deadpan as usual. "Pity."

"What did you do to your hands, anyway?" I asked, glancing at the bandages covering both knuckles.

"Glass. A goblin crashed a hover bike through the front of a shopping centre on Valeria."

"Really? Only you could say that and not sound totally insane… wait. I take that back."

He let go of both my hands and pushed, so suddenly I almost tripped over my own feet.

"Quit it." I righted myself, glaring at him. And then shook my head, unable to keep from smiling.

Then we were both laughing. I'd been on edge since

leaving Central, and once I started, I couldn't stop. I leaned on the wall, giggling helplessly while Kay looked on, shaking his head in amusement.

"What d'you think?" I said, when I'd caught my breath. "You wanna start over? Because I don't like fighting with people."

"Really? Could've fooled me."

"Ha. Okay. I don't want to fight with *you*."

A heartbeat's pause. Our eyes met, and I hadn't seen him look at me like that since… since we'd kissed in New York. I was pretty sure the tingles racing up my arms had less to do with magic than the way he'd been holding my hands. And I wanted to hold his again.

I wanted more than that.

"Yeah?" he said. "Sure. We can start over."

My heartbeat kicked up, and then slowed just as quickly as he turned away, opening the door to Earth. The ordinary street appeared before us, the sharp profile of the Alliance's headquarters outlined against the grey sky.

"Kay…"

"We're late already. Hopefully they won't have sent people after us." Kay crossed the threshold, muttering a curse as raindrops spattered both us and the Passage floor.

"Gotta love London," I said, wishing I had a hood and wrapping my coat tighter around me. At least it was water-proof. "I'd emigrate to Aglaia if the locals were a bit friendlier."

"Not my top choice," said Kay. "They're in a drought now. Something to do with the magic."

"Really?"

"I have no idea. Just something one of the mages on the council said."

The washed-out grey sky was dull compared to Aglaia, but at least there were no centaurs hiding between the run-down houses. We reached the back gate, and he retrieved a key from the inside pocket of his coat.

"Uh, did Ms Weston say everyone on Aglaia has magic?" I asked. "Like, every single person?"

"Yeah, it's the way magic works there." He unlocked the gate, and we went through to Central's car park. "Every human has the potential. It's external, though."

So they weren't like us. They didn't have magic somehow living *inside* them.

"How high is the level?"

He paused, re-locking the gate. "Same as Valeria. Second. But it isn't used to attack other people. That's illegal, actually. They use it to... change things. Like they manipulate the weather, that kind of thing. I imagine it's pretty useful."

So magic for the Aglaians wasn't a threat? I pondered it as we went back into Central.

"Wow. How does that work with the Balance?"

Kay pushed his now-dripping-wet dark hair out of his eyes. "Well, they probably caused the drought by summoning up a storm or something. The counter-effect rule still applies. Read the files Ms Weston sent you. I think you'd find it interesting."

"Sure, I will." Of course, since the mission had been sprung on me the moment I arrived at Central that morning, I'd only had the chance to learn the basics. But now we were out of the danger zone, my curiosity rose again. "I skimmed it, but I don't remember it saying anything about magic."

"That's mostly classified," said Kay, in a low voice.

Like that source. No wonder Markos didn't want people finding out.

But what if someone already knew?

"They have files on every world?" I asked, as we climbed the stairs to the first floor. I talked to fill the silence, though I couldn't find words for what I actually wanted to say.

"Near enough. Ms Weston said you had a pretty good basic knowledge of offworld, actually."

"She did? Wow. I'd got the impression she hated me."

"It's what she does. Just don't poke her with a stick, and you'll be fine."

"What, you aren't planning on trying your invisibility trick?" I flashed him a grin.

"I'm not sure it works on Earth. Damn, that would be priceless, though." He laughed quietly. "I'll save it for a special occasion."

But his expression blanked when we reached Ms Weston's office. He knocked on the door.

"You took your time," she said. "Another hour and I would have sent backup."

"There was a hitch," said Kay. "We had to skirt around a group of unfriendly Anthos tribe centaurs. They were trespassing on royal ground."

"And?"

"Magic did it, but not Aglaian," said Kay. "Magi-tech."

"I see." Ms Weston spoke as though we'd just commented on the rain outside, as opposed to an imminent offworld war. "Where is Markos?"

"He stayed behind, to tell his sister about his cousin's involvement. Sounded like Tryfon is somehow involved with those Anthos centaurs we saw," Kay said. "So Markos was hoping it would make his sister listen to reason and step in as queen. I tried to get him to come back to Earth, but understandably…"

"Yes, we need to do everything we can to avoid outright warfare. The centaurs have yet to make an open accusation towards the mages, but it's only a matter of time. If there was a way to expose whoever is working with offworlders… a magic scanner wouldn't be enough, especially if they used technology to do it. It's a clever plot. Someone is playing us—the whole Alliance, not just Aglaia."

"Exactly," said Kay. "The next meeting's in two days, right?"

"The treaty renewal. Supposedly. It's looking doubtful at the moment that Aglaia will want to renew its membership in the Alliance."

"Can't exactly blame them," Kay muttered. "Dammit. This is a lose-lose situation all around. Unless we prove someone got through from offworld. At the moment, I'm inclined to think Cethrax. And someone mentioned that bloodrock solution was stolen from West Office?"

Ms Weston gave me a sharp look. "And have you forgotten I told you to keep those details quiet?"

My heart sank. I guessed he wasn't supposed to tell me that.

"I already knew," I said quickly. "Um, my guardian's friends used to trade in the stuff. They know some of it went missing. That's all I know." *It's not a betrayal,* I told the stab of guilt. The Alliance knew the Knights dealt in bloodrock solution. Used to.

"As it happens, after Cethrax was fined for helping the Campbells, they were also forced to give up what little bloodrock they possessed… which suggests someone is offering them the solution for a price. But that's beside the point. Someone intends to stir up trouble on Aglaia and they have no qualms about straying into dangerous territory to do so."

"Yeah, that's why I think someone else is working with Cethrax," said Kay. "Is the council looking into it?"

"As much as they can. Remember that Aglaia is not Earth's priority."

"I figured." The corners of his mouth pulled down. "Can I

keep the earpiece on for now? I don't know if it works across long distances, but Markos will still have his."

I'd totally forgotten I still wore the invisible earpiece, too.

"Ah," I said, and they both turned to me. "It'll stay invisible, no one will know he's wearing it."

"I hope not," said Kay, "considering the centaurs' opinion on technology. But if anything were to happen to Markos, it'd be the only way he could get a message to the Alliance."

"By violating his own laws," said Ms Weston, a challenge in her expression.

Kay's eyes narrowed. If it came to a staring contest between the two of them, I honestly didn't know who would win.

"He's our colleague," he said, his expression becoming even harder. "Your employee."

"The contract between an individual and the Alliance is always beneath the laws of their own world."

Really? I hadn't known that. So if my own world claimed me, they'd be able to override the Alliance?

"That's ridiculous," I cut in, before Kay could speak. "What if that world's overthrown by a maniac dictator? Don't human or cross-species' rights come first? That's what the Alliance is founded on." I might not have Kay's seemingly encyclopaedic knowledge of the Alliance and the Multiverse, but I did know *some* things.

"Exactly." Kay's glance barely flickered towards me, but I sensed his approval. "First principle. I think you can trust I know every word. And I have license to travel offworld with or without direct Alliance approval. Unless you want me to take it to the council."

"That *won't* be necessary," said Ms Weston. "And I'll thank you to remember who you're talking to. *Both* of you. You may keep the earpiece, but Ada, I'll take yours back. The tech team need it."

"Right." I fumbled with the device. My hands were shaking. Though her tone of voice hadn't changed, it didn't take a genius to see she was really pissed off. And as for Kay, the last time I'd seen him that furious, it had been when I'd left him in the Passages when he'd tried to get me to go to a shelter rather than helping my family.

"You can both leave. Just remember your own loyalties are with the Alliance now. Go."

Kay's jaw clenched, and he swept out of the office without a backwards glance. I was kind of nervous to follow after, but neither did I want to stay in the room with Ms Weston. I made for the stairs. Kay was already out of sight. *Jesus Christ.* I mean, I was pretty angry that Ms Weston appeared to be unperturbed about one of her employees being stuck on a hostile world... but Kay, well, I kind of felt sorry for those virtual monsters. This definitely wasn't the time to try and make up for all the crap I'd said to him.

Typical. Even if we'd almost been getting along back in the Passages. If his scaring me half to death counted as *getting along.*

He could become invisible. He hadn't denied his abilities out of fear like I had, even after he'd apparently lost control of it and almost killed Aric. And he'd killed Skyla, and Janice. I hadn't seen how he'd learned to use it so quickly. He'd been a magic-wielder the whole time, though.

I'm not at all interested in magic-wielders, he'd said to me once. At the time, I hadn't known he was one himself. And now he appeared to actually be embracing it. But then, you couldn't change what you were. Even with bloodrock solution. Under the surface, you were the same.

Magic-wielder. Adamantine.

13

KAY

L ustre. That was what I'd seen on Aglaia.

I hadn't said the word in front of Ada. I knew it for what it was immediately, because I'd been looking at pictures of it when researching the Alliance's most up-to-date information via communicator. Sure, it looked like adamantine, but it *felt* different. Like it made the magic living under my skin even more intense. As Amanda had said: only magic-wielders could feel the difference between sources. And according to the notes I'd read, only lustre grew in those particular formations.

There was a whole magic source right there, and the humans didn't know anything about it. They'd never been that far onto the mainland, because the centaurs had been there before they'd even come to the continent, nigh on a thousand years before.

Not a word from Markos had come through on the earpiece. It was possible he'd forgotten he was even wearing it—hell, I'd forgotten about the damn thing myself. And so had Ada.

What a blasted mess. So that was why the centaurs were

so uptight about humans impinging on their territory. If the Alliance found out, a dozen or more worlds would want to cash in on it. Maybe they already had, if there really was someone offworld working against the centaurs. With the rebels.

It seemed too big a coincidence that we'd seen them so close to the source. It was near the royal grounds, so those rebel centaurs shouldn't have even been there. Did anyone outside Markos's family even know about it? Usually, the important people had the information, while the others were left in the dark to avoid potential conflict.

Ms Weston had given me the option to come into Central or not the following day. I still wasn't allowed into council meetings, and the blasted Aglaian fiasco was postponed until the next morning, so technically, I didn't have anywhere I was supposed to be.

So I didn't particularly appreciate being woken at five in the morning by a message reminding me—again—that I was expressly forbidden from interfering in Aglaia today. Nights where I actually managed to get a decent amount of sleep were rarer than a sunny day in Cethrax, so the interruption put me in a raging bad mood. I took my new motorcycle out for a ride, winding up at the training complex. But even beating the crap out of virtual monsters became dull after a while, even if it took the edge off my frustration about not being able to do a thing about Aglaia. I'd tried contacting Markos a couple of times through the earpiece, only to be greeted with static. I didn't know if that meant he'd taken it off, or if it wasn't safe to talk without antagonising the centaurs.

I'd never been able to deal with boredom. Especially when I was irritated as hell that Ms Weston had once again put a wrench in my plan to talk to Ada, who would be at Central right now with the boss hovering over her shoulder.

I didn't especially want to head back to my apartment—I barely lived in the place anyway. I wanted to do something useful.

After picking up coffee and food from a local cafe and checking I had my offworld credit card on me, I made up my mind. I had my Ambassador's pass, and my first payment in offworld credits had come through.

I knew exactly what I planned to do with *that*.

London's main Passage was now open again following the fiasco at Central, and more crowded than the tube at rush hour, with people from a hundred or more universes traversing from one gleaming metal door to another. Each door led to a different part of a different world, and even the presence of countless guards wasn't enough to deter some people from trying to sneak a free pass. My Ambassador's coat ensured I got through the crowd easily, and I found Raj by the public entrance to Neo Greyle, in conversation with the Valerian guards.

"Everything all right?" I asked. "Not been any trouble, has there?"

The guard shook his head. "Nothing new. Just had to restrict access to non-Ambassadors. You two are fine to go through."

"Any reason you're here?" Raj asked me as we passed by the guards. This doorway led to one of Neo Greyle's endless main roads, this one alongside the main Alliance branch. The building was virtually a twin of Central in London, the black adamantine covering standing out amongst the other skyscrapers.

"I'm gonna apply for a license for a hover bike."

"And a crash helmet?"

I rolled my eyes. "I did check their manuals first. What're you doing here?"

"Meeting people in the offworld district, seeing as we're off-duty."

"If we don't run into any more goblins."

"I'm holding you responsible if we do."

Judging by the number of guards patrolling outside the Alliance building, they were on the alert for trouble. But even ravegens wouldn't dare use the main entrance. For one thing, they'd probably get trampled in the rush, invisible or not.

Speaking of which... I had the Chameleon with me for a reason, clipped to my sleeve. Even with the battery dead, I could still turn invisible just by touching it. When using the lustre's amplifying effect, it was like being tuned into a low-frequency radio only I could pick up on. Once I'd found the signal, I could control whether it was switched on or off in the same way I could pull on magic or release it. Like a sixth sense impossible to explain to anyone who wasn't a magic-wielder.

As for what else I could do with it... I planned to find out.

"I'm going to put a deposit on one of those bikes," I said, at the street corner near the hover-depot. "Don't suppose you want to join me?"

"I'd prefer to stay in one piece, thanks," said Raj.

While he went in the direction of offworld district, I picked out a sleek silver hover bike and put down a deposit. One provisional license application later and I was at the racecourse, in a fierce one-on-one race with an overeager Valerian kid who could barely steer in a straight line. They were insanely lax with who was allowed to drive—everyone over the age of thirteen. Only their hover-transport's built-in collision shields stopped the number of accidents getting out of hand.

"Not fair!" he wailed, as I cut across him and managed to

steer the bike to a stop at the finish line without tipping over this time.

"Bad luck, kid," I said. Out the corner of my eye, I saw cash exchange hands, and a blond woman—couldn't tell if she was Earth or Valerian—gave me a *come over here* smile from behind the bordering fence.

Ordinarily, I'd have taken her up on it. But my thoughts strayed to Ada before I could stop them. Irritated at myself, I parked the bike properly in the hover-port. Better to leave it there, where no one would be able to steal it when I wasn't here. My communicator started buzzing as I left.

"Simon?" I flicked the touch screen. Thanks to time zone differences between Aglaia, the UK and New York, where Simon worked at the main US Alliance branch, I hadn't heard from him in a while. "What's the deal? I was buying a hover bike."

"You're joking."

"Nope. I'm in Neo Greyle right now."

"Tell me exactly where so I can come and kill you. Can you even drive one of those things yet?"

I glanced back at the gleaming rows of bikes in the depot. "On automatic, yeah. I'll figure it out."

Simon snorted. "Of course. Don't go causing any more traffic accidents."

"You heard about that?"

"One of our Ambassadors was in the city at the time. I knew it was you he was talking about."

"Hey, I'll have you know I caught the criminals. Both times."

"Both...? Jesus Christ, Kay. What are you even doing there? On a mission, or what?"

"No. I'm dealing with crap on Aglaia, but that's on hold until tomorrow. So I decided..."

"...to buy a hover bike. Of course." I heard Simon's exasperated sigh through the phone. "Dammit. Why do we mere mortals have to go through admin before we can make Ambassador? I'm dying here."

"What, no monsters yet?"

"A few dreyverns. Got some of those invisible what-d'you-call-its, ravegens, too. Near another Valeria door on this side."

"Damn," I said. "They sure are persistent. That's kind of why I'm here, to keep an eye on things. Plus, there's the hover bikes, of course."

"I get why so many Earth Ambassadors transfer over there. Epic, Kay. You're living the dream."

Yeah. Except for the slight issue of a potential war on another world, and no word from Markos yet.

"Guess so. How's New York?"

"Same as ever. Which is to say, awesome, if I could get the hell out of this office. Still, can't complain. Everyone knows I helped set up those Passages to Enzar. Dunno how it got out, but I'm drowning in female attention."

"Not a terrible way to die," I said.

"Ha. I suppose it isn't. How's Ada, anyway?"

Dammit. "Okay, I guess. I've been offworld most of the past week."

"That's not good. I thought you two were, like…"

"Tara showed up at Central."

Simon swore. "What? Seriously?"

"She's at London's West Branch, and that bastard Aric decided to go over there and tell her stories about me—of course Ada had to show up when she was causing a scene."

It was as much my fault as hers. I should have just told Tara to back the hell off, or talked to her somewhere else. I didn't even want to get into what Ada's brother had said.

"Damn, Kay. No offence, man, but Tara's kind of a bitch."

"Yes, I think I realised that a while ago," I muttered. "Ada has enough crap to deal with."

"Like what?"

"Working at Central with Ms Weston breathing down her neck, for a start. And you know what the Campbells did to her." I'd only told Simon the basics—it was Ada's business, after all—but I reckoned he'd figured part of it out.

"You've heard of, I don't know, talking to her about it? Seeing as you were there?"

"She won't talk to me about it. Can't say I blame her."

"Damn," said Simon. "Guess being kidnapped would screw a person up. She seemed okay when…"

"Yeah. Seemed." I stifled a sigh. "She has her family, anyway, and god knows they have enough to deal with, the way the Alliance upended their lives."

"I guess so. Still. You're an idiot."

"Cheers."

"I gotta go, anyway. I'm on the next patrol and I'm thinking of checking up on the Enzar Passage—you've been there recently?"

"Over the weekend. I've been kind of occupied by this offworld assassination," I said. "You must have heard about Aglaia by now. It's not classified."

"Wait, you're involved in that? Bloody hell, Kay. No wonder. *And* the ravegens? No world is safe from you."

"Yeah, thanks, Simon," I said. "I should get away from this place. They'll start trying to sell me hover boots next. Not that I'd refuse, but…"

"Ha. Got it. You stay out of trouble… I don't know why I bother saying that anymore. Just don't crash that bike."

"I won't make any promises." I clicked off the phone.

No hover boots this time. But I did have an idea. First, I headed into an alleyway between two buildings to make sure no one saw me. Then I tapped into the magic ever-present in Valeria, and disappeared.

The invisibility-effect could last as long as I wanted it to. The lustre in my blood amplified the magic that was already there. And I had the Chameleon clipped to the inside of my sleeve at the moment. Even on Earth, I could tap into it. The magic inside *me* responded to external sources. It must depend on skin contact, because I'd never got the same reaction from any other magic-powered object I'd been near. That explanation made sense, given that the Chameleon only worked if you were touching it. And so did bloodrock.

I'd checked the laws on human enhancement. The Alliance had updated them twelve years ago, to rule out any kind of experimentation involving pure magic sources. I was fairly sure Klathica frequently flaunted those rules, but it didn't sound like I'd run into anyone with the same ability as me anytime soon. Because the other three were dead.

Maybe others had died in the process.

Restlessness burned in my blood. It wasn't worth my while to try and track down who, exactly, had been the one to inject me with magic. Their trail would be covered up like everything else. Besides, they weren't the perpetrator. No, he was on a world beyond reach.

Stop it. Don't bother looking for answers where they don't exist. Whatever my father's intentions had been, he'd handed me a weapon I'd be an idiot to ignore. Maybe I'd been able to control it all along. Magic responded to the wielder's intent. The Academy had decided that I'd used it against Aric in self-defence. I hadn't contradicted them, because it was partially true. But now, I had to wonder.

Stop being ridiculous, Kay. If I hadn't killed with magic, then I'd be the one dead. I should know better. *You strike first, or you die. There are no other options.* You could call a dagger an ornament, but you'd be a damn fool not to use it if someone was about to cut your throat.

I watched the crowds passing by from the side street with a vague sense of detachment. Nobody could see me. In fact... I could sneak into places I'd never been able to get at before.

Including the Campbells' main base, only a short walk away from here.

A prickling sensation crawled between my shoulder blades as I slipped underneath the tape sealing the entrance to the wide-open concrete space. The twin warehouses were still there. The place I'd killed for the first—and not last—time. The place Ada had been trapped.

The sudden, searing urge to set the place ablaze rose within me. *Get on with it, Kay.*

I headed for the spiralling office block which had once been the seat of the Campbells' power. A powerful family based their empire here. A family who turned their children into killers. Whether brainwashing had been involved, I didn't know, nor did I particularly care. It all came down to the same thing: choice. They didn't have to obey without question even when asked to kidnap a girl and turn her into a weapon against Central.

Ada's panic-stricken face flashed before my eyes, and my hands clenched into fists. I wished they'd all fucking died.

Rage blacked out my vision and I slammed a fist into the metal wall. The sharp pain brought me back to reality, breathing heavily, shoving the memories behind a wall. The glass cuts across my knuckles were bleeding again.

I skirted the building, which twisted like a double helix pattern with windows curving around the sides. Doors all closed, as I expected. I checked no one was around, then found a likely window on the floor above. And I tried to *push* on magic, like I'd tried in Aglaia. The subtlest movement barely disturbed the air with a faint ripple. Magic was stable here.

The window opened with a quiet click, and I jumped, pulling myself into the room. A meeting-room, by the look of things. This place was seventy-odd floors high. But there'd be a floor plan somewhere.

It didn't take me long to find it, in the corridor outside. I memorised the locations of the likely rooms I'd need to check out, and headed for the stairs. Three floors up.

The Campbells' tech labs covered this particular floor. I didn't hold out much hope for finding anything useful. Their speciality was offworld communications, but that had been a front for their illegal smuggling operations. They'd pretended to help Enzar for altruistic reasons when they were really looking for power. They had the links to get hold of illegal substances like bloodrock, but what they'd been planning to do with it, I couldn't say. They'd been intending to use Ada to attack Central because they wanted revenge on the council for limiting their offworld trade...

Something didn't add up. They'd been involved in illegal operations for years. They could have attacked the council at any time. Why now? The offworld trade laws had only been updated a few months ago, which must have been the trigger to put their plan into action.

Most of the rooms had been cleared out. I guessed it had been naive to assume I'd run into a blueprint for their plans or something. How many people had worked here? Had they even known? I'd asked a few questions in offworld district and at the Alliance base the one time I'd been, but after the Campbells were jailed, no one had wanted to associate with the place. I imagined a lot of them would probably have been imprisoned. *Tough shit.* Ignorance was no excuse. But there had been a *lot* of employees, and they'd had connections with other offworld tech suppliers. Neo Greyle's Enforcement

Squads had been occupied with chasing down those ravegens the past few days, so they clearly weren't guarding this place efficiently. And hidden cameras didn't mean a thing when bloodrock solution was involved.

I searched the rest of the labs, finding nothing, and then headed for a particular boardroom I'd made a note of, three floors above. Still nothing. Someone had done a thorough job stripping this place of anything useful. Even the furniture was stacked against the walls. I backed out of the room, cursing the place. For all I knew, it was empty, but I had to be sure. My options now were to leave it alone, stay here all day and search every goddamned room...

Or find a way to draw out anyone who might be hiding in here.

I was setting records for law-breaking already. But if anyone was here, *they* were breaking the law, and then some.

I headed downstairs, leaving via the window I'd come in by. At a safe distance, I gathered magic in the palm of my hand, aimed for the roof, and fired.

The first level shot rippled down the building. It wasn't strong enough to break a window, of course. That hadn't been my intention. But the magical aftershock sent a second ripple through the building's foundation. Anyone inside the place would be able to feel it.

They'd think they were being attacked.

At first, I thought my paranoia had been for nothing. The building quieted, the magical backlash fading.

And then, finally, two figures came out the front door.

I went very still. Two men, I couldn't see their faces, but they were arguing, looking wildly around, but I was safe. Magic beat beneath my skin like a second pulse. I pulled out my communicator. I'd never used the face-scanner before, but it was soundless and had no flash. I took an image of their faces.

Gavin Conner. Albert Conner.
I drew back in shock, staring. Those were *Conners.*
Aric's family.

ADA

Paperwork was incredibly dull after the excitement of yesterday, but Ms Weston was in council meetings all day. Probably for the best. She'd been seriously pissed off.

So had Kay. And he hadn't materialised either. I smiled at my mind's choice of word. He could turn *invisible.* Without a Chameleon. I wouldn't lie, I was kind of envious.

It wasn't a dangerous, world-destroying power. And yet the whole time we'd been on Aglaia, I hadn't felt magic trying to tempt me. Kay had said it was part of their lives there. Incredible. I'd read the files. A million mages, all with the power to kill in their hands, and yet there'd been peace for a hundred years. They didn't kill each other or enslave one another. The conflict with the centaurs was over resources, and how centaurs hated magic and technology while humans embraced it. Yet the last recorded magic-related death was a *century* ago.

Until now. Someone wanted to stir up conflict.

But for the first time in over a month, I wanted to use magic again. *I think.* Yesterday, even when invisible, on enemy territory, climbing for my life, I hadn't panicked. So it didn't happen all the time. Just when I was vulnerable, like when I was sleeping. Maybe I should take Kay's advice.

If I survived my next patrol.

≈

"You doing okay, Ada?" asked Carl, as our group assembled in the entrance hall.

I nodded, but inwardly cringed. The last thing I wanted was what Ms Weston would have called *preferential treatment.*

"Yeah, I'm good."

"Shouldn't be any trouble this time," he said. "We're heading through the main Passage and then back the same way. Pretty straightforward."

"Really?" I hadn't been there before, because I'd only ever used the between-world illegally. But Central was built practically on top of Earth's main connection to offworld, where people crossed in both directions to pass between London and the various equivalent entry points on the other worlds on the first level. I supposed Kay, as Ambassador, must use that Passage a lot now, as it offered the quickest route between places within the same time zone as the UK.

I didn't expect it to be quite so *loud.* For me, the Passages had always been quiet, almost spookily so, because I'd sneaked around back roads, or the equivalent, to help refugees onto Earth. But the background-noise of a crowd grew louder until we reached the busiest stretch of Passage I'd ever seen. It was like a high street, only lined with doors instead of shops, and each was guarded by at least two Alliance people. I stared, drinking in the brief glimpses of other worlds. A smoke-shrouded city. A desert guarded by two women with claws in place of hands. A group of blue-skinned security guards besides a door which appeared to be the only thing holding back an entire ocean, arguing with a group of damp-looking people carrying old-fashioned Earth cameras.

"The Alliance had better pay for damages!" one of them

yelled loudly. "This is a hoax! We didn't see so much as a scale."

"What was that about?" I asked Carl.

"Unauthorised tourists trying to get a glimpse of Zanthar's infamous sea monster," he said, shaking his head. "With Earth technology, no less."

"They're the fourth this week," said a passing blue-skinned woman with sea-green hair. "I showed the first lot what happens when you take Earth tech into a high-magic world. Now they're threatening to sue the Alliance."

"Figures," said Carl, elbowing through a contingent of people with hair dyed in eye-watering neon shades I was pretty sure were impossible on Earth, who were demanding access to Alvienne to collect their family's griffin ("I've learned not to ask," said Carl).

Carl led us down a side-tunnel between a door opening onto a mountain with winged creatures soaring across the sky and another which looked like a seaside town, and turned to make sure the rest of us were keeping up.

I'm here. I'm offworld. That was why I'd joined the Alliance in the first place.

"What d'you think?" asked Carl. "A little different to what you're used to?"

I grinned. "Just a little. No monsters?"

"They wouldn't dare. There are a hundred or so Alliance guards from different worlds in that corridor alone."

Holy wow. I shook my head. Even here, I couldn't fully grasp the extent of the Multiverse. Maybe it really was as infinite as the stars in the sky.

Carl led our group down corridors which were at first unfamiliar to me, but gradually, I started to recognise parts from when Kay and I had met with Simon from the New York branch. Including the staircase to the second floor. No longer off-limits entirely.

People could get out of Enzar. Start new lives on other, safer worlds. Just like I had.

Shouts echoed from up ahead, and Carl indicated us to slow down. My heart rate kicked up. I knew the sounds of a fight from a mile away.

And this sounded like a big one. Snarling noises were interspersed with the clash of something striking the Passage walls.

Crap. A shiver ran through me as I took my stunner in hand, like the others.

"Those aren't dreyverns," said Carl. "Sounds like something feral. Be careful, everyone."

Right. Of course we were going to walk *towards* the scary noises. Not that I used to pass up an opportunity to fight monsters... but that was before.

Blurred, indistinct shapes moved in and out of the shadows, striking at several people in the dark. Carl swore and took the lead to join them, firing a warning shot with the stunner. It struck the nearest shadow—what the hell *was* that? Electric sparks filled the air and the shape became even more indistinct.

"Daggers won't work!" Carl's shout rang out. "Use the stunners!"

I barely had time to tighten my grip on mine before one of the shadow-things came at me.

It was more smoke than shadow, reddish smoke sparking and howling. A blurred, clawed hand lashed out, and I struck with the stunner, slamming my hand on the switch. The recoil sizzled through my veins and I fought back a wince as I remembered just how much getting zapped by one of those things hurt. Shaking the feeling off, I aimed a shot at another monster bearing down on several other guards, which caused the shadow to break apart, becoming smoke, and then nothing.

One last zap from Carl's stunner took care of the final monster. When it died, it kind of... faded. Like *magic*. They were the same colour as high-level magic.

"What in the Multiverse were those things?" I asked, joining the others.

"Bad news," said Carl grimly. "Nice shot back there, by the way."

"Uh. Thanks." I looked around at the others. There'd been at least two other patrols caught up in the fighting. No one appeared seriously injured. *Thank god.*

Except one of the others was Kay's freaking *ex-girlfriend.*

Oh. Crap. And she was looking at me again. Not unfriendly this time, more curiously. I turned away. I didn't want to get into another fight. She worked at West Office. We were bound to run into each other at some point.

"Let's head back. We need to report this," said Carl.

Apparently, the Multiverse was on a mission to turn my life into a series of severely awkward situations. And I wanted to know what those creatures were. But Carl refused to say, and no one else knew.

"Your name's Ada, right?"

Oh, great. She was actually starting a conversation with me.

"Yes." I gave her a sideways glance, unsure if she was going to opt to attack or insult me. Either way, I still had one shot left in the stunner.

"Aric said."

"Uh-huh. Why so friendly all of a sudden?" I said.

Tara shrugged. "Guess we got off on the wrong foot. I was just pissed because Aric's a lying dick. Not much of an excuse, I know."

Wow. It really was a conversation. *Wonders will never cease.* Not that I'd be giving her gossip on Kay.

"I guess I'm sorry," said Tara, after a short pause. "Especially when I got nailed to the ground by my supervisor for leaving West Office when I was supposed to be checking on the stores."

"And you're telling me this... why?"

"Didn't you rob Central once?"

How the hell did she know?

"Hey, quit giving me that look. I'm pretty sure everyone in London's Alliance knows."

"Right," I said. "What does that have to do with anything?"

"Someone broke into our stores. My fault for forgetting to check, but I just wondered how you got in."

"It's classified," I said, thinking of the Chameleons. *Someone stole bloodrock solution.*

"Oh. All right. So... are you and Kay a thing?"

"That," I said, "is none of your business."

"Suppose not. I was just curious. He—"

"I don't want to hear it."

"All right," she said. "I suppose you know about the whole wyvern incident?"

"About Aric nearly killing him? Yeah."

"Hey, I was there, I knew what happened. Aric and his sister—their family's dodgy as hell, and I'm pretty sure some of them are magic-wielders, too. He's in your office, right? You should avoid him."

"Now you're worried about my safety?" I said, incredulously. "Jesus. I'm seriously confused right now. Just so you know."

"Hmm. I was curious. You're a celebrity at West Office. You stopped the Earth from being destroyed."

I shook my head quickly. "That's... not how it happened."

"Kay did, then?"

"Didn't he already tell you it's classified?" My patience was wearing thin.

"All right, chill out."

"Well, it's true." Jesus, how had Kay put up with her? "If you're gonna keep asking me questions, then why'd you tell me not to trust anything he said?"

That got her. She paused. "I didn't mean it."

I glanced at her. "So why say it?"

"I wanted to annoy him. He lies by omitting information, then acts like it's no big deal."

Huh? "So you thought you'd wind *me* up? Thanks for that, by the way."

She shrugged, tossing her hair over her shoulder. "Better you find out beforehand. Did you know he's a magic-wielder?"

"Wait, that's what he didn't tell you?"

"Amongst other things. You might have better luck getting answers than I did. Sounds like you have a secret or two of your own."

"Maybe I know it's rude to go poking into people's businesses," I shot at her, my brief curiosity extinguished.

"All right," she said, raising her hands. "So I might have overreacted a little when I found out he'd been arrested and used magic on Aric. What's done is done. Don't suppose you know what attacked us back there? They weren't from Cethrax."

I shook my head. "No clue."

I had an idea, but I wasn't about to say it in front of her. It had felt… like raw magic. Creatures made of pure magic. I'd never heard of anything like it. They hadn't really been alive. But they'd acted like it.

And from the expression on Carl's face, I had a feeling he knew, too.

14

KAY

So the Conners were involved. Damn. I knew Aric's family were shady. He'd pulled strings to even get through the Academy, and land a job in the Alliance. He wouldn't be the first, either, even if nobody particularly liked him. But this was something else.

The aftereffect of magic lingered after I'd fired the shot, tugging at me like the residual magic in the Passages, but I ignored it, my gaze following the two guys as they walked to the gate, still arguing quietly. My mind was racing.

What did Aric's family want with the Campbells? Power, I thought. Political power, for sure. But maybe magic, too. Cethrax had worked with the Campbells and it didn't take much for those treacherous vermin to switch allegiances. Anyone who hated the Alliance would probably find support there. True, Cethrax didn't have magic, but it did have a seemingly-unending supply of foot-soldiers and other monsters and they didn't know when to quit. Cethrax had used bloodrock solution stolen from the Alliance to create a diversion... so had these guys used it to get into the building?

Too many questions. It appeared to have nothing to do

with the pressing problem of Aglaia... but maybe it was *all* interconnected. The person who'd killed the centaur king had used magi-tech. And the Campbells had specialised in that kind of technology. The Conners could have easily got hold of it. Why they'd want to start an offworld war, though, was a mystery.

I followed the two Conners out the gate, where they were swept up in the crowd heading for the city centre. Still invisible, I stuck close behind them. I could take them out, for sure, but unless I got a confession out of them, I'd be the one to fall under suspicion. And then no one would know about it at all.

The Conner family was spread across three universes. If they all came after me, I had no chance. And that wasn't counting Cethrax, who everyone knew hated the Alliance. Hell, any of the monsters that had escaped into the Passages might have been a diversion. It would be the perfect cover-up. The obvious enemy was right in front of us.

But the Conners? How far was Aric involved? He'd certainly put his family's reputation to good use at the Academy. I'd never had the pleasure of meeting the other Conners, but his sister worked at West Office and the two men I was following were his cousins. They worked in Valeria's Alliance, like his father... Mr Conner, alongside his two brothers, ran a multi-universal technology company similar to the Campbells. They weren't the only ones to cash in on trading technology between worlds before the Alliance had upped restrictions. I couldn't say I paid too much attention to it, but the Campbells had been furious enough to attack the Alliance. Would Aric's family do the same?

Aric was the youngest kid and although he might have been an entitled prick, he'd been packed off to the Academy most likely because his father wanted him out the way. At Central, I was pretty sure everyone knew he was a thick-headed idiot, but nobody knew that two years ago, he'd proven he was willing to kill innocent people who got in the way of a grudge. If his family asked him to kill someone...

Yeah. He'd do it. Just like Ada's friend.

Lucky I was still invisible, really. I had to calm the hell down before I punched out the next person to get in my way. Trying to calm my breathing, I walked close enough to keep them in sight. I was unarmed, but invisible, I had the advantage.

I'd never be blindsided again.

They headed into an empty side road alongside a hover car station. Damn, the last thing I wanted was to cause another traffic accident. But this was one of the few uncrowded spots in the city. I sprinted after them, and tackled one of the guys from behind.

"What the hell?" he said, as he hit the ground, face-first. "Dude—something's attacking me!"

"Damn ravegens," said the second guy, looking madly around before the side of his face met my fist. "Shit!"

His reaction made the pain in my already-busted knuckles worth it. Pity I'd had to hold back, because if I did serious damage, I wouldn't be able to question them.

The first guy got to his feet, gaping at his companion, who rubbed his bruising jaw.

"How many are there?" he asked. "Crap. I know we weren't supposed to leave. Seriously, let's just—" He cut off in a yell as I kicked him sharply in the back of the knee, and he rolled on the ground, howling. Then I kicked the second guy in the shins. Both were down.

Easy, and entirely too much fun. I almost laughed. But I had answers to get, and these bastards only answered to violent threats. I moved in and caught the first guy in a chokehold.

"If I were you," I said in a low voice, "I'd stay put."

He froze. So did the second guy, still sprawled on the ground.

"Who—what the hell are you?" the second guy asked, his face twisted in pain.

"When I let go of this son of a bitch, the pair of you are going to go to that police station and turn yourselves in for trespassing on private property," I said. Quiet. But they caught every word. "Before that, you're going to tell me, *quickly*, what you were doing at the Campbells'."

The guy I held made choked noises, while the other went deathly pale.

"Shit," he said.

"I'd hurry up." I tightened my grip, pressing against his windpipe. "Talk."

"We were searching, okay? For their weapon. There was a weapon."

"Enlighten me."

"It was meant to be a super-powered magic weapon, I don't know! Just a rumour. My dad took it dead serious, though. We had to set up a base there."

"With the ravegens' help?"

"What? I thought *you* were—" His eyes widened as his companion fought for breath.

"Tell me how they became invisible. Did you give something to them?"

"I—it was bloodrock solution. Please…"

"Where from? Answer quickly."

"West Branch. London."

Crap, it made sense. Aric's damned *sister* worked there.

"And why Cethrax? What's your plan?"

"I don't know the details, dammit! My father doesn't trust us. Cethrax owed us a debt, they helped us. They hate the Alliance."

My hostage's face was turning blue. I let go, and he crumpled. "Take him to the police station. I'll know if you don't. And tell them. *Everything.*"

"Who… who are you?"

"Let's just say the Campbells might not be as gone as you hoped."

The guy swayed on the spot, mouth hanging open. I fought back a smirk. He made for the street again, dragging his semi-conscious brother. I tailed him the whole way to the nearest Enforcement Office. There was no shortage, given the sheer population of Neo Greyle. Inside, he started babbling about a ghost, confessing everything. I listened in a half detached way, making a mental note of everything he said. So Aric's sister was in on their plan, meaning he must be, too. Conner Senior himself hadn't told them exactly what they were looking for. Didn't trust them, I guessed. He was based here on Valeria, but where exactly, I had no idea. They were a huge family, and in an overpopulated city like Neo Greyle, even the Enforcement Squads would have their work cut out tracking them all down. Here, it was easy to disappear with or without invisibility.

And the Conners had been after the *weapon* the Campbells had hidden. Except I had a horrible suspicion the weapon in question… was a person.

Ada.

15

ADA

I followed Carl to the guard office once the patrol had been dismissed. The room was bigger than I'd expected, though most of the space was given over to a huge cabinet. I caught the door as it was closing, almost impaling myself on the end of a giant wyvern claw someone had drilled a hole in and mounted on the inside of the door.

"Ada?" he asked, surprised. "Is there something wrong?"

"No," I said, a little too quickly. "I just wondered if you could tell me about that magic-creature." He didn't respond, setting various devices down on the desk. Not just stunners, but an odd, rectangular metal object with flashing blue lights and a thin black rod with a gleaming sheen. I stared, unable to help it. That looked like…

"That kind are bad news." Carl scratched the scar on his face. "They're a rarity, usually formed of built-up residual magic if it gathers over a long period of time, or if there's a mass use of high level magic that isn't taken care of. In some worlds, the magic in the atmosphere is too dense for the backlash rule to properly work, so it builds up, resulting in those… monstrosities."

I blinked. "Really?" I knew magic was drawn to itself, to high-magic worlds, but not that residual magic could form something *living*.

"It isn't common knowledge on Earth, obviously," said Carl. "I can trust you won't spread this information around, Ada? We don't want mass panic. The guards are twitchy enough as it is, thanks to those invisible ravegens."

"Yeah, of course," I said. "What's that?" I pointed at the glinting black rod.

"That isn't something we usually show to guards."

"I won't say a word," I said. "I just thought... it looks like adamantine."

"Similar, but not quite," said Carl. "Most magic-based substances look similar, which doesn't help with identifying them. Adamantine looks the same as the material used in stunners for instance, but it's used for something quite different."

I hadn't known that. "So, what's in that...?" I indicated the gleaming rod-like device.

"World-key," said Carl. "To use the simple term. It can be used as a shortcut from the Passages to anywhere. Like any magic-charged device, it isn't effective on Earth, but it works in the Passages. The world-key only links to one world at a time."

"World-key." My hands itched to touch it, just to see if it felt as icy-cold as the Passages. "Wow. Is it made of the same stuff as the Passages?"

"Talk to an offworld physicist if you're interested in the substances that make up the Multiverse," said Carl, looking amused. I guessed it was pretty obvious I wanted to get my hands on the thing.

"Makes my head spin just thinking about it," I admitted. "What do you have to do to get authorised to use that?"

"It's for emergencies only," said Carl. "West Branch has

another for long-term use. Ambassadors rely on it for access to precarious worlds over a long period of time. I believe someone recently tried to steal theirs."

"They were robbed," I said slowly. "Um. Someone said." Tara did. So she was telling the truth.

"Yes," said Carl, his expression darkening. "It was… audacious. Rather similar to something that happened here at Central."

Yeah. Me. I was willing to bet bloodrock solution had been involved. But who would do that on Earth? Was there another traitor?

Carl tapped his communicator screen. "Trouble all around. Have you seen Aric, by the way?"

I shook my head. "No… should I have?"

"He didn't react well when I restricted his patrols," said Carl. "Damned idiot. I think he's skiving off somewhere."

"He's not in the office?"

"Not when Danica last checked. Ms Weston," he added, in response to my puzzled look. "She expects me to keep an eye on all the novices. If we hadn't lost Alan and Linda in the attack…"

Twenty guards died, I remembered, with a flash of guilt for forgetting. No wonder everyone here seemed so highly strung. "Anything you need my help with?"

"Don't worry yourself about us, Ada," he said. "You're a damn good fighter, but I can tell your heart's set on offworld, right? You don't want to join us boring senior guards."

I smiled at that. "Boring?" I jerked my head in the direction of the wyvern claw mounted on the door.

"Compared to offworld, most people would say so. This is hardly a treasure trove." He indicated the cabinet. My gaze drifted to the familiar cuffs hanging on a hook inside it. I remembered too well the shock of having my magic cut off when the Alliance had arrested me.

"Those cuffs," I said. "Are they antimagic?"

He picked up some keys from the desk. "They're double-sided. Magic on one side, antimagic on the other. They blocked your magic, right?"

"Yeah."

"Non-magic-wielders wouldn't be affected by the antimagic, but if things got violent, these cuffs also have obsidiate on the outside. Just enough that the antimagic doesn't stop it working."

"Like a stunner?"

"Exactly like a stunner. It's a precautionary measure, though we've never had a prisoner give us half as much trouble as you did."

"Do I get a medal?" I said, but smiled. "I get why you need that rule. Are there any prisoners in here now?"

"Actually, no," said Carl. "Like I said at the induction, it's rare that we have to apprehend anyone for a serious offence here on Earth. Most trespassers in the Passages tend to make for the high-magic worlds." He closed the cabinet door. "But as I said, we try to prepare for any eventuality."

"Even hiring a criminal?"

Carl paused in the act of locking the cabinet. "Are the other guards giving you trouble?"

"Nah," I said. It seemed petty and stupid to confess my worries that I'd never fit in here. I was no stranger to being an outsider. "Except Aric, but he's a shit to everyone. Though I could do without the stares."

"It'll die down," said Carl. "On my first mission, I fell down a hidden staircase and woke a sleeping chalder vox. I reckon I'd rather be remembered for being an infamous criminal."

I smiled. "Those hidden staircases are hard to spot if you aren't looking for them."

He turned the key in the lock. "True. I have to explain that to some of the novices at least one a week. I reckon you know the Passages better than most of them."

"Not as well as Kay does," I said, wondering what he was doing right now. Sneaking around the Passages scaring the crap out of novices, maybe. "Doesn't look like he minds the attention."

Carl's expression was a little too assessing. "I imagine he's used to it by now. I admit, I'm not overly fond of the other guards following his example. I meet a lot of Academy graduates, and in general, their sense of danger is a little skewed. They tend to run into dangerous situations without thinking. But Kay tends to consider the danger and then do it anyway."

I shifted, not sure what to say to that. Of course he'd always get attention, because he had a name everyone knew. I was lucky *my* real name hadn't got around. Adamantine...

"Can I ask you a question about magic?"

Carl nodded.

"Uh. Well, I know our uniform's magicproof. But we can still use magic, right? How does that work?"

"There are different levels of antimagic, too," said Carl. "I've often wondered about that. It does depend on skin contact to some extent. The uniform's laced with pure adamantine, as much as it's possible to weave into fabric, anyway. It won't protect you against a higher level of magic, and it isn't as potent as the stuff this building's made out of. That's seven layers of antimagic, enough to absorb even a magical assault."

"Damn." I glanced at the ceiling as if I expected it to reveal hidden powers. "It isn't magicproof on the inside though, right?" I recalled the double assault on Central. Skyla had used magic in here and it had rebounded off the walls and floor.

"No. There's a certain amount of adamantine built into

the walls, but it does tend to wear off over time. Same with your uniform."

I turned this over in my head. "So… that's why third level magic can get through."

Carl's expression darkened. "Yes. It's impossible to block. This building could probably take it, but I can't speak for the collateral damage. If the Campbells' machine had gone off…"

Then we'd all be dead. Even I might not have made it through that one alive. Because if it was true, if there were different levels of antimagic, then mine had to end somewhere. The amount of energy I'd channelled during the fight with the Campbells had sent me into a coma.

"It won't happen again," said Carl, with unexpected sharpness. "Maybe we got complacent about our safety before the attack, but with our new precautions, this is the safest building in London. It's unbreakable."

I swallowed at the unfortunate choice of words. *I* wasn't unbreakable, not really. And the adamantine in my blood didn't mean I couldn't be harmed. In fact, that definition wasn't right, at all, because if it was, I wouldn't be able to use magic at all.

Right?

"You should go home, anyway," said Carl. "Let me know if I need to yell at anyone."

I grinned. "Will do."

After checking out, I headed to the tech labs, where I found two of the tech team in conversation by the doors. Andy and Vic.

"What the bloody hell is his problem?" Vic was saying to Andy. "I thought he was going to hit me."

"You're lucky he didn't," said Andy. "I still have the scars from where he beat the crap out of me one time at the Academy—hey, it's the prisoner."

"Um," I said, guilty at being caught eavesdropping. "Is Jeth in there?"

"Should be on his way out soon," said Vic. "Jesus. This big scary guy—what's his name? He came and threatened us."

"Aric Conner," said Andy.

"Oh. He threatened me the other day, too," I added. *And told me Kay was a criminal.* "He beat you up?" I asked Andy.

"Four years ago," said Andy, looking annoyed. "He started on everyone at one point or other, was always picking fights. What issue did he have with you? Aren't you in the same department?"

"Yeah. What did he want?" I asked.

"Wanted in on our Chameleons," said Vic. "Said he had authorisation, but I checked and that was a blatant lie. We can't go handing out classified tech."

My heart dipped uneasily. "Seriously?"

"Yeah," said Andy, "but we only have one left, don't we?"

"Keep it down, he might still be out there," said Vic.

I'd handed that Chameleon in. What did Aric want with it?

"Is that Ada?" asked Jeth, coming out of the office.

"Hey," I said.

"Hey. You didn't run into the crazy guy, did you?"

"He cleared off," said Vic. "Good riddance."

"I don't trust him," said Andy. "You did lock the back room, right?" He made for another door.

"Of course," said Vic. "Come on. He wouldn't break in."

"If he wanted to…" Andy looked up and down the corridor, clearly rattled. "Thought I was well shot of the bastard."

"I'll double-lock it, then, if you're paranoid," said Vic, pulling a key from his pocket. "He's an employee, for god's sake. You don't honestly think he'd break Alliance code?"

"He would," said Andy. "Seriously. I'm not being paranoid. He's capable of murder, that guy."

"What?" said Jeth. "You're joking."

Vic's expression said the same.

"Stop looking at me like that." Andy hitched his bag onto his shoulder. "No one talks about it because we can't prove it was him, but you can ask anyone from our class at the Academy in confidence and they'd tell you. There was this... incident in our third year. It's kind of a long story, but some of us were in the Passages—we shouldn't even have been in there, but that's beside the point—and a wyvern attacked us. We couldn't prove Aric was behind it because wyverns are usually drawn to magic, and there wasn't any evidence someone had lured it out. But it's true, and I almost fucking died. Don't try to tell me that guy isn't capable of murder."

Everyone stared, open-mouthed. I shivered. So Andy must have been the other person who'd been with Kay and Simon.

"Jesus Christ," said Vic. "How the *hell* did he get away with something like that?"

"Effing family connections," said Andy. "I'm off. For the love of god, don't go spreading that story around!"

And he took off. Jeth shook his head.

"Damn," said Vic. "Okay, that's some scary shit. I'll see you tomorrow, all right, Jeth? And you, Ada."

"Bye," I said awkwardly, as he headed down the corridor.

"Yeah," said Jeth. "We better go, Ada."

We came out onto the second floor corridor and headed for the lifts. I still felt completely shaken up by what Andy had said. Simon had told me Aric must have lured the wyvern from Cethrax somehow, but it had slipped my mind until now. What did he want with a Chameleon?

"Uh," I said to Jeth, belatedly remembering why I'd gone to the second floor. "I was going to tell you, I wanted to head for the training complex for a bit. I want to get in some practise. I'll only be like an hour or so. You can go home if you want."

"Nah, I'll hang about in a coffee shop or something."

"You sure?"

"Ada, you forget I'm your bodyguard now."

I narrowed my eyes.

"I'm joking, sis, chill out. Or better, go and blow off steam hitting virtual dreyverns."

"That's the plan." I smiled. "You sure you don't want to come and try it out?"

"Hmm. Maybe another time."

You're in control of the environment, I told myself, waving to Amanda as I entered. She gave me kind of an odd look, like... worry? Crap. She must know about the way I'd screwed up the other day. "Hi, Ada," she said, coming over to me.

"Hey," I said. "Thought I'd try simulation for a bit." I'd had the presence of mind to bring my guard uniform and a change of clothes just in case I got called out last-minute on patrol.

"Sure thing," said Amanda. "You go change, I'll find a free room for you."

"Thanks."

Maybe I could learn to fit in at the Alliance, after all. Admin was kind of dull, but then, all the action was offworld right now. Kay had escaped admin pretty fast, though I was told that wasn't the norm. I expected to wait several months before I had the chance to go offworld... unless they needed my help for anything else on Aglaia.

Damn. What a week. And it wasn't even over yet.

The nerves kicked in again as I found myself alone in a cubicle with a virtual helmet in hand. *Come on, Ada, get hold of yourself,* I thought, putting on the helmet. The world blanked to the cliff scene again, before the menu screen unfolded. I needed to face dreyverns, because they were what had kicked it all off. It was like exposure therapy. I could control this.

I'm in control. I'm in control. I launched into action with an abandon I hadn't felt in weeks. Since before the Alliance, before everything, when I'd lived for the Passages, taken a fight as a challenge. Like that time a band of dreyverns had tried to attack a group I was helping, and Skyla and I had beaten them down. She'd had my back, then.

I faltered, surrounded by a heap of dreyvern corpses. Maybe that was the problem. My former friends turned out to be the opposite. I no longer felt like I had someone to watch my back. But that was stupid. I'd fought alone countless times. It was the way Nell had raised me.

"Are you okay?" Amanda asked, as I left the changing rooms later.

I shrugged. "Just tired. I don't know."

"If ever you want to talk, Ada, I'm happy to. I mentor novices, remember? I know you didn't get in here the usual way. You don't have to be ashamed."

I swallowed. "Thanks. I'm not—" Of course I was struggling. Why bother denying it anymore? It was just too big a change to handle, after what I'd been through.

My communicator buzzed in the silence. I flicked the screen. A message from Ms Weston.

"You're needed on Aglaia tomorrow. The council will make its final decision, and if the situation turns hostile your abilities as a shield may be needed."

I sagged against the wall.

She knew. Everything.

"Ada?" said Amanda, alarmed. "What is it?"

I shook my head. "I have to go."

It was finally happening. The Alliance planned to use me as a human shield.

I stopped halfway to the gates. There was only one thing

to do. I pulled out my communicator again, found Kay's number, and hit the call button.

"Hey," I said, quickly. "Sorry for calling you like this. I—I don't know if you've heard, but Ms Weston just sent out a message."

"Yeah, I got it," said Kay. "Wait, she sent it to you?"

"She wants to use me as a shield, Kay." I closed my eyes. "I'm not okay with that. She *knows* it nearly killed me. Was this why the Alliance hired me?" I was babbling now. "They just wanted to use me? Seriously, Kay, tell me this isn't some huge mistake."

"What exactly did she say?"

I repeated the message.

"That can't be right," he said. "Aggressive magic is forbidden in Aglaia by law—you know that."

"Yeah, and I know there's likely to be a war. You said so yourself. I'm not being anyone's shield. I absorb magic, I can't control if it gets out again. That's how I killed—I killed." I sank down onto the ground, my breath catching.

"Ada, you're not going to kill anyone. The Balance had tipped, remember? Earth's levels aren't usually that high. Neither are Aglaia's. You won't lose control. I'll talk to her, but she's obviously got some kind of plan… God*dammit*. Why would she even suggest that?"

"About time!" I said, my voice rising in pitch. "I'd leave the Alliance first. I'd *die* first. I almost did die when I absorbed magic last time. She *knows* that." I took a deep shuddering breath.

"I said I'll talk to her." He cursed under his breath. "It's all I can do. Where are you?"

"Training grounds, going to meet my brother. Dammit, Kay, I can't do this."

"Then we'll figure it out. Talk to her tomorrow. I'm in

Valeria, dealing with—look, I'll get on her case soon as I can, but you need to speak to her yourself."

"Yes, I'm aware of that!" I snapped. "I just don't have a lot of options at the moment, and as it happens, I'd rather lose my job than go out there again."

"You knew you'd have to go into the field, Ada. I'm just saying—"

"Not as a weapon!" I said. "You want to know why? I'm scared. I'm terrified out of my freaking mind that I'll kill people again, and I am *not* being the Alliance's shield."

A pause.

"You, scared?" said Kay. "Whatever happened to the person who refused to let a tiny thing like being imprisoned in a magically-secured building stop her from escaping and taking out half the Alliance's guard in the process? Who risked her own life for the sake of the Multiverse even when she was being used against her will? Jesus Christ, Ada."

I jerked back like he'd hit me. My eyes stung. "You know, not all of us can walk away unscathed from murdering someone."

A long pause. "Unscathed?" said Kay, his tone harsh. "Look, you have two choices, Ada. You can let this break you, or you can get the hell over it. You made your choice. You have to live with yourself either way."

"So that's it?" I said. "That's all you have to say to me? Why I ever thought you had the tiniest bit of sympathy—I've no idea. I thought I could *talk* to you." And now the floodgates were opening. "There's no one else in the whole Multiverse who has a goddamned *clue* what I went through. But oh no, you're too busy saving the Multiverse to care about someone else, right?"

"That's *not* what I said," he said. "This isn't the best time to talk. I'm in the middle of a situation. Look, you have other people on your team. Your brothers, for one. Your guardian. Right?"

Dammit. He just had to remind me.

"Actually, my guardian called me a *monster*, so I'm not exactly well-inclined towards her at the moment."

"She said *what?*" He sounded genuinely shocked.

"She implied it. I—she said Central would do to me what they did to Skyla. That she was a monster. But it's the same thing that happened to me."

And Kay. I gritted my teeth, hand clenching the communicator, waiting for him to hang up. I'd reminded him of something he most likely wanted to forget. To *get the hell over*. Was it really so easy for him?

He didn't hang up. Didn't say anything, either.

Then: "Is *she* a magic-wielder?"

"No. No, she isn't." I closed my eyes, loosening my grip.

"Then she doesn't know a damn thing. I know she's your guardian, but no one has the right to talk to you like that."

He didn't acknowledge the implication that she'd said *he* was a monster, too. God, I was an idiot. Could I blame him for being annoyed at my calling him in the middle of a mission to offload my problems onto him?

"Right," I said, my voice cracking. "Sorry I—I'm sorry I called."

"Don't be. We'll sort this out tomorrow." This time, he did hang up.

People on my team. *Oh, god, I'm an idiot.* I was so wrapped up in everything, it had never even crossed my mind Kay might have had just as much trouble dealing with the aftermath of last month as I had. I might not know much about his past, but I knew he didn't have any family or any kind of support network outside of the Alliance. And he was an Ambassador, saddled with responsibility, and entirely too good at hiding what he was thinking.

I'd wiped the worst of the tears away before I met Jeth, but he could tell something was up.

"Panic attack," I muttered, and refused to answer any more questions.

The last thing I wanted was to confront Nell, especially now I had proof the Alliance were as underhanded as she'd thought. They really intended to use me.

"Ada, you're starting to worry me." Jeth unlocked the front door to our house. "Did something happen? Seriously. That guy who threatened you—Aric. What did he say to you?"

"It's not that." I followed him into the hallway. "Honestly. I threatened *him,* actually. Kicked him in the balls."

Jeth raised an eyebrow. "Wow. Glad I'm on your side."

I wanted to tell him. But that would mean betraying Alliance secrets. I was trapped on both sides.

"What's up?" Alber came out of the living room. "I thought you'd be back now. Nell's cleared off again."

"She has?" I said. "What is it this time?"

"She's at the Knights'. Someone's been threatening them. Word got out about their old bloodrock supplies and someone wanted to buy some. But it's all gone."

"Really? Threatening them?"

"I don't know," said Alber. "Nell's pretty angry though. Why do you two look so serious?"

"I'm trying to get Ada to tell me," said Jeth. "Want to try?"

"Honestly," I muttered. "It really isn't a big deal."

As I passed by Alber, I noticed he wasn't wearing his contact lenses, and his purple mageblood eyes gleamed in the dark hallway.

"Why no lenses?" I asked.

He shrugged. "No one's been around. Why?"

I'd never asked before. But then, I always kept my own eyes hidden. Even if it wasn't linked to my power, it was conspicuous on Earth. I knew exposing my real eyes wouldn't destroy the planet, but still.

"What's it like?" I asked Alber. "Being mageblood?"

He blinked. "Uh… What brought this on?"

"Just wondered what it feels like to be a magic-wielder who doesn't have the power to destroy the Multiverse living in your skin." And now I wished I could staple my mouth shut.

Alber blinked. Jeth asked, "Is that what this is about?"

"Yeah." I threw my bag down with a sigh. "There's no way I can risk using magic anymore. But the Alliance will expect me to. And even if they don't, it's part of me. I can't ever be rid of it."

"Ada, you're being stupid," said Alber. "You know any of us can use third level power in the Passages, right? *Anyone* who can use magic can use it to destroy the world, if they wanted to. You *don't* want to. You almost killed yourself trying to stop it."

"What he said." Jeth nodded. "Ada, you need to stop blaming yourself for what the Campbells did to you. It was their doing, not yours."

"I know." I closed my eyes. "But the magic came from me. And I killed people with it—killed Delta. I meant to."

Jeth sucked in a breath. "Ada, I don't care and neither does Alber. You think either of us wouldn't have done the same? You saved the planet, plus the Balance. You don't have to use magic again, if you don't want to."

"Listen to us, because you're being a complete twat, Ada," said Alber.

"Ha." I shook my head. "Thanks, guys."

Kay was right, I did have people on my team.

16

KAY

"Good news," said Ms Weston, to Ada and me, as we stood in her office the following morning. "The centaurs were able to come to an agreement. Markos's sister takes the throne."

I stared at her. Of all the things I'd expected her to come out with, that was so far from my expectations I honestly didn't know what to say. After the ruckus on Valeria yesterday, reporting the Conners and trying to get a cross-world arrest warrant sent out without anyone ending up killed—including me—I hadn't had the mind-space to think about Aglaia. Really, it seemed an unnecessary distraction. Aric was still here somewhere, as was his blasted sister. And I hadn't known until now if Ms Weston had heard about the Conners' arrest. Apparently not.

"Yes," she said, her expression unchanging. "Markos's cousin was colluding with rebels. They were found in possession of a substance not naturally found on Aglaia, pure obsidiate. It seems they intended to create magic-based weapons to use against the mages. Tryfon was executed at dawn, as were all rebels found on centaur territory."

Ada gasped. "No way."

What? "Just like that?"

"Centaurs are remarkably efficient."

No kidding. Given how close Ada and I had come to being killed by them, I couldn't say I was sorry.

"What happened to the obsidiate?" I asked. "The Alliance took it, right? Because that alone might spark a war." Literally, given that it had such a high recoil level.

"The council took it from them, yes. There is to be a discussion on what to do with it. In any case, despite this unpleasantness, the centaur and human communities have agreed to a renewal of the treaty between their species and with the Alliance regardless."

Seriously? "They have? Not a word about magic, and the king's murder... the other centaurs are just accepting it?"

"They are none the wiser. It seems we have averted a war, for now. But your presence is still required to oversee the treaty signing."

Of course. Couldn't let me do something actually useful, could you? I wanted to say. And why the hell had she told Ada she'd have to act as a shield?

Ada herself was plainly thinking the same. I'd almost feared I'd gone too far, pushed her over the edge. She'd bared her soul to me and I'd...

Why I ever thought you'd have the slightest bit of sympathy. But what choice did I have? She was in the Alliance now. I'd rather drive her away than see her get hurt again.

I clenched my fist—re-bandaged, seeing as I'd managed to open up the wounds again—and looked at Ada as she stepped forward.

"So, do we still need to go?" Ada asked. "I got your message yesterday."

"Oh?" Ms Weston's expression was a challenge. *Dammit.*

"I'm not your shield, or your weapon," said Ada, looking

her in the eyes. "Firstly, it wasn't in my contract. I'm under no obligations." She drew in a breath, and Ms Weston raised an eyebrow, inviting her to continue. "And more importantly, I have no control over magic. Whatever you think I'm capable of as a shield, I can't guarantee that it wouldn't destroy the Alliance along with everything else. Are you willing to put your own people at risk?"

She kept eye contact with Ms Weston the whole time. Kind of impressive. But I felt like a dick for not intervening, even if it would have made things worse for both of us.

What a freaking mess.

"You certainly make a good case for yourself. I confess I expected an immediate response."

Damn her. "What, you thought I'd to call you back?" asked Ada. "I'd have thought this would be the sort of thing you'd discuss with your employees face to face first."

I almost thought Ms Weston would shout at her. Instead, the boss shook her head. "You did have the option to call into the office out of hours. I've been in contact with Aglaia constantly, thanks to your brother's… earpiece."

"Markos?" I raised an eyebrow, forgetting I wasn't supposed to be interfering. "You talked to him?"

"He was the one who informed me of the situation, yes." Ms Weston turned her disapproving stare onto me instead. "He seemed reluctant to discuss the nature of the traitor centaurs' bargain with outsiders. At least, I assume bargaining was involved."

Oh. Shit. The source. She knew *something* was up, though I doubt even she could guess at a hidden magic source. Had she thought Ada knew, and tried to blackmail a reaction out of her?

"I have no idea," I said, keeping my blank, professional Ambassador expression on. "Centaurs are secretive by nature, and easily offended. They don't take kindly to their sort liaising with offworlders. I'm amazed Markos's sister let him stay around long enough to witness the execution."

Ada's face paled slightly to hear me speaking casually about someone's death. Well, we'd had a lucky escape from Tryfon's lot.

"Neither of you know?" Ms Weston's laser stare managed to spear both of us at once. "If not for the new Queen's swift actions, war might have broken out on Aglaia within the week. For either of you to keep vital information from myself and the council, however noble your motives, would be a direct violation of your contract with the Alliance."

Damn. Now ninety per cent of her glare was levelled on me. And I had a creeping suspicion I knew why.

My family had a history of violating Alliance code.

"So," said Ms Weston slowly, "I hope you'll both consider my words carefully. If the situation is irredeemable, you should leave Aglaia immediately and not interfere further. As for your ability, Ada, there are a few things I want to discuss further with you, but now isn't the time."

No. It isn't. I only hoped she hadn't told the council the extent of Ada's ability with magic, and was doubly glad I hadn't brought *mine* up. I'd barely scratched the surface, really.

"So you want us to go to the meeting?" asked Ada. "Even though I'm not an Ambassador?"

"Yes. You're one of the few people aware of the situation on Aglaia, and we need more witnesses for the signing of the treaty. I think you'd benefit from sitting in on the meeting."

Ada frowned. "What about whoever killed the centaur king? It wasn't just the rebels."

She didn't know the half of it. The Conners. Cethrax. Even though I'd forced those guys to hand themselves in, I didn't know if their confession was enough to put the whole family behind bars. Given their connections, probably not.

I'd relented and called up Carl yesterday, and he'd said no one had seen Aric at Central that day at all.

"Have you spoken to Carl recently?" I asked Ms Weston.

"No, I haven't. The council is waiting for both of you, so if you will..."

Ada shifted to leave, but I stayed put.

"I left you a message," I said, "Several members of the Conner family were arrested on Aglaia, and confessed to crimes that suggest the entire family was involved."

Ada turned to stare at me. Damn. I'd have to explain this to her, too.

"Yes, I received it," said Ms Weston, "but that's a matter for Valeria, not for us."

What? "Really? Aric works here."

"His tracker disappeared yesterday, and we've been unable to contact him."

"Wait, what?" I said.

Ms Weston's eyes narrowed. "We do have people looking for him, but we don't have the staff to spare to go chasing after every rumour while the council's offworld. We'll have to wait until they get back."

"It's not a rumour," I said. "Neo Greyle's Enforcement Officers took a statement from the two men who were arrested, implicating their whole family. Aric might come back to try and steal something again."

Out of the corner of my eye, Ada shifted position, looking from me to Ms Weston with her brow furrowed in confusion. *I'll tell her later.*

"As I said: it's Valeria's problem, and I can assure you that our security is tighter than it's ever been. Kay, I know you feel you have to intervene in everything after what happened last month, but we are capable of defending ourselves without you here."

"Wynn Conner works in West Office," I said. "I'm pretty

sure she's in on this, too." I hadn't met his sister. She'd been three years ahead of us at the Academy.

"Kay, whatever you think *this* is, being a magic-wielder does not entitle you to give me orders. If you have a concern about security matters, then Carl is the person to speak to."

I clenched my teeth to avoid saying something that would get me into a world of trouble. "Yes, I understand."

Don't say I didn't warn you.

"Then leave, both of you. The rebels are no longer a threat, and you'll be going to the meeting place on neutral ground."

"More blasted meetings," I muttered, as Ada and I headed downstairs. "What a joke."

"What was that about?" she asked, still looking at me in total confusion.

"Later," I said, heading for the stairs.

Ada made an impatient sound. "I'll hold you to that," she said, catching up with me at the top of the stairs. "That was underhanded of her."

Yeah. It was. I'd never thought even Ms Weston would suggest something so ruthless and cold. Quite apart from the fact that Ada couldn't control her powers. And, as was all too clear, they scared her. But there was no time for another confrontation with the boss.

"She's never gone that far before," I said. Did she want to push Ada into quitting? She had to be considering it by this point. But of course, it was the Alliance or her bitch of a guardian, who'd better hope we never met face to face again. It was none of my business, really, but the last thing Ada needed was her own guardian guilt-tripping her when she had enough crap to deal with already.

Last time I'd seen Nell was when I'd showed up at the hospital while Ada was in a coma. Nell had caused such a ruckus yelling at me about how it was all Central's fault Ada was in there in the first place, she'd drawn the nurses' attention and they'd kicked me out. I didn't think Ada even knew about that, but still.

"Yeah. Guess I asked for it by joining the Alliance. Never mind."

"What?" Her guardian had really done a number on her. "Don't let anyone tell you it's your fault. Have you talked to Nell?"

"No, I haven't," she snapped. "Because she's never at home, she's always out. The people who ran the other shelter here in London are struggling because of the pressure the Alliance has put them under, and she's dead set on blaming all of you."

Like things couldn't get any worse. "I'll look into that once we've dealt with this meeting. I can have a word with the council—"

"You don't have to do a thing," said Ada. "She's wrong. It's *not* your fault, it would have happened no matter what. Anyway, what was that about Aric?"

"Long story," I said. "I caught a couple of his cousins acting shady in Valeria yesterday... you know, I'm going to have a word with Carl before we leave."

We reached the foot of the stairs, and I made for the guard office. Luckily, Carl was in the office and not patrolling. He looked up from the desk as I entered.

"Kay? Aren't you going offworld?"

"I'm going there now, but I wanted to check if you'd seen Aric."

"This again?" said Carl.

Of all the times for him not to believe me. "You must have heard by now, about two of Aric's cousins being arrested on Valeria for illegal trespassing. They suggested their whole family's in on their plan, whatever it is." I didn't want to bring up the Campbell family in front of Ada when we didn't know for certain. Ada herself was openly frowning at me now. Maybe even she wouldn't believe me.

"Valeria's doors are closed," said Carl. "They finally decided to take extreme measures against Cethrax. No one's allowed in or out for the next twenty-four hours. Last I heard there were three more ravegens running around in the capital."

I swore. "Why did no one tell me this?"

"Because I'm the head of the guards here, Kay, not you."

Damn. He was right. I didn't have a counter-argument to that, because the Conner brothers hadn't known it was me who'd forced a confession from them.

"Ms Weston said Aric's tracker disappeared," I said.

"The idiot probably broke his communicator," said Carl. "I can't send people chasing after Aric when no one knows where he is."

"Dammit," I said. "Okay. What about Cethrax? The Conners were the ones who gave bloodrock to those ravegens."

"Kay... what?" Ada stared at me. "You think Aric's working with *Cethrax?* When did that happen?"

I sighed inwardly. We were running late to the meeting already. "Tell you what, never mind. Just keep an eye on him if he shows up. Ada, you go and meet with the rest of the Ambassadors. I'm going to make a quick call."

I left Carl's office, skimming through the contacts on my communicator.

"Hello?" Tara's suspicious voice rang in my ear. "Kay, why are you calling me?"

"Because I needed to speak to someone from West Office." *And, unfortunately, you're the one person who might listen.* "Wynn Conner's family are involved in something shady, offworld. I need someone to keep an eye on her to make sure she doesn't try and get into the Passages. I think Cethrax is involved."

"What? I haven't seen her, Kay, but what you're saying is—"

"It's true. Ask anyone from Valeria's police force. I'm heading to an offworld meeting, and I reckon Conner's going to play his hand while the council are gone. Just keep an eye out."

"Right. If you say so. But—"

I hung up, cutting off her response.

Ada said, "I'm completely lost, Kay. You think Aric's family are dealing with Cethrax?"

"Yeah, they are, but I don't have proof." I lowered my voice. "The story's too long to tell right now, but let's just say I spotted them doing something illegal while I was invisible."

"*Oh.*" Ada nodded, the confusion clearing from her expression. "You aren't telling anyone that."

No. Maybe my paranoia was running in overdrive again, but considering what had happened to the only other people with the same ability as me, I wasn't about to tell even the higher up members of Earth's Alliance. They only knew the basic details of the experiment, not what the outcome had been, and I intended to keep it that way.

"Now I've convinced three people I'm off my head, let's go and deal with this bloody meeting."

Outside the building, Raj and the other Ambassadors waited with the council, all of whom gave the pair of us disapproving looks for showing up late.

"She's authorised?" Raj queried, with a glance at Ada.

"Yes, Danica thought it would be good experience for her," said Mr Sanders.

It took a second for it to click that he meant Ms Weston. Who, I was starting to think, was playing some serious mind-games with Ada. I never should have hung up on her yesterday, but I'd been at Valeria's police office at the time. All I'd managed to do was act like a complete dick, again. For all I knew, trying to snap her out of the guilt would only make things worse. But Ada didn't deserve to suffer for what someone else had forced her to do. Even if it made me a monster in her eyes.

~

Aglaia's council meeting room was wrapped in tension so thick, even magic felt more potent. Perhaps it had to do with the heap of glittering black rock on the table. The obsidiate the council had confiscated from the centaurs. It didn't escape my attention that the mage kept glancing at it. And we were unarmed, too. Ms Weston had given me the magic-tracker again, and a stunner with one shot, just in case. But that wouldn't stand up to an army of mages *or* centaurs.

I got the vibe that no one thought the centaurs would give in so easily. But the terms of the treaty were laid out, and both humans and centaurs signed in triplicate, one for mages, one for centaurs, and another copy for the Alliance, communicator-scanned for permanent records. Markos wore an expression of absolute relief when Eidora signed her side of the agreement, and some of the tension in the room eased.

Except there was still the obsidiate. Only one world openly traded in the volatile substance used in the Alliance's weaponry, like the stunners: Valeria.

"If I may interrupt," said Ikor the mage, "it seems a tad unbalanced to only permit the use of such a substance on certain worlds. Aglaia has no such method of defence."

"Nor does it need one," said one of Valeria's council members, a sour-faced man with a metal replacement for one hand. "The peace on Aglaia is due in no small part to the absence of such substances as this." He indicated the obsidiate. "In any case, this is the property of Valeria's Alliance now. I trust that the queen would never permit the use of this by her people?"

"Certainly not," said Eidoria, looking affronted. "Tryfon and the Anthos tribe were unnaturals." She glared at her brother, which broadcasted her opinion on any links with offworld. But with her as queen, at least there was no danger that the centaurs would take advantage of a volatile magic-based substance.

Pity I couldn't say the same for the humans. Valeria's head didn't appear to be acting suspiciously, but after what had happened yesterday, I wasn't about to let him out of my sight. I kept one eye on the mage throughout the rest of the meeting, too. He might have had a point that not having access to magic-based sources put Aglaia at a disadvantage, but it wasn't as though they were defenceless. No, everyone put their own world first, and it was a bloody miracle we'd found any solution at all.

But for now, Aglaia was united alongside the Alliance, and the obsidiate now in the hands of Valeria's council. Whoever had wanted to cause a war had failed. I scanned the room as the meeting broke up, and the mage caught my eye, and beckoned me to follow.

"Yes?" I said once I was sure no one was listening in.

"I merely wanted to ask after your success with the advice on magic I gave you."

Like hell was I telling him a thing. "I fail to see how that's relevant here."

"I was simply curious. Is that so hard to believe?"

"As it happens, yes. There are an awful lot of untrustworthy people around."

"And you don't trust me."

Sure. As much as I'd trust a rabid chalder vox.

"Well," said the mage, my silence having spoken for itself, "it is a relief that this business is dealt with, at least. It seems the centaurs had a traitor in their midst."

Yeah. I needed to speak to Markos. The horse-men had been the first to disappear after the meeting. I pointedly walked down the corridor, which like every other part of this building, was panelled in wood. Though the place had most likely been built by humans—centaurs conducted all their meetings out in the open—the doorways and corridors were wide enough to accommodate centaurs.

"Apparently," I said. "Is there anything else?"

"Only that I hope you enjoy the celebrations."

By the strident sounds of what could only be centaur-music drifting through the open windows, he seemed to be right. Dammit. I wanted *off* this world.

After following the pathway to the mainland, I caught up to Markos at the clearing.

"What happened?" I asked.

The centaur raised an eyebrow. "By the gods, human, calm yourself down. My sister executed the traitors."

"And the rest?" The king's murder. Magi-tech. Damn. Why did there have to be so many people around? Crowds gathered under the trees. Every world's council had brought at least three members, and it looked as though a few curious centaurs had wandered into the clearing, too. There hadn't been that many of them at the meeting.

"I am returning to Central once I have sorted my affairs here, human. I'll talk to you then."

"Right." I narrowed my eyes. "And Eidora gave in easily?"

"She's always had a taste for leadership. Human, you don't have to involve yourself here anymore."

I shook my head. "It seems too easy."

"My cousins think the occasion merits entertainment."

Judging by the discordant sounds of some kind of harp

screeching out over the forest, I'd figured that much out myself.

"Right," I said. "I can't say I'm a fan of this song... if it is one."

"It's appalling," said Markos. "I never did like classical music."

"I think Valeria's train-wreck soundtrack is more like actual music," I muttered, scanning the clearing for Ada. There were a few centaurs roaming around handing out glasses of what looked like wine.

"You'd better go, human. I'll catch up to you."

"Yeah." I spotted Raj, who looked like he wanted to disappear as much as I did.

"Don't drink the wine," said Raj, as I caught up.

"What, you don't think it's poisoned?" I said this in an undertone, just in case.

"No, it's potent as hell and makes you lose all reason. One glass and the next thing you know, you're skinny-dipping in the river and have a hundred centaurs pointing their spears at you and threatening to have you arrested."

"That didn't happen to you... did it?"

The look on his face said it all. Despite everything, I laughed. "Really?"

"I'm surprised you haven't heard the story yet. Even the council members like to tell that one at parties."

"I can imagine." I glanced around and caught sight of Ada, hovering awkwardly on the side-lines.

"We're allowed to leave now, right?" I asked Raj.

"Sure hope so."

I beckoned to Ada, who came over. A glass in her hand.

"Don't drink that," said Raj.

"Uh... why?"

"Because you'll make an idiot of yourself like this guy," I said. "We need to go, anyway."

EMMA L. ADAMS

Get back to Central. Deal with Ms Weston. And then... I didn't know. Check up on the Conners. I was still no closer to figuring it all out.

"Mr Sanders said we have to wait for the council to leave first," said Ada.

Raj sighed. "Typical."

The last thing I wanted was to hang about this blasted forest. Ada set the wine glass down, but she swayed slightly already. Oh, crap.

"Kay?" She turned to me. "Can—can we talk? Alone?"

My eyebrows shot up. Seriously? This was neutral Alliance territory, so it was safe. In theory.

I kind of wasn't paying much attention, though, because she'd taken hold of my hand.

"Don't disappear on me," she said.

"I wasn't planning to." Admittedly, I'd been tempted to go invisible and sneak out of the meeting, but it would have been a little conspicuous if people had seen me vanish into thin air. The irony.

"Good." She pulled on my arm, and I was too surprised *not* to let her lead me after her, down one of the paths, until trees blocked our view of the clearing. I still heard the music, though, and I scanned the surroundings—nothing disturbed the leaves around us. We were alone.

"Ada... *how* much of that wine did you drink?"

"Don't spoil it," she muttered, turning around, still holding onto my left hand. The non-bandaged one, though it was still marked with half-healed cuts from the glass. Her eyes weren't, as I'd expected, unfocused, but oddly clear.

"Ada..."

"Just kiss me."

I could do nothing but gape at her before she'd thrown her arms around me and kissed me full on the mouth.

She tasted sweet, and it lit a fire in my veins. I knew she

was probably half unaware of what she was doing—god knew this was a bad idea all around—but I kissed her back. It was impossible not to. My hands were moving of their own accord, one hand cupping the back of her head, the other sliding around her waist.

Damn. This was way out of line. We were colleagues. She was half drunk... and trying to take off my jacket.

"Ada—"

She cut off my words by kissing me again, her hands now somehow inside my jacket and sliding under my shirt. The skin contact about drove me over the edge.

God*damn*, I wanted her.

Yeah, Kay, this is a seriously bad idea, shouted what was left of rationality, but the part of my mind telling me that was drowned out by the part which was more interested in how to get her out of that uniform.

A sudden *neigh* echoed around the forest, making the earpiece vibrate so loudly I jumped, and my head collided with a low-hanging branch, knocking me back to reality.

"What the hell?" I pushed the offending branch out the way. "What's going on?"

Ada let go of me. "I can't hear them..." She shook her head dazedly.

Damn. She was right. The music had stopped.

"There's been an attack on the humans' capital!" Markos yelled into the earpiece, almost deafening me.

"Jesus Christ." I turned to Ada, who blinked at me.

"Kay?"

"Oh, shit," I said intelligently. "Can you walk?"

"Of course I bloody can." She took one step forward and tripped over a tree root. I caught her arm in time to stop her falling.

"We have to get back." I felt like I'd been clobbered by a branch, and the throbbing lump on the back of my head reminded me that was exactly what had just happened. "What attacked the capital?" I said into the earpiece, beckoning Ada to follow me to the clearing.

"I have no idea, but it's on the rampage," said the centaur, and cursed loudly in Aglaian. "Where in the gods' name *are* you, human?"

"Here," I said, spotting him across the clearing. The council had scattered, and most of the centaurs had gone. Those who remained were arguing in groups.

"Go," said Markos. "All non-Aglaians have to leave, before they blame you for it."

"What?" I stared at him. "They can't seriously blame us."

"One of the council members took the obsidiate. It happened so fast."

"*Where?*"

Markos pointed, and I sprinted down the forest path. I'd cleared a hundred metres before it caught up with me that running into the forest alone was a damn *stupid* idea—but if someone had got hold of the source…

An explosion of sparks took me off my feet, my back slamming into the ground. My skin buzzed all over. Swearing, I stood, climbing over a tree root. Reddish smoke pointed me in the right direction.

Ikor the mage lay sprawled on the ground, as did the Valerian council member who'd taken the obsidiate. No, that wasn't him. Not anymore. A fair-haired, sharply-dressed man got to his feet, dusting off his suit.

Bloodrock solution.

He had to be Aric's father. And he held the obsidiate. Or what was left of it.

The mage trembled all over, and I recognised the tell-tale effects of magical aftershock. Magic burn. *Hellfire.* Ikor must have chased him down. Either the guy was on our side, or he wanted the obsidiate for himself.

I turned invisible, before either of them saw me. I had to get that source away from Conner. He'd already turned his back on the mage and was in the act of using what looked like a communicator. I aimed carefully to avoid the obsidiate and sent a bolt of magic at him from behind, hitting him square between the shoulder blades.

"What the devil—?"

"Close enough," I said, and the side of my fist struck him down. *Great plan, Kay.* I hadn't knocked him out, only dazed him, and the buzzing magic forced me to drop the invisibility. As he stirred, I zapped him with magic, kicking the communicator out of his hand. With difficulty—like his son, Conner Senior was built like a chalder vox in human skin—I wrapped one arm around his neck and used the other to divest him of two Valerian-style guns. Couldn't see any other weapons, but it was difficult enough to keep hold of him.

"No you don't," I snarled, zapping him again to stop him hitting me.

"Kay... Walker?" The mage had staggered to his feet.

"Give me a hand over here," I said, attempting to drag Conner through the thick undergrowth. As tempting as it was to leave him out here for the wolves—well, centaurs—this was a matter for the council.

The magic burn had Ikor shaking so hard, he couldn't walk in a straight line. Cursing under my breath, I tapped the earpiece. "Could use some help, Markos."

I zapped Conner with second level magic again, and this time he shook so hard, it became doubly difficult to keep my grip on him. His eyes rolled back in his head.

The sound of hooves. I froze, automatically pulling on magic ready to defend myself, but it was just Markos, and the other two centaurs who'd been with him and Tryfon at Central.

"We'll take him to your council, human." Markos grabbed

Conner and lifted him bodily into the air. Lucky for him he wasn't awake enough to be aware of the indignity of being carried by a centaur. The other two centaurs kicked the thick undergrowth out of the way, and I ran ahead, back to the clearing. I had to find Ada and get Conner under close watch before the bastard pulled another trick. He'd used bloodrock solution, and no one had even noticed. How many times had the Conners got away with that? Might they even have impersonated centaurs? *Not Aric.* No way was that imbecile a good enough actor to pull that off.

My heart sank when I saw most of the council members had gone. The open Passage door swarmed with people leaving, while the remaining centaurs stood with weapons at the ready.

"What the hell's going on?" I demanded of the universe in general. "Who was attacked?"

"The humans," said Markos. "Speaking of whom—" He gave Conner a shake. The bastard's eyes were half open. Damn. He'd be pissed with me.

Ada, who stood apart from the crowd, rushed over to me. "Kay, we have to go." At least she sounded sober enough to run.

Before I could respond, a long, drawn-out scream vibrated through the earpiece—from Markos's expression, I guessed the same noise came from his earpiece, too. Even Ada jumped.

"What the hell was that?" I said.

"I don't know." The centaur fiddled with the earpiece, and I did the same. It vibrated in my hands, and my ears rang with the sound of the scream.

Ada made a strangled sound. "Did... who has the other earpiece? There were three."

Oh, crap. "It was with the tech department, at Central, right?"

That scream…

"What? My brother's there." Ada sagged against me, the colour draining from her face. "Someone tried to steal it from them yesterday. Aric. I forgot…"

I looked from her to the Chameleon and back again at Ada. "Aric. Damn."

The earpiece vibrated again, so intensely I dropped it. A deafening scream, followed by gasping, the sounds of someone in terrible pain.

"Shit." I crouched down to search. "I can't find the damn—"

My hand closed over the metal object as another scream rang out. Then sobbing. "Ada," whimpered the person on the other end. "Please…"

Then the noise went dead.

Ada dropped to her knees, too. "That was my little brother," she said. "Alber."

17

ADA

The scream rang through my head, cut through me like a swinging blade. Alber.

Kay was speaking to me, saying something. I shook my head to clear the ringing in my ears.

"Ada. Ada. Dammit, we have to go." He took my arm and pulled me to my feet. The strength had gone out of my limbs, the glow from the wine burned away.

"Come on, Ada."

"By the gods, humans, leave now!" The centaur had reared up on his hind legs, and kicked at a—*what* was that? A snarling bundle of smoky red fur and claws, moving too quickly for me to make out any more, and then it vanished.

Crap. It was the same as those creatures I'd fought in the Passages yesterday.

Kay swore. "Markos—"

"Get out of here!" Markos shouted, as the smoky creature slammed into him and knocked him back. What could possibly do that to a centaur?

And then Kay was steering me after him, across the leafy floor, through the opening in the rock and into the Passages.

The magic struck, cold and tingling under my skin. "Alber," I gasped.

"I know." Kay hadn't let go of my arm. I pulled it free as my legs remembered how to walk again.

"Ada," said Kay, walking alongside me as I strode ahead, right through the groups of council members scattered in the Passage. "Ada. I know. Here." He pressed the earpiece into my hand, and I stared at him for an instant. "You use this. I'm going to see if I can pick up a signal." He had his communicator out, hitting the offworld roaming button, but of course, Earth was unreachable out here.

"Alber," I said into the earpiece. "Alber, please, please tell me where you are. I'm coming, I promise—Alber!"

Nothing. I pressed a hand to my mouth to stifle the scream building inside me. Someone was hurting my brother, and they could be anywhere, on any universe. I couldn't move fast enough, even as I kept pace with Kay, who knew where he was going in this effing maze.

How had this happened?

"Ada. I'm going to need you to calm down. You said Aric tried to get the Chameleon from the tech rooms? It might help us find him."

I swallowed. "Yeah. The tech team said he threatened a few people. They locked the door for precautions. But Alber's never been near Central."

"Your older brother works in tech, though," said Kay. "Is there any reason he might have given your younger brother the device?"

"No clue," I said. "It was the only one left, Ms Weston said. Oh my god…"

The walls were closing in. *No, not now.* I swallowed, hard, concentrated on breathing.

"You're all right." Kay's hand closed over mine. "Come on. We're going to help him." I looked up at him, and his dark eyes gleamed in the blue light of the Passages. "I think Aric's family's involved. The Conners—they've been using the bloodrock. And if he knew about the Chameleon already... dammit, it doesn't add up."

"What?" I said, some of the fog in my head clearing. "The Conners? Aric's family?"

"They were trying to cash in on what the Campbells left behind," said Kay, speaking quickly, regarding me like he expected me to collapse. "On Valeria, they had Cethraxian foot-soldiers, the ravegens, creating diversions while they raided the Campbell place. Aric was looking for the Chameleon... but it does just the same thing as bloodrock solution, and they already had that. So why would he need it?"

"The solution isn't permanent," I said. "Wait—my brothers said someone threatened the Knight family, too. About the bloodrock. They were the ones who used to help Nell make the formula, and the Alliance confiscated all of it. There was none left."

"Nell made it?"

"Yeah..." I stopped dead, the world tilting under my feet. "I haven't seen her since yesterday. She was out, I assumed till late, but I never heard her come back. And—and I didn't check on Alber this morning. He might have already been gone..."

Kay's hand on my arm steadied me. "Ada. Focus. We need to move."

One foot in front of the other. I concentrated on him, instead, his total calmness of manner despite our urgent pace.

"The Conners," he said. "I caught two of them in Valeria yesterday. They handed themselves in to the police, confessed everything, but I've no bloody clue where the rest of their family is. There's no way they can't be involved in this, the timing's too close to be coincidence. So now the police know, Conner had to strike first. But how in hell is *Aglaia* involved? Why would they need them?" He was tenser, more agitated with each step, and fighting to keep his cool. "Get your communicator. We'll be in signal zone soon."

He was right. I'd been listening with numb, detached horror. That wouldn't do if I wanted to save my family. I hit the button to call Jeth with shaking hands, over and over again.

Finally, it connected.

"Ada? What's up?"

"Someone's taken Alber," I gasped into the phone. "He's hurt. I don't know who, or where, but someone's—they're torturing him, Jeth."

"What?"

I had to repeat it twice before it sunk in. "Shit. Ada... guys, be quiet!" he yelled at what I assumed were the other people in the tech office.

"I think it might be to do with the Conner family," I said, and now, hearing his voice, I was properly sobbing. "They searching for something, after the Campbells, I don't know what. Did Nell come back last night?"

"I didn't hear her, but I was running late. Damn. Ada, where are you?"

"In the Passages, on my way back. I don't even know if he's on Earth!"

"Earth or Valeria," said Kay, who was one-handedly typing on his own communicator screen. "Damn. Aric's father lives in Neo Greyle half the time. He might still be there. The Enforcement Squads who arrested Aric's cousins didn't find him, but it's possible in a city that size. Especially for a resourceful bastard like him."

"God. Alber…" The communicator slid from my hand, and Kay's hand shot out and caught it.

"You ask around the office," he said to Jeth. "Ask if anyone's seen Aric, or the other Conners. Do *not* leave Central. You might be another target."

I didn't hear what Jeth said in reply.

Kay clicked off my communicator and passed it back to me, digging in his pocket. "I have this." He pulled out a rectangular metal object I recognised from Carl's office. "A tracker. It can trace magic use… is your brother a magic-wielder?"

I nodded. "Mageblood."

"I thought you told me that once. If he used magic, I can use it to trace him. On Earth, there are few enough magic-wielders that these things can trace an individual."

Yeah. If he *was* on Earth. I pushed back the sob in my chest and concentrated on power-walking like hell itself was on my tail.

"Wait," said Kay. "Your brother was at your house? Did he use magic there?"

"I—yeah. All the time. It drives Nell crazy." *Walk, Ada. Don't think.*

"Then we can pick up his trace. We'll have to use the hidden Passage near your place. It's the quickest way, and it isn't sealed."

"It isn't? Jeth…"

"Call him." Kay paused, assessing the route, and then took off again down a side tunnel so fast I had to hurry to keep up.

I took out my own communicator, called Jeth's number. "It's me," I said. "We're headed to the house, through the Passages. If you can, tell someone what's happening. Ms Weston. Our boss. Kay and I are going back home."

"Yes," Kay cut in quickly. "This merits an emergency call

to the Alliance. I already sent an alert, but the connection's limited in here. I don't know if it reached them."

"What he said," I gasped, my legs protesting at the speed I pushed them to. "The Conners. We think it's the Conners. Aric."

"Dammit." He swore in Karthonic, then English. "Someone *did* break into the tech room early this morning. Someone inside Central."

"Ada." Kay caught my arm. "The stairs—"

We'd reached the tunnel with the hidden staircase to the lower levels. Damn. I didn't have any weapons at all. And neither did Kay.

We just had magic.

He nodded to me. "After you."

In the lower Passage. Blood streaked the walls, old wyvern blood from the time I'd been chased through here. The stench of Cethrax was everywhere. Doors often opened to their swampland in the lower levels. God help us if there were any monsters about now...

One way back, and I took it breakneck pace. I all but held my breath the entire time, until we came to the door which had started everything. Kay shoved it open.

I ran, flat out, leaping clear of the fallen remains of the wall a chalder vox had destroyed, pelted down the street, to my house. The door hung off its hinges. A humming sound behind me made me spin around. Kay had activated the tracking device, and the air around it shimmered as he approached the door, frowning.

"Got it," he said. "Magic signal—just the one. It's definitely not yours?"

I shook my head. "I haven't used it since."

Kay tapped buttons on the device. "Should be able to trace it." He pulled out his communicator and lined the flashing ends of each device together. "I've never done this before, but it should link to the GPS. Damn thing's only ninety per cent accurate, but it should... Shit, it's out of range. Offworld."

I sagged against the wall. "You're kidding me!"

Kay swore, hitting the device over and over. "Can't get a reading. Wait a minute." He looked down at the screen, then at me. "I can try... we need to get back in the Passages."

"Huh? Why?"

"I think I can amplify this." He indicated the tracker. "It's dangerous, but we don't have an option." He shook his head. "The tracer in this is made of a magic-based source. I can use it."

I nodded frantically. "Do it."

"I'll need you to be there, Ada, in case it goes wrong. If anything happens, go back to Central, go to your brother. Get the addresses of all the Conners' places, they can have people sent in. Then—Ada, I'm sorry, but you'll have to let Ms Weston know. About the deposits on Aglaia, even. Everything."

I swallowed. If it helped get us out of this nightmare... but the possibility of anything happening to Kay, too...

Back in the Passages, he hit the button on the tracker again. And then he turned to face me. Looked me right in the eyes. The breath punched out of my lungs. He was risking his life to help me save my brother.

My hand gripped his like that would express what I couldn't in words, as the magic swarmed around us in a blur of red, and his hand was wrenched away.

KAY

Awareness flooded me like an electric charge. Even though I'd become accustomed to the way magic felt, this was different. A heightened sense.

The light cleared. Ada watched me from the other side, eyes wide, hand outstretched where she'd let go as the magic hit both of us.

"Can you feel that?" she gasped. "It's Alber."

I shook my head, slightly dazed. Magic left blurred imprints on my eyelids, but a sensation tugged at me, coming from deeper in the Passages. Like a radio signal, but one I felt rather than heard.

The tracker. I'd tapped into the tracker... but Ada shouldn't be able to feel it, too.

"You can absorb magic," I said, as it hit home. "You can feel the tracker, because you were touching my hand. Somehow it transferred over."

"It's that way." She pointed with a shaky hand.

And once again, we struck out through the Passages. I cursed this damned maze for having no shortcuts. Nothing we could do but move as fast as humanly possible. Ada's face was set, and I hoped it wouldn't turn to panic. But she held it together.

Once we were out of the hidden Passage, I led us through a shortcut to the Valerian door that led to an alley, and pushed it open. The tracker-sense deepened instantly. So it was true. It came from Valeria.

Apparently, being arrested wasn't enough to keep the Conners out.

I'd thought the door was under guard, but the quietness gave me the sense that something was wrong. I gestured to Ada to stop as she caught up.

"Hold on. I can go invisible and—"

"Try and transfer it," she said quickly, grabbing my hand. "If the tracker works—"

Of course. I shook my head, amazed she could think clearly, and tuned into the Chameleon's energy. Instantly, the effect took hold. And both of us vanished.

"Holy hell," said Ada's voice. She gripped my hand. "Come on."

I stepped through the door to Valeria, Ada at my side.

No one guarded the doorway. The alleyway was as deserted as before, even though I'd told the police about it when I'd caught that ravegen. *Something's wrong.*

It became apparent what, exactly, when we reached the street. It was all but deserted, but the few people about headed towards smoke rising from the east.

But that wasn't the way we needed to go. Someone had caused a hell of a distraction to drive everyone far away from the doorway entrance, which meant there were people here who shouldn't be.

The Campbells' place was unguarded, though the police tape remained. But anyone could force a lock, even on a building like this, if they had magic on their side. Once we were properly inside the grounds, I saw the limp bodies of several people in Enforcement Officer uniform. Fury surged through my veins. We'd got here too late.

The magic level rose without warning, the static in the air buzzing so intensely it was like standing next to a speaker set to full blast.

Ada gasped in alarm. "What was that?"

"No clue. We'll find your brother." I knocked open a window with a subtle magic shot. Nobody appeared to be inside, but a building that size could hide anything. Lucky I remembered the way to the stairs.

Our path was blocked by... a screen? The image of a forest path covered the space where the stairs should be, as if a piece of reality had been torn away.

A doorway. It took a second to grasp it. Someone had *opened* a doorway. To Aglaia.

"Shit," I said.

Ada's hand gripped mine tighter. "What the hell?" she whispered.

The doorway extended from floor to ceiling, leaving no way around. Underneath, something gleamed cold and black, and the magic under my skin buzzed in response. They were using a source to power it.

The last time I'd been near a source like this had been when the Campbells had taken Ada. Every drop of blood in my veins turned to ice. *Not again.*

"Other stairs," I said, calmly as I could. "Come on."

We backed downstairs and hurried down the corridor to the other staircase. As we reached the third floor, the tracker pulsed more insistently than ever. Ada's brother was in one of these rooms.

"That one," I whispered to Ada, turning visible again to point at the right door. "Set your brother free, now."

Footsteps sounded and I quickly turned the chameleon effect back on. Magic sparked from where Ada was still invisible, knocking open the door. She disappeared inside, just as two men came around the corner, both smartly dressed and armed with Valerian-style guns. Magic-based weaponry, and highly illegal. I moved so I was between them and the open door. No way in hell was I letting them near Ada and her brother.

"Blasted woman won't say a word," one of them was

saying. "Not one. We're gonna have to try something else. How long will that thing hold open?"

"Not long," said the other.

The first man cursed. And then dropped like a stone as I punched him in the temple, an instant knockout. As the second man spun around, searching for the target, I knocked the weapon from his hand and caught him in a chokehold.

"I'm not playing games here," I said. Quietly. "You're going to tell me what the hell's going on here right now, or so help me, I'll kill the pair of you in a second. Don't think I won't."

His legs spasmed as I squeezed his throat. *He tortured Ada's family.* He'd get no mercy from me.

"For starters, what's that door for?" I released my grip slightly and he gasped for air.

"Shit! It's that ghost! Gav was right!"

"You have three seconds." I twisted his arm, in such a way that indicated I knew exactly how to break the joint and put him in a world of pain. He wailed, and I tightened my grip around his throat, just long enough for a warning.

"It's so we—we can take this tech through from here. We needed a source, our dad needs a source, and it's the only one we haven't tried."

"For what, exactly?" Damn, how many Conner kids were there?

"I don't know!" he howled. "Stop. Please stop!"

"Tough shit," I said. "What have you done with Nell Fletcher?"

"On Aglaia," he sobbed. "She's on Aglaia. Helping. She makes… disguises."

Shit. "You need those disguises. Why?"

He sobbed again. "To infiltrate the councils… offworld."

"Okay," I said. "So, let me get this straight. Your family's after sources. You arranged the assassination of the centaur king?"

"My sister went to talk to the centaurs, in disguise." He sobbed again. "She killed the king—when he guessed she wasn't her." So he must be Aric's older brother.

"Where did you get the bloodrock solution?"

"West Office. They confiscated it."

"And the door? How did you do that?"

"Magical fairy dust, I haven't a clue. We stole everything West Office had." His voice rose in pitch as my grip reflexively tightened. "My father took some of it with him, said it was ob-obsidian or something."

"How the hell did you open that doorway?"

"Magical fucking fairy dust. Let go of me!"

I kicked him, and he whimpered. "No screwing around," I said. "Do you know how they opened the doorway? With a magic source?"

"Yeah, yeah, it all looks the bloody same, doesn't it? I just turned on the machine, it's supposed to link up with a source on the other side."

Goddammit. This was worse than I'd feared. And he was dead right that all magic sources *did* look identical. He was no magic-wielder. But I was getting an entirely different vibe from the doorway than from any other sources I'd been near.

"Why Aglaia?"

"Nobody claimed their source yet." He squirmed in my grip. "If the Alliance gets hold of it, they'll bury it underground where no one can ever use it. It's a freaking *amplifier.* They're rare as hell and my dad needs it."

"To do what?"

"Sell, what else? The Alliance's new laws crippled us. A source will get our family out of debt."

"Or it might blow you up," I said coldly. "I'm not impressed. Didn't you learn from what happened to the Campbells?"

"They were deluded," choked the guy. "They wanted to

destroy the Alliance, they didn't care who got in the way. We want to build things. To change. Upgrade. Wynn's already proof it works on non-magic-wielders. Why shouldn't people from Earth have magic, same as everywhere else?"

"That's not for you to decide," I said, adjusting my grip. "Not by stealing a dangerous source from a contentious world. All that'll do is bring an army of pissed-off centaurs on your tail."

"They don't have magic," he said. "It's no use to them."

I gave him a shake. "Still not impressed. Isn't the bloodrock enough? You got that from here?"

"Campbell's kid gave it my uncle, yeah. So what? It's not potent. The power drains out of it within minutes."

"Tell me something I don't know. Who else used the bloodrock?"

"Just… my father."

So no one else was running around in disguise… but someone must have impersonated one of Aglaia's council on more than one occasion. Even the centaurs. I couldn't think of any other way they could have found out about the source.

"Who killed those Enforcement Officers? And distracted the others?"

"My sister. She used the last of the source to attack one of the Alliance's bases."

Damn. So she must be a magic-wielder.

"And Aric? Where's he?"

"Went after Wynn, through the door. He brought the woman. And the boy."

"And you? What did your father tell *you* to do?" The words came out before I could stop them, though I knew the answer already.

"To make them talk."

Magic surged into my hands, crackling in lightning waves

made ever-strong by the presence of the open door. The second level shot had him on the floor, convulsing.

"Still think magic's so great?" I raised my hand again, and an answering sound kicked up in the background, a roaring in my ears, a surge of adrenaline and fury. He'd kill me if I let him go. He'd kidnapped and tortured a teenager. Who else was here to stop them?

I let the invisibility drop, so he could see my face before I struck him dead—

A noise behind me. Ada and her brother came out of the room, him half-conscious against her shoulder. She stared at me in abject horror, and for an instant, an image rose up of a cliff's edge, and her on the other side, slipping further and further away, out of reach.

"Kay, *stop!*" Her voice was louder than the roaring, louder even than the magic crackling around me. My gaze dropped to the limp form of the guy I'd zapped. He wasn't moving.

Reality slammed into me like a wave. Her guardian was trapped in Aglaia. Which was still under attack. And the door wouldn't stay open forever.

I dropped the magic, shaking inwardly as I moved away from the fallen Conners and towards Ada. I shoved the thoughts away. There'd be time enough to think about what I'd almost done later.

"I have to get through that door," I said. "Nell's somewhere there. I'll save her, you get your brother out."

"No way am I leaving," she said, without looking me in the eyes. "I'll do what I damn well like." She pulled out her communicator and punched buttons. "Jeth. I've got Alber, he's at the Campbells' place on Valeria. Get someone sent over there now. I'm going to…"

The magic started to fade, the buzzing from the door reduced to a faint hum. The door would close any second now.

"You can follow later, but you have to keep your brother safe. I'll find your guardian. The door's about to close."

She glanced at her brother. Then back at me. She nodded. Once.

And I ran. I left the Conner brothers, pelted for the stairs, at the rapidly disappearing doorway, and flung myself through it.

18

KAY

I rolled over on the rough ground of the forest, firing up the invisibility again just in case.

Ada's guardian was held hostage somewhere here. There had to be a clue... though the tracker wouldn't work if she wasn't a magic-wielder.

There was no sign of anyone. Of course not. But the door had been opened for a reason, and Aric and his family would be here somewhere. Nothing but trees all around. I guessed the Conners hadn't known exactly where the source was. But I did recognise the area. This was the spot where the mage had caught Mr Conner escaping with the obsidiate. The trees bore the marks of the aftermath, and tiny fragments of gleaming black were scattered on the ground. Was that why the doorway had opened here? The two sources... I bent to pick up the pieces of metal, and dropped my hand as it burned. It was obsidiate, all right, though broken into too many fragments to be of much use to anyone. Maybe the Conners had intended to set up a doorway here all along, because even Tryfon hadn't told them the exact location of their source.

Voices came from nearby, drifting through the trees. I was less than a hundred metres from the clearing, where that magic-sourced monster had been attacking the centaurs. They called it the kimaros, according to the files, a mythological monster predating the arrival of humans, though what exactly they were, no one knew. Fitting for a magic-fearing species like the centaurs. But the voices didn't sound panicked from here. They must have got rid of the creature, somehow. At least, I hoped so.

I fired up the tracker, even though I knew it wouldn't do any good here. As I predicted, the general buzz of magic in the air increased, making it impossible to distinguish an individual signal. I swore in a low voice, taking a few steps along the track. And then stopped as a figure appeared on the path ahead.

Aric.

"Yeah, real funny, Wynn," he muttered. "Damn forest. Back where I bloody started."

He stared around, then kicked a tree, viciously. Lost, I assumed. Typical of the idiot, really. At least he couldn't see me.

It didn't mean he wasn't dangerous. And right now, he was the only person around who might give me answers about his family's plan.

I switched off the invisibility. Aric started, gaping, steadying himself against a tree to keep from tripping over the tangled undergrowth.

"The hell?"

"Aric," I said. "Fancy meeting you here."

He shook his head, probably wondering if he was hallucinating.

I took a step towards him. "Don't suppose you could tell me where your father's holding Nell Fletcher?"

"Who? Where the hell did you come from, Walker?"

"That's for me to know. Where's your father?"

"I haven't a fucking clue, have I?" His glare deepened. "You were invisible. You handed my cousins over to the police!"

"So you do have one more brain cell than I gave you credit for," I said. "Now, tell me where Nell Fletcher is. You kidnapped her, didn't you?"

"That Enzar woman?"

"That's right, Aric. Now you're going to tell me where she is, and I might just let you walk out of Aglaia alive."

My hands shook with fury again. Conner gave the orders, and he obeyed. Without question. They all did. His mouth half opened, and he shook his head. I turned invisible again, leaving him blinking at the spot where I'd stood. I crossed the path swiftly, and swept behind him to close my hands around his throat.

Magic crashed into me like a wave, throwing me off my feet. I slammed into a tree, sliding to the ground, and then the backlash hit. The second level shock flared through every nerve in my body, and I was so shocked I let the invisibility drop. Aric turned around, teeth bared in a grin.

"Surprised?" he said. "Not all of us magic-wielders have a death wish, Walker."

No freaking way. I pushed away from the tree, ignoring the static after-shock, and faced him. *He's a magic-wielder? How long?*

"I never used it in the Passages," he said. "But damn, it feels good."

"You're a moron," I said idiotically. *Crap.* This was bad. Aglaia was second level, and weakened. Aside from turning invisible, I had no advantage. So we were evenly matched, magic-wise at least. I'd always been able to get the better of him on the rare occasions we'd been unwisely paired up in Academy combat training, but with magic thrown into the equation, all bets were off. Especially when he, of all people, needed a goddamn rulebook to keep him from doing something stupid.

"I can do whatever I like." He held out a hand, magic crackling around his palm. I turned invisible again. It couldn't block magic, but it was the one advantage I had left. The question was: was he a natural-born magic-wielder, or had something—had his father—?

I gave myself a mental shake. Now wasn't the time to speculate. I had to attack first, but using magic would immediately give away my position.

Damn. I ran for the nearest tree, out of Aric's sight. I climbed, letting magic flow towards one hand as I did, and before Aric could turn around and figure out where I was, I'd hit him in the back of the head with it. He stumbled right into the backlash, which I, aboveground, avoided, and fell flat on his face, twitching. The impact paralysed him long enough for me to jump out the tree and slam down on top of him. I shifted, hands around the back of his neck.

"I really wouldn't." I switched off the camouflage and zapped him with magic again.

Aric cursed, repeatedly. I kept firing first level shots, aware that if I hesitated for a second, he'd throw me off him. I couldn't keep him pinned down for much longer.

"Tell me where Nell Fletcher is. No bullshit."

"She's in the council meeting place," Aric spat into the ground. "They cleared the place out when that monster got loose." He twisted his head, and I zapped him again. "Get the hell off me, you murdering bastard."

"You're shitting me, right?" I said. "You kidnapped and tortured two people."

His head shifted. "No," he rasped. "I didn't. That was Wynn. My sister."

"Your sister," I repeated. "Is she here? With your father?"

The faintest nod.

"Anyone else in your family here? Your mother?"

"Dead," he said. "Six years ago."

I went still, as did Aric, though magic still buzzed through my veins.

"I'm telling the truth, Walker," he choked into the dirt. "I knew you'd try to kill me again. You goddamned psycho."

"Yeah, I got that part," I said. "And what you did with that wyvern back at the Academy? You weren't trying to kill us? Because it sure looked like it."

"That was my sister's idea," he said. "A wyvern was attacking guards, and Wynn lured it to the Academy's Passage."

Shit. Was he telling the truth? At the time, I hadn't looked into it. I'd almost died, I hadn't exactly been in any state to ask anyone if they knew who in his family worked at the Alliance. I'd wanted to put the whole thing behind me. But the quickest way to draw a wyvern's attention was to use magic. Which meant...

"She's a magic-wielder, too." *Hell.* Like I needed any more enemies.

"Yeah. We both..." I gave him another sharp magic-shock before he could throw me off his back.

"Both what? You weren't born a magic-wielder, were you?"

"What's it to you? It's normal on Klathica." He moved one hand, to indicate the metal stud in his ear.

That was the source? How in hell had he got away with it?

"We blindsided you," said Aric. "It's coated in adamantine, so it won't set off the scanners at Central."

Shit. His father had thought of everything.

"What part of following your father and sister here doesn't say you're a psychotic bastard, too? I'm having a little difficulty understanding you, Aric. Perhaps your stupidity is rubbing off on me."

"Real funny, Walker."

"You haven't answered my question. You wanted in on their plan? A bit of power of your own?"

"Who the hell wouldn't? Our family lost everything when the Alliance stopped our trade. This source is worth more than money."

"You don't know what you're doing with it," I said. "If you use it, you'll wipe Aglaia out of the Multiverse, and six million lives with it."

"You lying bastard, Walker. My father said—"

"Say no more. He said you deserved to take what was rightfully yours? Something along those lines?"

A ringing silence. I'd got him. I figured he'd have heard that speech. I'd heard it half my life, back when my father's insane conspiracy theories made any kind of sense. But then, Aric had actually volunteered to be 'upgraded' to a magic-wielder. Nobody had forced it on him.

"Did I get it right? Might have missed the part about the Multiverse not owing you a fucking thing, Aric. I don't give a crap whose orders you were following. If you lived here on this world, you'd be executed for conspiracy and murder. As it is, the Alliance will be more than happy to give you what-ever punishment befits the crime."

Aric swore, over and over. *Enjoy your reality check.*

One movement, one shot of magic would take his life. But as furious as I was, magic didn't surge around me, didn't pulse alongside the anger in my veins. I wasn't in the Passages. I was in Aglaia, where magic was stable. For now.

"You're gonna stay put, Aric," I said. "If you want to live."

He nodded.

"If you fight on your father's side against me, don't expect any mercy." I jumped, sending another shot of magic behind me. Just enough to stop him firing an attack after me. But he didn't move.

I hit the ground at a run, trees whipping past, without stopping for breath until I reached the clearing. People and centaurs moved around between the trees. Swearing, I went invisible again, and slipped around the outskirts of the clearing. Save Ada's guardian first. Figure out what the hell was going on here later.

~

ADA

I watched Kay disappear through the door with a feeling of unreality. This was it. I'd put Nell's life in his hands. After watching what he did to those two men…

Alber groaned. His face was bruised all over, and by the way his feet dragged, I could tell they'd really hurt him.

I wanted to hurt them back. But I had to take care of my brother. Propping him up, I began the slow task of getting both of us downstairs, while updating Jeth on the situation. Telling him Alber was hurt, to meet me outside the Passages if possible.

"Hey, Ada," Alber said softly. "Did I mention you're awesome?"

I blinked tears out of my eyes. "Alber… I'm so sorry."

"Not your fault." He coughed. "I kicked the bastard good. Took… the earpiece they stole from Central."

"That's… amazing, Al. I wouldn't have thought of it."

He half laughed, which turned into a coughing fit. "Think the buggers broke a rib or two," he said between coughs. "Who knocked them out?"

"Kay did." My heart lurched unpleasantly. I'd seen him fight before, of course, seen him slaughter monsters and kill both Janice and Skyla with magic, but that had been in self-defence. The man who'd stared at me with eyes like fathomless black pits, the blazing red magic sharply outlining his face... hadn't looked like Kay at all.

Don't think about that now. I had to make sure Alber was safe first. The strong magic presence had faded with the door, and the tracker-sense had switched off now. And I wasn't invisible anymore. Not that it mattered.

By the time we reached the ground floor, several people had run into the building's lobby. Police force-types. They zeroed in on me immediately.

I didn't have time for their probing questions. "Take me to the Alliance," I said loudly. "A call should have gone out from Central, London. Earth." Even through the panic, I managed to get into my pocket, get my Alliance ID. "For heaven's sake, my brother's been tortured!"

"Let her through!" a guard shouted from the entryway. Orders were barked, and I was hurried back through the streets, two guards on either side. The wail of sirens cut through the general background noise of Valeria's capital, but I could only concentrate on helping Alber, averting my eyes from the bodies of fallen officers. People the Conners had killed on the way through, I guessed.

The way to the doorway to the Passages was guarded, but someone had already sent out an alert and Alber and I were allowed through. A path had been cleared through the blue-lit corridors.

"I'm at the entrance," Jeth said through the communicator. "They won't let me any closer, but hand him to the guards. He'll be fine."

As we reached Earth's door, Carl, head guard, hurried to meet me. "I figured something was up with Aric," he said, and took Alber from me, passing him on to two other guards. My brother groaned, and my chest tightened as they helped him cross the threshold to Earth, leaving Carl and me alone. "It's why I suspended him. We've sent teams out to his family's place. They didn't cover their tracks well. But his sister got away."

"They didn't need to," I said, urgency rising within me again. "Is Conner still on Aglaia? We didn't have the chance to hand him over to the council. He had a magic source. Kay's gone after them, but my guardian's with them. I can't let him go alone. Please believe me."

"I do." He steered me by the arm so we moved away from the door to Earth. "As it happens, we got a call from the West Branch not long ago, warning us that Wynn Conner had gone into the Passages unsupervised, and she'd been talking to her father on her communicator shortly before. Seems Kay asked someone to keep an eye on her. Tara Franklyn."

Hell. She'd actually kept her word.

"I need to go to Aglaia," I said. "Kay's out there alone."

Carl nodded. "This is far off policy, but what the Conners have done—there are fifty arrest warrants out on Valeria and the other Alliance branches are up in arms. Looks like they were involved with illegal trade on Klathica, too. Our other magic-wielders are over there, and we don't have backup at the ready. I can send you on ahead, but this is charged for one-use only."

He took something from his pocket. It was the thin glass-like rod I'd seen in his office, and it gleamed black, reflecting the blue Passage light in fragments.

"World-keys are rarely allowed for use even by Ambassadors," he said. "But Ms Weston tells me you can handle this. Let's hope she's right."

He drew a symbol on the wall, shaped like a sideways arrow, and leaned in close to sketch three smaller symbols besides the end. A humming sounded with a surge of magic —like in the Campbells' place—and a door opened where there hadn't been a door before.

On the other side, a familiar forest waited.

"You can handle it from here?" He gave me two daggers. "Just in case."

I nodded, pocketing the weapons. "Thank you."

"Good luck, Ada. You only have a minute to get through that door."

Like I'd hesitate when Nell was out there. I stepped through the door to Aglaia.

19

KAY

The council building was quiet. I used magic to open a likely window and climbed in as silently as possible. No one was about. But Aric's family... I was willing to bet at least one of them would be here.

Even if not, if the way back was blocked, I hadn't a freaking clue how I was going to get Ada's guardian out of here without getting both of us killed.

I slipped down the corridor, following the path I remembered. There were holding cells in this place, for people on trial who needed to be held on neutral ground for whatever reason. Like suspects for crimes against the Alliance. I headed downstairs, my skin prickling all over. Ignoring all instinct to get the hell out of the confined, dark space, I tried every door. Most were open.

One was locked.

Child's play. I shot magic at the lock on the door, breaking it. Before I could open the door, it opened and someone ran into me. I stopped, almost letting the invisibility slip, as the dishevelled figure of Nell, Ada's guardian, fell to the ground. I took in the bloodied cuffs on her wrists, her drawn face, now looking around in open confusion.

"What in all the Multiverse are you?" she asked, as I pulled her to her feet.

"Central's monster." I switched off the invisibility.

"You're Walker." Her eyes blazed in the darkness. I examined the handcuffs and carefully directed magic into one part of them. The metal shattered in a second, and she jumped.

"The name," I said, "is Kay, and I'm here for Ada's sake, not yours."

She recovered herself, looking at the shattered cuffs with a slightly dazed expression. Aside from her wrists, she didn't appear hurt, at least. I guessed they'd needed her to be able to help them.

"This is your doing. All of it. Thanks to you, they *tortured* my son." She took an unsteady step towards me.

"Yeah?" I said. "The Multiverse is more than you and your family. This is something that's been going on a long time, and if we don't get a move on, I won't be able to stop it."

"Is that how it is?" said Nell. "You arrested my daughter. You're the reason we're involved in this."

She might as well have stuck a knife in me. "Maybe you aren't the only person who thinks that, but I don't give a crap. *You* called your daughter a monster. If we get out of here alive, the first thing you're going to do is apologise to her if you ever want her to talk to you again. Get the hell over yourself and quit taking it out on her."

She said nothing. Her jaw hung slack.

"Follow me, and keep quiet."

She didn't protest. I still hadn't figured out the next step. Find somewhere to hide. Maybe. Or I could get us to the doorway. Use magic—that was my only option now.

"Did you do it?" I asked. "Did you help the Conners?"

"No," she said, through clenched teeth. "I refused. The

Conner girl left to help her father. What is your game here, Walker?"

"I told you not to call me that," I said. "I'll take care of the Conners. But it'd help to know what I'm up against."

Apart from an amplifying magical source. But if they'd tapped into it already, I was pretty sure I'd know about it. We were on the mainland now, the clearing only a short distance away. I wished I could transfer the chameleon effect, but that only worked with Ada, because of her ability. This woman had no magic of her own.

"They had bloodrock solution," I said. "Some of them disguised themselves... did you see Mr Conner himself?"

I'd never met the guy until now. He'd probably been involved with the Walkers at some point, but the Conner family were mostly about developing technologies on worlds close to Earth. The idea that something like *this* was going on —who had even told them about the source in the first place?

"No. Only the girl. Wynn."

I swore. Of course. "Right. I'm gonna try and get you back to the Passages, but there are centaurs blocking the way and they don't look too friendly." I glanced at her. "You can fight?"

"Of course."

Yeah. I figured where Ada got her stubbornness. I was willing to bet neither had wanted to give ground and apologise... a pretty familiar situation.

Except two humans against a bunch of aggravated centaurs was hardly a fair match without magic. And using that would risk both our lives.

Wait. I'd forgotten the blasted earpiece. *Idiot, Kay.* I'd been so focused on getting Nell out of there, it had slipped my mind. Tapping the device, I said, quietly, "Markos? Are you there?"

Did Ada's brother still have the other earpiece? I hoped not. He was hurt, anyway. Tortured by Aric's sister.

This whole thing was fucking insane.

"Human," said Markos's voice. "By the gods, you have awful timing."

"What? I need Passages access, *now.* Where are you?"

"With my family. They can hear you."

Shit. "You're in the clearing? What happened to those monsters?" I was nearing the clearing myself by this point, Nell on my heels.

"We killed them. There may be more. We're by the Passages, but—" I had to raise my voice over the yelling in the background—"They're not letting anyone through."

"Oh, for crying out loud," I said. "Tell them it's a goddamn emergency! And make sure Ada knows her guardian's safe."

"She's not on Earth," said Markos. "Carl just got a message through. She's coming here."

"What?"

I spotted him in the clearing, then, surrounded by other centaurs. He tapped a hoof, while several of the others circled him, tails swishing. All were armed with crossbows and spears. Shit.

"I have no idea where she is, human. Our communication was cut off."

They must still be in the Passages. Dammit.

"Can you get away and find her?" I said to Markos. "I'll divert their attention." I switched on the camouflage, indicating to Nell to stay back.

Then I let magic surge through my fingers, up into the sky.

ADA

I ran through the forest, cursing every step. The area I'd come out the door in was right by the clearing, but the centaurs gathered around the Passage entrance killed all notion of asking for help. They were probably there to make sure no one else got in.

I needed to find Nell, if Kay hadn't already. But I had no idea where he was. Wandering into centaur territory alone would likely get me killed.

The coast. Head for the coast. That was neutral territory, so supposedly safe. But without Kay, I couldn't turn invisible.

Hell. I was in trouble.

I skidded to a halt at the edge of a cliff. A narrow path led the way to a large building—the council house, Kay had told me—and beyond, the islands the humans lived on. A distant glow surrounded the island facing me, and the smell of smoke mingled with the sea breeze. Fire. There'd been an attack on the capital.

A crackle of thunder made me spin around, in time to see a fork of lightning surge through the trees. The sounds of angry centaurs drifted out of the forest.

Crap. Someone had used magic in centaur territory. I froze up. It must be one of the Conners, which meant they were close by.

Move it, Ada, I thought, and aimed for the bridge.

And then hands grabbed me, lifting me off my feet—*way* off my feet. I yelled, my cry cut off as a hand clamped over my mouth.

A centaur held me, right over the cliff's edge, over the churning waves.

"If you want to live, I'd get away from there."

I went limp with relief. It was Markos.

The hand lifted from my mouth. "What're you doing?" I said. "I'm here to save my guardian. Did you see her?"

"I didn't, human." The centaur sounded weary. A long scratch marked the right side of his face. He must have caught me staring, because he said, "The kimaros haven't been seen on this world in a hundred years."

My heart plummeted. "Was that... what you were fighting? There were some of those in the Passages yesterday, too."

"Yes, I believe they came through the illegal doorway."

"I thought so," I said. "Listen." And I summarised the situation. "Conner is going after your source. He might already be there!"

Markos bristled in alarm. "By the gods, human." And he drew back, putting me down, and began to canter off into the woods.

"Wait!" I hurried after. "You can't fight him alone. He'll have this magic source. Centaurs—you can't use magic."

"I am aware of that, human." He slowed, agitated.

"Kay's here somewhere. He might be going up against Conner. I have to go there." But he still didn't let me go. "I have adamantine in my blood," I said. "I can absorb magic. I'll be your shield. Please. Let me help."

The centaur went very still. "You *what*, human?"

"There's no time to explain," I said. "Please. Help."

Then, in one motion, he lifted me by the scruff of my coat and placed me on his back.

"Hold on tight, human."

And he ran, with me clinging on for dear life.

20

KAY

Naturally, the instant I entered the clearing, I became the centre of attention, and the group of furious centaurs turned on me.

"We need Passages access," I said to Eidora. Or the queen, now. If *she* guarded the door, then they must be dead serious about keeping people out.

"You shouldn't be here, human," she said, hoof tapping the ground.

I looked her in those furious eyes. "Tough. I am here, and if you don't want the Conners to burn the forest to the ground, I'd suggest you let me pass."

"You humans are responsible for attacking our world," Eidora spat. "Because of you, my brother betrayed us. How dare you come here?"

"We haven't got time for this," I snapped. "The Conners are after your source. Where the hell is Mr Conner?"

"The human escaped," said one of the others. Leonid. "We're searching the forest. He's unarmed, he cannot have gone far."

"And who brought him here?" Eidora snarled. "You humans bring chaos wherever you go."

"I'm not the one pointing spears at people."

I stepped back as several centaurs closed in, spears out. My heart sank. Nell was unarmed, and I'd never risk her getting caught in the backlash if I used magic. And Markos was gone.

I raised my hands in surrender. "I'm not going to attack you. Are the council still behind the door?"

"Nobody is allowed in or out, human. Those monstrosities came from the Passages."

"This woman was captured and tortured." I glanced at Nell, who appeared dazed but defiant. "By the Conners. Under Alliance law, I demand access to the Passages."

A pause. Not even the centaurs' queen could deny that. I knew their laws allowed for circumstances like this.

The centaurs moved aside, and the Passage door slid open. Immediately, a group of what looked like several worlds' Alliance council members and guards tried to emerge, only to be pushed back by the centaurs' spears.

Hell.

"We are allowing access for this one individual." Eidora gave me a contemptuous look, and I turned to Nell, who glared at the lot of them. Pretty bold of her.

"The Conner family captured and tortured her," I said. "As part of some kind of insane plan involving a magic source. Warn the Alliance, in all the worlds, to prepare for the backlash if I can't stop them. Unless you're willing to change your minds." I glared at the centaurs.

Instead of replying, Eidora shoved Nell, roughly, through the doorway. As she crossed the threshold, she turned back and stared at me—as were all the others behind the door—which was already sliding closed.

Shit. "There's a threat to your entire world," I said to the centaurs, as the door closed with a final *click*. "I don't know where the Conners are, but they're on Aglaia somewhere. They were colluding with the Anthos tribe, with Tryfon, and they're after your source."

"You blasted Alliance people want it," Eidora said. "I knew it. You were after the source all along."

"Are you out of your mind?" I said. "Your whole world dies if we don't stop Conner. Who apart from you knows about the source? You notice I didn't tell the council members? I could have. The entire Alliance would know."

As it was… only the people in the clearing did. Most of whom had probably known already, even if they didn't know the name. Lustre.

Three spears pointed at me, close enough to brush against my jacket. For a heartbeat, I thought it was game over for me. And then Eidora gestured to the others to lower their weapons, still eying me with distrust.

"Until now, only the royal family."

Crap. "Including Tryfon? He was trading something with offworlders."

Her eyes narrowed. "If it wasn't for Markos and his arrangement with the Alliance, human, you'd be dead now."

"Yeah? We're all going to be dead soon if you don't answer my question. Do you think I'd be wasting my time here if I wasn't trying to help? Someone attacked your world already. You might be next. Tell me what you know about your cousin's involvement with offworlders."

"I did not know any of this," she said haughtily. "The traitors are dead."

I indicated the other centaurs, who pointed spears at me, too. "Any of you want to contribute?"

No answer, but they came closer, until I was pinned to the spot. Even if I turned invisible, if I moved in any direction, I'd get speared. I didn't like my chances here.

"Okay. The source, then. Do you use it? Because someone's planning to turn it into a weapon. How much is there?"

Something in my voice seemed to get through to her. "Tryfon was a fool to think he could trade with offworlders. We don't use the magic, humans, we do not destroy."

Okay... "Either way, I reckon at least one of your family was impersonated by someone using bloodrock solution at some time or other. That's disguise-magic."

The tip of a spear touched the back of my neck, and it took all my self-control not to flinch.

"It's true. Someone set you up. Somebody must have told the Conner family about the source in the first place. They aren't in the council. None of them have even been here, as far as I know."

Unless they'd used those doorways before. But that thing had carried a hell of a lot of magical energy. No way could they have done that under normal circumstances without drawing attention.

"Tryfon was foolish. Like my idiot brother, he decided to travel offworld, to a human city, and talk to them. He thought he could win us glory through sharing the information."

"With Conner?"

"With humans. You're all the same," said Eidora.

"Not all of us want to blow things up with magic sources," I said. "So Tryfon decided to trade it for obsidiate. For what purpose?"

"For revenge," said Eidora. "He was attacked by a mage when he was a child."

Obsidiate was used in Alliance stunners, so I supposed that was where he'd heard about it. Even centaurs, who couldn't use magic, would be able to create a hell of an explosion with it.

"Where is the obsidiate now?"

"The Alliance confiscated it," said Eidora. "Tryfon confessed to speaking with an offworlder, and trading some of our source in return. He could not recall who this individual was."

"That's it?" I said, disbelieving. "No details? He just handed the information over to a random offworlder? Where?"

"In the Valerian capital. I believe there were threats involved," said Eidora. "I can assure you that *I* would not cave in so easily."

Yeah, right. Valeria's population of offworlders was so high, it might apply to anyone. It was beside the point now.

"And the Conners?" I said. "I suppose they'd have got the information out of whoever they told..." Offworld politics at its finest.

Magic surged through the air, without warning, and all the centaurs turned to face the direction it had come from. Somewhere in the middle of the forest. It split the sky in two, rippling outwards, opening to show... a blue-lit corridor.

The Passages. And a smoky shape emerged from the doorway.

"The kimaros!" Eidora shouted.

Holy shit. The air hummed with residual magic, the after-effects of a spell gone horribly wrong. It was a warped creature, more shadow than living, a larger version of the creature that had attacked Markos before.

The centaurs all turned towards it, weapons levelled. Apparently unconcerned, Eidora aimed a crossbow at the creature, and it hit home.

The beast didn't flinch, but the impact rippled through the whole forest. The centaurs were already charging towards the monster, leaving me an opening.

But the kimaros was between me and the source. Where the Conners must no doubt be.

"Damn it all to hell," I muttered. It was use magic, or die, and the centaurs would just have to deal with it.

I ran back to the official Passage door. Pushed it open.

"Anyone up for a fight?" I asked the perplexed council members.

~

ADA

I was too surprised to yell as the centaur pelted through the forest, kicking undergrowth aside. I lay flat to avoid hitting low-hanging branches and getting tangled up in foliage.

"Wait!" I gasped. "Slow down—" My words were cut off as a branch smacked me in the face. "Ow."

"You told me to hurry."

"Yes, but…"

I didn't know for sure what we'd find when we got there. Could I really trust myself not to let magic swarm out of hand? Kay had said the magic level here was the same as Valeria, and there, too, it didn't feel like the Passages. It didn't pull at me constantly like a wicked temptation that might blow up the world.

I had to believe it wouldn't. I could absorb it.

Markos stopped so suddenly, I almost went flying. Clinging to his back and gasping for breath, I saw the cliff edge ahead. And the site of the source.

People were there. I counted at least four of them, setting up a metal structure exactly like a bigger-scale version of the metal-plated bomb Delta's father had strapped to me. I wouldn't forget it in a hurry.

That was what they'd been making at the Campbells' place.

"Oh, shit." I gripped Markos's back. "They're making a bomb."

Could I counter something on that scale, even with antimagic? If I threw myself in the way, I didn't even know what would happen. I'd almost died last time. And the thought brought me out in a violent shivering fit. My breath came too fast.

"Human. Calm yourself down."

"Bit difficult," I gasped. "What the hell am I going to do?" If I used magic, I could destroy everything. Wipe out the whole world, without the Conners needing to do it.

I scanned the people moving about. Most were gathered around the machine, but others were holding something, lifting it out of the ground and carrying it to a spot at the foot of the cliff I'd almost fallen off. A gleaming black multi-sided shape. *The source.* It was smaller than I'd expected, but if they put it in that bomb... No. I had to stop them.

Energy surged through the air, sending me flying from Markos's back. I wildly shot level one magic at to the ground to stop myself hitting a tree and landed on my feet, the backlash fizzing through my skin.

Using magic to take down the Conners would be the obvious solution, but if that source got hit, we'd all die. I couldn't risk it.

I felt the magic before I saw it, awakening in my veins, and surging upwards in a spiral of red smoke from somewhere ahead in the forest. Tearing the world in two, into another door. In the air, above the trees.

The magic slammed into us like a wall. Markos reared up on his hind legs, and the trees around us were ripped from the ground. But I wasn't sent flying this time.

Adamantine was a built-in shield, and the magic couldn't get through to me.

A fearsome shape appeared from the doorway, taking form in the air as a raging red cloud, with vaguely defined limbs and a long, muzzled head like a lion. It crashed through the canopy somewhere ahead, and cries of alarm sounded. It must have attacked the centaurs. I spun around wildly, looking for Markos, and found him staring up at the door in horror.

The forest came to life around us. Rustling noises sounded and centaurs ran past, all heading towards the doorway and the monster. To defend their home from the beast.

Hit it. With magic. The humans hadn't managed to kill it. But… that would risk everyone in the forest, everyone in this world. Unless I managed to control magic.

Ignoring Markos's shout, I pelted through the trees. God help me if I ran into any centaurs, but they had a far bigger problem to worry about right now. I ran, pulling magic towards me. The energy within me buzzed in synchronisation with the magic in the atmosphere. In the monster.

Before I had the chance to consider my options, I'd already run right into the middle of a battle.

Ruined trees lay everywhere, scattered and torn. Centaurs were amongst them, relentlessly firing arrows and hurling spears at the monster. They'd driven it back, but it was closer to the cliff now.

To the source.

Magic pulsed from it like a malevolent energy. Wild as the Passages. Uncontrollable. Pit-like dark eyes locked onto me.

"Shit," I whispered, seeing my own death reflected back at me. The centaurs were too close. If I used magic, I'd take them all out.

No. Aglaia's magic was still there, beneath the chaotic trail the beast and the door had left. Stable. Controllable. And I could absorb it. As much as I needed.

I splayed out my hands, and *pushed.*

Magic surged through the air, and the beast's smoky form faded then became distinct once more. I hit it again, hardly able to believe this was happening.

I pulled on Aglaia's magic, and the beast pushed forwards with its lionlike paws. I stumbled, barely keeping my feet, and trees were ripped from the ground. The centaurs staggered and as magic surged out from the beast, they fell.

"NO!" I screamed, and pushed again. Energy surged from my skin, and the monster fixated its attention on me. I stepped forward. One foot. Then another. I pushed against it, sweat dripping down my forehead, magic rising to a static pitch. No way could I keep this up forever.

The beast stopped, snarling, as though stopped by an invisible force. Something bolstered me, helping me push the monster.

Someone else was using magic. More than one person...

Mages. Aglaia's magic-wielders. And there were others, too, appearing amongst the trees. Alliance members. Not just from Earth. Someone had let them into this world.

I wasn't fighting alone anymore. I pushed, and this time, the monster moved, its smoky form forced back towards the place where sky and earth were divided. The doorway.

We had to get it through before it closed, and the monster was trapped in the forest. Which was probably the Conners' plan.

It yowled and struggled against the force but to no avail. Sweat dripped down my face, and I staggered despite the antimagic in my blood. One final push sent the monster through the door in a torrent of smoke.

And then someone held me from behind, supporting me.

"We've got this, Ada."

"Kay." As our hands touched, I felt the magic inside me bolstered in response. He was amplifying it.

I drew in a shuddering breath, stumbling into Kay.

"Holy hell," I gasped, tilting my head to face him as he switched off the camouflage. "Did you just amplify *my* power?"

"Honestly? I'm still not sure how it works. But we took out the monster."

"Yeah. We did." I looked around, only now becoming aware of just how many people had gathered behind us. Mages and centaurs alike stared at the doorway, which remained even with the monster gone. Other Alliance members conversed. Even Eidora had come to stand at her brother's side.

"Ada. The source. We've got to take down the Conners."

"Really?" I brushed sweaty hair out my eyes with a shaking hand. "That sounds like suicide."

"Before the council get to the other side of the door. If they see it, I'll bet Conner will attack, and using magic near a source…"

"Crap," I said. The door itself was more like a *split*, from earth to sky. And the Conners were behind it.

Magic sparked up my left arm as Kay took my hand and turned us both invisible.

"Right," he said, in a low voice. "What was your plan? I'm guessing you weren't just running through the forest at random."

"Act as a shield," I said. "Stupid idea, I know. But I don't know how to fight a force like that without magic. We need to destroy their weapon."

"Yeah," said Kay. "We do."

"What *is* it?" I asked. "It's not any source I know, right? Not bloodrock." *Or adamantine.*

"It's called lustre," he said, quietly. "And few people know that. It's an amplifier. I don't know if it *can* be destroyed, but it isn't antimagic. If someone hit it with magic, even an Alliance stunner, it would be enough to turn it into a bomb. I guess they planned to take it through that doorway. If they activated it here, they'd die, too."

Crap. We needed to move even if we had no solution. Still invisible, we made our way as fast as possible through the trees. Down below the cliffs, the four people working on the machine were regrouping, by the look of things. One man shouted something, agitated, but their backs were turned on their work. We navigated our way down the cliff, approaching the machine carefully. Interlocking metal plates encased a gleaming multi-sided hunk of metal-like black rock. I would have taken it for adamantine if I didn't know the difference now. This source didn't absorb magic but enhanced it.

"What the devil did you bring that here for?" That was Conner. I recognised him from when Kay had dragged him into the clearing.

Another man shouted, "I told you, they took the Campbells' base! If we'd left the rest of the machine there, Enforcement would have taken it. I haven't heard from Leroy. I'll bet they have him already. Wynn, you drew too much attention."

"Oh, so it's my fault?" a woman shot at him. "You're the one who said we couldn't leave it at the Campbells'. The Alliance will be there by now. We can open another door and get it out of here while they're preoccupied."

"And so are you," Kay muttered, almost too quiet to hear, as we got close enough to reach the machine.

The rocky ground had been split open down the middle. There was no more lustre. They'd taken all of it to put into their machine.

"Ada." Kay spoke, the faintest whisper. "I think you can

get it out of there. Most people wouldn't be able to touch it. But—"

"I can absorb magic." Whatever defences they had, I might be able to absorb them. If I was willing to take the risk. "Okay."

He squeezed my hand, pressing something into it. "The earpiece. I contacted Markos already, but just in case. Can you take care of those guys?"

"Take care of?" My heart beat fast.

"However you want to."

He meant, I could kill them or silence them another way. Like he'd knocked out those guys in Campbell HQ. Which I'd choose depended on how merciful I felt towards the people who'd captured and tortured my family.

"Wait…"

But his hand slipped from mine. "I'm still drawing on its power. I don't know how much I have left. I'll divert their attention. You get that lustre out."

"Kay—no!"

Too late.

I hope that didn't mean goodbye. I climbed the rest of the way down the incline, towards the machine.

The lustre was in the direct centre, surrounded by a tangle of wires I could only assume activated it as a bomb… but the lustre was the only place I felt the magic coming from. Which meant one of the Conners had to be able to use magic to activate it. If I took the lustre out, they wouldn't be able to use it anymore.

I dropped down the incline and reached for it. Magic seared through me, but as heads turned in my direction, a fork of lightning shot from the sky on the opposite side of the plains.

A voice rang out. "Show yourself, magic-wielder!"

My heart dropped. A tall woman had broken away from

the group, and headed in the direction the lightning had come from. Towards Kay. She must be Aric's sister.

Kay appeared, directly beneath the door, fury etched on his face.

"You," he said. "If any of you people interfere, you're dead."

~

KAY

So this was her. Wynn. Aric's sister, who'd been behind the wyvern incident. Who'd tortured Ada's brother, and killed a dozen officers on Valeria.

"You're Walker," she said, predictably. I didn't even bother arguing, just fired a shot of magic at her. She dodged, but I meant her to.

I'd already turned invisible again and charged her, slamming her into the ground. Magic sparked around her, sending both of us rolling across the plain into a gap between the rocks. I landed on my feet, pinning her to the wall as the backlash shot over our heads.

And then she held a dagger to my throat. An Alliance-issued, adamantine dagger. Magicproof.

Fuck. I hadn't prepared for this. I was backed against the rock, no room to manoeuvre, and even magic—

She grinned. "Gotcha. Never expected that, did you, Walker?"

There was maybe half a metre between her and the opposite wall. Magic sparked around her dagger hand. The blade was icy-cold.

I took in all these details in the split-second I made up my mind.

I pushed at the air, the magic forcing her to back against the opposite wall. As her dagger swiped again, I raised my left arm to block the blade, and grabbed for the handle with my right.

Her eyes widened. *Never expected that, did you?*

Thanks to her and the wyvern, I couldn't feel the blade slice into my skin, even as blood dripped down my arm, and her surprise was enough to give me the advantage. My fingers closed over the wyvern-hide handle and I pulled, hard. She only resisted a second before letting go before I broke her fingers.

I could kill her now. But I wasn't about to risk being trapped again. Grabbing her arm, I dragged her out of the incline. Magic sparked around the dagger as I held it to her throat, and pressed.

Something flashed in the corner of my vision. In a second, everything seemed to slow down, details hitting me all at once—the doorway had disappeared, ten or more centaurs gathered on the clifftop, and a dozen spears were flying right at us.

ADA

Again, I extended my hand towards the lustre, and met an invisible shield that set every nerve in my body vibrating. Like second level magic. I jerked to the side, sweating all over.

Was this what it felt like to be killed with magic, burned from the inside out?

No. I'm adamantine. I'm unbreakable. I pushed through the invisible shield, and closed my hand over the cold, gleaming black metal.

Magic seared through my veins, and I clenched my teeth to keep from crying out. My hand shook, the rock pulsing with power, but I held on. My other hand locked around the lustre at its base. The buzzing rose to a fever pitch as I pulled all the magic towards me. Into me.

Like before. No. Not like before. This time... I could control it.

I let the magic flow through my fingers. I was the conduit, and the magic flowed out of the bomb, through me, into the atmosphere. I dug my heels into the ground, and gave one last tug.

The lustre came free of its casing with a sharp noise, lost under the sound of the fight. My hand tingled with heat, but didn't burn. The lustre's black gleam was fading. I'd drained the magic right out of it.

Kay and the woman were still fighting. Both alive. My heart beat faster.

And then Mr Conner turned around. Saw the dismantled machine, and shouted.

Shit. I froze on the spot. Rustling noises sounded in the trees, and a thrill of dread went through me. Centaurs emerged from the edge of the forest, on the cliff-top, spears and crossbows pointed. At Kay, who still grappled with Aric's sister.

I cried out, but too late.

A spear soared towards them, plunging into Wynn Conner, and Kay, pressed to her back, went still.

❦

KAY

The spear pierced Wynn through the heart, stopping only inches from mine. I held my breath, blood streaming from my arm, as she fell.

At the same time came the sound of several other bodies hitting the ground. The three men, the Conners, all fell in a haze of blood, speared by the centaurs' crossbows.

"Ada!" She wasn't amongst the dead. She must still be invisible…

"Justice," said a voice, in Aglaian, and other centaur shouts rang out in agreement.

21

ADA

oly hell. My knees went weak with shock. That spear... had almost hit Kay.

The bodies of the Conners lay only metres away. The centaurs had already re-armed themselves, led by their new queen. She'd been the one to throw the spear.

"Ada!" Kay scanned the fallen bodies, eyes wide.

Breathe, Ada. I concentrated on the magic still swarming around and switched off the camouflage. Instantly, a dozen spears pointed in my direction.

"Stop," said Kay, taking a step forward. One arm was dripping blood. "Lower your weapons."

"That's enough." Markos stepped up besides his sister. "Let them go."

"Kay," I said, taking that as the cue to run to him. "You're bleeding. Holy *shit!*" It was a wonder he was still standing. Blood seeped down his left arm.

"I'm all right, Ada. We have to get out of here."

"You—seriously." He didn't object when I took his arm and pushed up his left sleeve to show a long, vicious cut, right across the wyvern scar. "Can you really not feel it?"

"Lucky I can't." He half smiled. "She didn't know. It was her goddamn wyvern that did it. Nice bit of irony."

"Jesus Christ, Kay. Not being able to feel pain doesn't mean you can't bleed to death, you idiot!"

He rolled his eyes. "Never mind that."

Markos waited at the cliff top, between us and his sister. Eidora regarded us with anger in her expression, but her brother must have told her to step aside. Markos filled us in on what had happened while we'd been stopping the Conners. The doorway they'd opened was nowhere in sight, thanks to the council, apparently, who'd used Alliance tech to close it. The kimaros had gone, back to whatever ghastly world they came from. And Aric had disappeared, too. Either he'd wandered off on Aglaia or he'd gone into the Passages through the open door. Either way, I didn't particularly care. I wanted to get back to my family.

And we had a long walk to explain it to the council. Doing that without mentioning the lustre source was tricky, but Markos and Kay managed to tell the story while glossing over that particular part of the explanation. The council were more concerned with the treachery of the Conner family.

"I can't say I'm surprised," Kay muttered. Though his arm was bandaged, he was still pale.

"Kay, seriously. Let someone carry you or something."

"Like hell."

"Piggyback on Markos?" I suggested innocently. The centaur glared at me. "What?"

"Aric bloody Conner." Kay glanced over his shoulder. "I've no idea if he escaped into the Passages. I still don't trust him."

"You let him go, though…" I said, slowly.

"Guess I did. He was kind of clueless about what was happening. But someone gave him a magic-boost." Kay's expression darkened. "His family were messing about with Klathican tech. I'll have to look into that when we get back."

"You're already thinking about the next crazy thing you're going to do?" I shook my head. "You're impossible."

"I prefer 'improbable'," said Kay.

Improbable. A human amplifier. I'd felt the same thing from him when he'd amplified my power as I did from the lustre. *Kay amplified the magic from the Chameleon to turn invisible.* So the experiment his father had orchestrated hadn't involved bloodrock, though that had kick-started all of this. Someone had stolen it from the Alliance, who'd confiscated it from the Knights. The ravegens had used it on the orders of the Conners... but how had they even known it existed in the first place? Maybe from Delta, whose family had been involved with Cethrax at some point, using the monsters as a diversion just like the Conners had.

It was all I could do to walk upright. I just wanted to sleep for a year and leave someone else to deal with the fallout. Go back to my family. And Kay... I glanced at him again. I wanted to know what else he could do with magic. But then, I barely knew what *I* could do. I'd never thought I had the ability to pull the magic right out of another source before.

Once we reached the main Passage, a crowd swarmed us. People from all the worlds, descending on the council, demanding to know what happened. Markos swore, grabbing Kay's non-injured arm. Kay shook him off, and Markos signed melodramatically.

"Come on, humans."

He cut a path right through the middle of the corridor, the crowd instantly shrinking away from him. Turning the corner to the corridor with the doorway to Earth, we almost collided with Carl.

"What the devil happened?"

"Later," I said. "Where are—?"

"I'm here, you idiot," said a familiar voice. I went tense.

Nell stood in the doorway to London. Unhurt. And she swept me into a hug for the first time since I was about five.

Guess it wasn't really my fault I was in too much shock to return the hug.

"Ada. I'm so, so, sorry."

And now she was making me cry in front of all these people. "Cheers, Nell," I muttered. "Is Alber okay?"

"Of course," said Nell. "He's with Jeth. Come on. We need to get you home."

I glanced back at Kay, who leaned against the wall.

"Go with them." He smiled faintly. "I'll be all right."

I nodded. "Don't you bleed to death on me, you hear?"

"That's not gonna happen."

~

Nell kept glancing at me, without speaking, as we walked through the disarmingly ordinary-looking London streets. The debriefing session with Ms Weston hadn't lasted long. She'd told me to come and give a more detailed report in the morning.

Good. I was far too tired to face questioning from the council. I felt kind of bad for Kay, having to deal with that when he'd almost died.

It was only when we were on the tube home that I remembered to check my communicator. I'd had a message from Ms Weston telling me I had the option to stay at work tomorrow or not, after making my report.

So I had time to make up my mind, then.

Nell still studied me as I put the communicator back in my pocket. "You're really comfortable with these people?"

"Who? The Alliance? Or Kay?"

"Either." She frowned. "That young man spoke to me in a way no one's ever dared to."

I couldn't help laughing. "That doesn't surprise me at all."

"He's really Walker's son?"

"Yeah… why?"

Nell shook her head. "The experiments. On children. He… was one of them, wasn't he?"

I swallowed. "I don't know the details. I wouldn't ask. But he's not on his father's side."

"I thought so. I've never seen magic like that before."

"Yeah…" I glanced around. The carriage was empty. "It isn't the same as what they injected me with. I don't know why, either. Why'd they do it to me? To make me a shield, or a weapon? Or both?"

A pause. Nell lowered her gaze. "To make you unbreakable. A Royal. To win their war, whatever the cost." She looked me in the eyes then. "You'll never have to do that."

"So what *am* I supposed to do now? Hide out on Earth, scared? Or live my life? It doesn't matter what they wanted of me, does it? Not now."

Nell inclined her head. "You're completely right there."

"Okay. Is that a go-ahead to carry on working for the Alliance? Because it's not their fault. What happened… it's horrible. I'm so angry about it, Nell. I'd have killed those Conners if the centaurs hadn't got there first."

I told her everything, from the beginning, and she listened patiently. No comments, though she was used to staying calm in a crisis. Nothing fazed her at all.

When I'd finished, she said, "You can access your potential on high-magic worlds. Is that what you want?"

"I don't know." I sighed. "It used to drive me crazy not being able to use it on Earth, but that was before I knew what I could do. You know I've always wanted to go offworld, and I still do. With or without magic."

"I could tell you it's dangerous," said Nell. "But I suppose that's never stopped you before."

I smiled. "Guess not."

~

KAY

To say Ms Weston was displeased would be an understatement.

"And you didn't think to tell me any of this?" She glared at me across the desk. At least Markos was here to take half of the effect.

"I did tell you," I pointed out, biting back a sarcastic retort. "And I left a message. Besides, you insisted upon us attending the ceremony."

And it looked like it wouldn't be the last. The narrow escape from destruction had caused the Alliance to order an impromptu meeting of all the worlds' councils for the first time in years. I didn't particularly look forward to *that*. Because I had to make a decision about how much to tell them. Someone had been asking about sources. Someone not in the Alliance. I had no way of finding out now the rebels were dead and the Conners were, too, but the Alliance clearly had an enemy. And it was bigger than anything they'd dealt with before.

"Well, at least it all worked out," said Markos. "Centaurs and humans have never fought alongside one another before. I think Eidora might have to revise her opinion on magic."

"Her stalling almost got a bunch of people killed," I muttered. I wasn't particularly in the mood to debate.

"Kay," said Ms Weston. "You can't expect everyone to cave into your every demand."

"I didn't demand anything," I said. "The centaurs and the

council chose to come and fight. And when I acted, I was thinking about how Ada's family were being tortured and the Conners were on the brink of destroying Aglaia. Doesn't that qualify for an exceptional scenario?" Raj and the other Ambassadors thought so, as did the council, though it was probably only a matter of time before people started asking the wrong questions. Like why the Conners had been on Aglaia. The Valerian Alliance had confiscated some burnt-out magic source Conner used to open that doorway from the Campbells' place, which Wynn had stolen from West Office. Sounded like Conners had found the Campbells' records of what they'd used to make the bomb and decided to try it themselves, using their connections on Klathica, the same place those magic-implants had come from.

Though no one had particularly liked any of the Conner family, they'd stirred up a lot of contention. West Office, for one, had started in-depth interrogations of all their staff. Central had already done that, of course, but paranoia was rampant. I just hoped they'd leave Ada alone. She'd been through enough.

"You know it does," said Ms Weston. "The question, of course, is what drove Conner to pick Aglaia in the first place."

Her eyes dared me to tell the truth. No, even the council didn't know about the lustre. Or my boss. I knew better than to let that information slip into the wrong hands, even if Ada had drained the magic from it so it was essentially worthless now. How the Conners even knew about it in the first place was a mystery I'd probably never know the answer to, seeing as the only survivor was Aric, and he was AWOL. Either he'd got stranded on Aglaia, or he'd sneaked back into the Passages while the fighting was going on. I was inclined to believe the latter. He had a price on his head now, anyway.

I couldn't say he didn't deserve it. Though I did wonder

what, exactly, had been in the source he'd been injected with. And his sister. But now the rest of the Conners were dead, there was no way to find out how, exactly, they'd found out about the lustre source.

I shrugged. "It's contentious. Doesn't like outsiders."

"The mages certainly seem to have revised their opinions," said Ms Weston. "Enough to request a more active role in the Alliance. We certainly need more guidance for our magic-wielders. Now more than ever."

She meant Ada. Now she'd shown control over her magic, I predicted the Alliance wouldn't leave well enough alone. The last thing she needed was more magic-related problems. After almost losing her family, again, I was amazed she'd elected to stay.

Because it turned out magic did give you a choice. It didn't make you a monster. And she'd seen what I was capable of *without* magic, under my own power. What she'd seen had made her look at me in genuine horror.

"Yeah," I said to Ms Weston. "We do. For sure."

When she finally dismissed us, I made for the stairs. I had a whole day free to go offworld and do whatever I wanted, and I was determined to put this goddamn mess behind me and master control of that hover bike.

Markos cornered me before I reached the stairs.

"What?"

"You didn't tell her," he said, in an undertone.

"Which part? The source? I'm not an idiot. Besides, it's gone." Ada had done a hell of a number on it. She'd drained the magic right out of the lustre, rendering it useless. Good job the centaurs had never planned on using it. I doubted they could tell the difference.

"Your magic."

Of course. He'd noticed. "She's not a fan of magic-wielders," I said.

"She knows what you can do?"

"Some of it. I can't pretend to be an expert. Hell, Earth doesn't have nearly enough information."

I'd taken off the earpiece, but I still carried the Chameleon on me, just in case. Technically, I could draw on the magic at any time, though it was partly dependent on the world's magic level and probably didn't last forever. And I hadn't told Ms Weston that, either.

Lustre. Amplifier.

The mage didn't know. I'd seen him in the battle against the kimaros, fighting alongside the other mages, the other council members. Fighting on *our* side. He'd done nothing to rouse my suspicion, but he'd said Aglaia had enemies. Someone had scared the centaurs into giving up information on the lustre source to someone from offworld. Whoever could threaten centaurs and magic-wielders alike was an enemy I didn't want to face.

But right now, offworld politics were out of my hands, as they bloody well should be.

"Yes," said Markos. "Well, it certainly helped in defending my world."

"Guess it did. But then, magic caused the problem to begin with, didn't it?"

"Bloody magic," he said, "Ada's over there, by the way."

I hadn't seen her come in, though it was fairly early. Ms Weston had insisted on my coming to the office as soon as I'd stopped bleeding everywhere. "Oh, right."

ADA

I glanced up as Kay approached my desk. "You're all right?" His left arm was bandaged, but he seemed otherwise normal.

"Yeah," he said. "I was just heading out, but... could we talk a moment?"

My pulse sped up. "Uh... is Ms Weston around?"

"In her office. She won't come after you yet, don't worry."

We found a deserted stretch of corridor. Kay faced me, absently fiddling with the bandage on his arm. "Is your brother okay? And your guardian?"

I winced. "Sort of. I wasn't sure whether to come in, but there isn't much I can do."

"And you?"

"Same as ever." Except for the new screaming nightmares which would probably be a regular feature of my nights. But I didn't want to talk about that now. Instead, my mind jumped to something a hundred times more embarrassing. "Uh. What happened in the forest. I wasn't... completely in control."

"You don't need to explain."

My heart dropped. I'd thought, well, hoped, he might... I didn't know what I'd hoped.

"I know I've said some shitty things. I shouldn't have taken Aric seriously."

His eyes narrowed a fraction. "He had a thing for stirring up trouble."

"He said... he said you tried to kill him because he found out you were a criminal and a psychopath."

"What? He really said that? Jesus." He shook his head. "I have no idea why he's so obsessed with me. Maybe I should invest in security cameras in case he shows up at my flat." He didn't even try to make the sarcasm sound genuine.

"Kay... I don't care about the crap he said. I know you're not a psycho."

He blinked, once. "Right. Good to know."

Though I'd never really been able to read him, I swore there was something self-mocking in his tone. Had Tara thought of him like that?

"Look," he said. "I'm sorry. I never should have spoken to you like I did. It was unfair. You don't have to stay here at Central."

"Now you sound like my brother." Crap. I didn't mean to start an argument again, but I didn't like the direction this conversation was headed in.

"I shouldn't have pushed you into joining."

"None of that," I said. "I made my choice. And I'm sticking with it."

"The Alliance will keep your family safe, Ada," he said. "Even if you aren't working for us. It's in our mandate. What happened—it shouldn't have. You've no idea—"

"It wasn't *your* fault." He tried to protest, and I interrupted. "No, it wasn't. You think me and my family haven't risked our lives every day we've been on this world? People have attacked me before, you know. And my family. The Conners would have come after us for the bloodrock no matter what, Nell had enough of a reputation for it amongst the shelters." It was true. Oh, I'd be having words with Ms Weston about why the Conners had been allowed to run around the Passages even after some of them had been arrested, but I wasn't pinning the whole blame on the Alliance. Even Nell wasn't.

Wonders would never cease.

"You," I said, "need to stop blaming yourself."

"If I do that," he said, "then tell me what you want from me."

What? "You're saying… it's not going to work. Us."

"Ada—" He ran a hand through his hair, glanced over his shoulder. "It's not the most important thing. You should look out for yourself first, and the last thing you need right now is to be around someone like me."

"I wish I could see inside your head," I said. "Then I'd know what the hell to say to that." *Smooth, Ada.*

"Ada… that isn't a place you want to be. Trust me."

"I trust you." And it was true, despite everything. "Do you trust *me?*"

Shouldn't have asked. My heart dropped several notches as he met my eyes, the answer clear on his face. I'd seen that look before. On people who'd been betrayed too many times. And I knew it went far deeper than us.

My heart sank into the carpet, right down to the entrance hall.

"What are you two doing?" The frowning face of Ms Weston appeared around the corner.

"Just talking," said Kay. "I'm on my way out now."

"Good. I need to talk to Ada."

I groaned inwardly. Guess it was time to give my own version of yesterday's events. As Ms Weston withdrew, I caught Kay's arm as he walked past.

"Wait," I said, in a low voice. "I'm not picking my family over you. I'm on your team, and I told you I'm sticking around." I gave him a small smile, and headed to Ms Weston's office before he could reply.

"What's up?" Jeth asked, as we walked down the road to our house. "You're being quiet."

I shrugged. "Just worried about Alber."

"Yeah. Nell said she's calling a family meeting, by the way."

Dammit. "I've had enough meetings today," I muttered. Kay hadn't come back to Central, so I assumed he'd already given Ms Weston an explanation that satisfied her without giving anything away about the magic source on Aglaia. She knew something was off, but she hadn't pushed me.

"Ada, what you did was incredible. I don't know how you held it together. When I heard... I couldn't have done it. Gone after Alber, and then fought a battle. No way."

I let out a shuddering breath. "I was just so *angry*. They had no right to hurt us." Too angry to be afraid, maybe.

I turned my key in the lock and jumped as Nell's face loomed from the shadow of the hallway. "We're moving."

"We are?" I supposed I should have expected it.

"Yes. Tomorrow, actually. I've found us a smaller house, since we don't need the upstairs flat anymore now we're not running the shelter from here."

"Oh," I said, unable to think of a more adequate response. Tomorrow?

Jeth closed the door behind us. "That was fast. Whereabouts?"

"Other side of the river. Closer to your workplace."

I blinked. "You're really okay with it? The money's not an issue? I'll pay my own rent."

"We're opening our business. Legally. With Alliance approval."

"Wait, you sorted it out today?"

"It's been in the works for a while, but given the circumstances..."

"Wow," I said. "I'm up for that. Except I'm gonna need to pack."

"Get a move on, then," she said, half stern, half affectionate.

I grinned at Jeth. "How about that?"

"I can work with it," he said.

"Yeah." Alber appeared in the doorway. He had a cut

across his forehead, but bruised ribs were the worst of the injuries. On the surface, at least.

"Right," I said. "Guess I'd better pack."

Or try to. My room was especially chaotic lately because I hadn't been around often enough to keep it clean. I grabbed a large bag and started snatching up things at random, predictably sending a stack of books toppling down the back of my bedside table. I shifted the table out of the way and found a treasure trove of objects I'd lost under the bed, including a Valerian puzzle game Delta had once given me. I glared at it and tossed it into the bag.

A buzzing sensation made the hairs on my arms stand on end. I spun around, startled. *Did the magic level just go up?* That wasn't supposed to happen on Earth.

The buzzing faded. I stayed still for a moment, then, when it didn't come back, returned to packing. Maybe I'd imagined it. Or I was extra-sensitive to every magic-related change now?

My communicator lit up.

"Kay?" I switched on the speaker-phone.

"Hey, Ada. This a bad time?"

"Eh. Never really a good time these days, to be honest."

"Your brother?" He didn't ask *is he okay?* He knew better, I supposed.

I exhaled. "Coping. I don't know. It's hard to tell. Did you just feel that? I swear the magic level just went up."

"No, but I'm on Valeria. Are you sure?"

"I think so... I don't know." It had faded by now. "That was weird."

"Well, never mind it. We can't deal with every magic-related problem. If there's an issue, leave it to the Alliance."

"Until it hits me in the face." I'd had more than enough of magic-related problems for the moment. For a lifetime, even.

"I have a question."

"What?" I said warily, annoyed when my heart rate automatically sped up.

"How do you and Alber feel about hover bikes?"

"Uh. Why?"

"Because I'm in Neo Greyle's hover-port right now, and I have two hover bike hire tickets in my hand."

Holy crap. "Two?"

"Yeah. Thing is, I already own a hover bike. So…"

"Oh my god," I said. "I'll ask Alber. But you get a hell, yes from me."

"Good. This weekend okay?"

I almost said, *it's a date.* Except it wasn't. He just… felt sorry for me? "Sure," I said, trying to inject enthusiasm into my voice. "I'll tell him."

"I can promise there won't be any goblins this time."

I laughed. "With you? I wouldn't count on it."

Maybe just friends was okay. He hadn't *said* he didn't like me in that way… which was a start.

"Hey, Al." I pushed open my door and called down the corridor, "Guess who got us a free hover bike ride?"

ABOUT THE AUTHOR

Emma is the New York Times and USA Today Bestselling author of the Changeling Chronicles urban fantasy series.

Emma spent her childhood creating imaginary worlds to compensate for a disappointingly average reality, so it was probably inevitable that she ended up writing fantasy novels. When she's not immersed in her own fictional universes, Emma can be found with her head in a book or wandering around the world in search of adventure.

Find out more about Emma's books at www. emmaladams.com.